ORDER OF THE SHADOW

ORDER OF THE SHADOW

LEGACY OF THE SHADOW'S BLOOD™ BOOK 5

E.G. BATEMAN

MICHAEL ANDERLE

LMBPN Publishing
PMB 196, 2540 South Maryland Pkwy
Las Vegas, NV 89109

First US edition, January 2021
eBook ISBN: 978-1-64971-441-1
Print ISBN: 978-1-64971-442-8

THE ORDER OF THE SHADOW TEAM

Thanks to our Beta Readers:

John Ashmore, Kelly O'Donnell, Larry Omans, Rachel Beckford

Thanks to our JIT Team:

Diane L. Smith
Wendy L Bonell
Dave Hicks
Paul Westman

Editor
SkyHunter Editing Team

I dedicated the previous book to my brother, Steve and his cat, Alan. While Steve was appreciative, I received no such response from Alan. He didn't call, he didn't write, nothing. Therefore, I dedicate this book to my dogs Max, Scruffy, and Sparky. Dogs are the best.
Woof!

— *E.G. Bateman*

To Family, Friends and
Those Who Love
To Read.
May We All Enjoy Grace
To Live The Life We Are
Called.

— *Michael Anderle*

CHAPTER ONE

The plan had been simple enough, although not what Lexi would have preferred. Azatoth had insisted on entering the front of the building alone, which had immediately triggered all kinds of inner alarms.

Still, she didn't think her unwanted partner would kill their quarry now that it was daytime. For one thing, the werewolf would have changed and last night had been the final full moon of the month. The demon suggested that the were would sense her and be forced to escape out the back of the building where Lexi waited, ready to whammy him with a sleep spell she had learned from Scott, a pouch of wolfsbane, and failing that, her trusty katana. She had sealed all the other exits magically and the only way out was the door in front of her, yet it remained suspiciously silent.

A little impatient, she leaned against the fence at the rear of the building and listened intently for signs that their target was running toward her position.

Her attempt resulted in nothing at all and she sighed.

Two minutes of staring at the door were long enough. She waved a hand over it to seal it and walked around the building. As she hurried along the side of the old office building, a loud bang shook the window when she passed. She settled immediately into a defensive stance as an arm slid down the inside of the glass and left a bloody trail. It was missing the body it should have been attached to.

Her shoulders sagged. "Not again."

I hate working with Azatoth.

The demon insisted on joining her in the field at least once a week but didn't seem to understand or care that sometimes, their remit was to detain, not dismember.

As she approached the front door, Azatoth emerged through it. Blood spattered the demon's face and something hung from her hair. The dark sorcerer tried not to look at her gore-covered hands—which were, of course, her sister's hands.

Azatoth grinned. "All done." She strode casually away from the building.

While she hated taking the demon on jobs, Lexi was trying to keep her away from Kindred headquarters as much as possible. The death count at base had dropped significantly since Azatoth had insisted she take part in missions. A few other legacies had worked with her but had not returned in one piece—or at all.

She hurried after the demon. "What happened?"

"He tried to fornicate with me. I did consider it, but I've decided I'm not that kind of girl."

Startled, she barely registered that her mouth hung open. She highly doubted the were would have had the time to think of such things before the demon shredded him. Although she tried to think of a response, nothing came to mind.

Azatoth pulled something red from her sleeve and looked like she might pop it into her mouth. Lexi's stomach flipped.

The demon paused and grimaced. "This vessel has such a weak stomach." She dropped the morsel on the ground and turned to her. "Let's get waffles."

"Yes. Waffles." She despised socializing with the creature but it seemed like a great diversion from either of the conversations about sex or eating werewolves she thought she was about to have.

"Come on then." Azatoth took her arm and stepped forward.

The air became heavy and humid and their surroundings gray and impenetrable. A moment later, they stood across the street from a waffle house in New York. Lexi shuddered. There was something creepy about the way the demon traveled. She seemed to translocate but it was as though she went through somewhere deeply unpleasant.

"You have something in your hair." She pointed vaguely at Azatoth's bangs.

"Oh, would you mind?" The demon remained still while she picked a piece of organic matter from her hair.

It gave her chills to be this intimate with the being who possessed her sister. "Perhaps a glamour for the rest of it?"

"I don't need to glamour it." The blood disappeared from Azatoth's hair and face and ran in rivulets down the clothes. Finally, as she moved to cross the street, she left a small puddle of blood on the ground. "Thanks, sis." She froze, then turned to her companion. "I didn't mean to say that. How curious."

Lexi's heart raced and she worked hard to not show her excitement.

Is it Alicia trying to give me a sign?

The last thing she wanted was for the demon to realize Alicia was still in there. She kept the hope from her face.

As they approached the eatery, a group of young men passed them walking the other way. One of them leered at Lexi and intentionally brushed up against Azatoth as he passed. "Sorry, sugar."

The demon froze. Her arm snaked out, caught hold of the man, and she stared intently at him. Lexi had seen the look before—this guy was about to be mincemeat.

To avoid the inevitable fallout, she took one step closer and punched him in the face. He fell with a faint groan. "Sorry, sugar."

She grasped the handle and held the door open for her unwelcome companion.

"Thank you, Lexi." Azatoth stepped in and turned to give her a brief smile.

They entered the restaurant, where a few people waited in line to be seated.

Her companion sighed. She had a distinct aversion to waiting.

"I suppose you must often find the…uh, vessel doing things automatically." She hated referring to Alicia as a vessel, but she needed a distraction before all hell broke loose.

The demon frowned. "What do you mean?"

Lexi raised an eyebrow and looked pointedly at Azatoth's hand and a shuriken that spun between her fingers. "I know many legacies who do that. I do it too."

The demon stopped spinning. "I have noticed these things. I don't like it. It feels as though I don't have full control of the body."

This conversation wasn't moving in a direction she was comfortable with. She shrugged and tried to redirect it into safer waters. "I guess none of us have full control of our bodies. Did you expend effort and concentration on walking and breathing in your body?"

"You mean before I crossed to your realm? No, that would be tiresome. I like you, Lexi. You make me think about things in a different way. It helps me to acclimate."

A young man interrupted. "Have you booked?"

Azatoth frowned at the interruption.

Lexi panicked. Something small like this could easily end in a waffle house full of corpses. She smiled and spoke quickly. "Table for two in the name of Lexi."

He went to the screen while she reached out mentally and

convinced him he could see her name displayed on the bookings list.

"That's great." His expression revealed no confusion. "It'll only take a few moments to get your table ready."

"Great. We'll sit at the counter and check the menu." Lexi walked ahead and was relieved to hear Azatoth follow.

They sat at the red-and-chrome fifties-style counter. She passed a menu to the demon and they ordered milkshakes.

Her companion glanced at the greeter, then at Lexi. "You fascinate me. Your magic is inconsistent at best, but it quite often comes through for you when I least expect it to."

She shrugged. "I'm still learning. I trained as a legacy and sorcery takes a completely different skill set."

"But you used Scott's magic before. What's the difference?"

"I didn't have to source it before or balance it. It's harder than it would appear."

"How is the handsome young Scott? Now he's a male I could—"

Lexi interrupted as quickly as possible. She didn't want to hear the end of that sentence. "I don't know. I haven't seen him."

"But you're bound to him. Surely you know if he's well."

"You said you would tell me about my mother." It wasn't exactly subtle, but she needed to change the subject before it delved into all kinds of uncomfortable details.

The demon tilted her head and smiled. "Ah yes. I did, didn't I." She paused.

Lexi thought for a moment that she wouldn't continue.

"Caleb was interested in her."

She screwed her face up in revulsion. "You mean—"

"No, not like that. He never physically met her. He had someone dig into the files when we met you in Palm Springs. All I know is what he knew—she appeared one day, pregnant and with no memory. She died six years later."

Azatoth slurped her drink, then opened her mouth to say something else.

A waiter joined them. "Ladies, your table is ready."

"Oh, goodie!" The demon slid off her stool and followed him.

Lexi swore under her breath.

When they were seated and the waiter had left with their order, she decided to prompt Azatoth to continue, but the demon spoke first.

"I have a surprise for you at the office. I can't wait to see your face."

She coughed when her drink went down the wrong way and couldn't help but think of the surprise the entity had left for Bryan at the chief's house in New Orleans. She felt through the bond that Scott was okay, but this announcement of a surprise was unnerving. She wondered about everyone else in her life—Dick, Dolores, the Braxtons, and Bryan.

"Smile. It's nothing bad. I think you'll like it."

Their waffles arrived and they began to eat, although Lexi had no appetite.

"Would you prefer to call me Alicia?"

"No. No, not even…uh, no thank you." She began to wonder if the demon was trying to make her choke on her food.

"Then I'd like you to call me Az."

"Az."

"I think we know each other well enough by now. Unless you think Azzy is better?"

Lexi managed to plaster a huge smile on her face to stop the horror from showing. "Az is fine."

"I have a meeting. I'll see you in the morning for your surprise." The demon vanished.

With the seat opposite her immediately empty, Lexi rolled her eyes. Azatoth had stiffed her on the bill again. She called the waiter and ordered a coffee, then considered the somewhat disjointed conversation they'd had. As usual, she moved her consciousness into her dimensional pocket and watched a video replay of their exchange. As it played, she stared into the demon's face in search of any sign of her sister.

She watched the screen as the demon asked about Scott but not Bryan. Did that mean she knew where Bryan was? The thought gave her a lump in her throat. She hadn't heard from her sister's husband and mage for a while. It was frustrating as he was central to her plan to contact Alicia, but Dolores insisted on giving him space.

When the waiter asked if she wanted the receipt, she nodded. "Oh yes. I will be sure to expense this." She shrugged mentally. *A small win is still a win.*

With a smile, she realized that by mentioning the meeting, Azatoth had given her a useful heads-up. She wondered who the demon's late meeting could be with and what it might be about.

Lexi had begun to return to the office in the evenings to snoop around and try to discover the demon's plans for the realm, and she still hadn't located the mystery Kindred man who had watched them outside the Paris hotel in Las Vegas. She checked the time and decided she'd given the demon enough of a head start to the office. When the waiter turned away, she translocated.

As planned, she appeared beside her desk. She was the only member of the Overseers team to have an office to herself. It was a corner office with an enviable view of the city if she'd been into that kind of thing, which she wasn't. It had belonged to the team's manager. She didn't want to imagine what had happened to the previous incumbent.

Before doing anything, she gazed around the room to make sure no gruesome surprises had been left by the demon. Finding nothing, she breathed a sigh of relief before she picked a marker up to update the whiteboard. She drew a line through the werewolf job, then put a red X next to it—which meant that a clean-up crew was required. The job disappeared from the list. She knew it would have appeared on one of the similar boards in the outer office.

For a moment, she thought of Scott. She knew exactly what he'd say. *What a waste of magic. You could do that with a computer.*

Lexi thought about his *Star Wars* magic trick and smiled. He was no stranger to wasting magic and she missed working with him. Of course, she saw him every day—which was more frequently than she would admit to Azatoth—but she was used to working with him, eating with him, and generally spending her life with him.

She closed her eyes and focused on the bond. It gave her comfort. She'd see her team shortly.

A quick scrutiny of the rest of the board reassured her that there were no other jobs Azatoth would be interested in, and she breathed another sigh of relief.

She stepped out of her office and glanced around. The silence told her that everyone else had gone home. As she read the boards out there, the werewolf job went from *Cleaning crew required* to *Cleaning crew at scene.* She went into the hallway and headed to the executive level in the elevator. The moment she stepped out, she knew something was wrong.

Nora sat with her head slumped on her desk outside Azatoth's office.

Lexi rushed over to the woman. "Nora? Are you okay?"

The secretary jerked her head up. "It's only water." She stared glassy-eyed at her.

Oh, man, she's sloshed.

"Has Azatoth seen you like this?"

Nora's eyes bulged. "Is she back?"

"She came back about half an hour ago."

"Ugh. She must have gone straight to the meeting." She dropped her head into her hands. "I can't cope with this anymore."

"Maybe you should go home."

"I can't. Millicent will be on the warpath. She got back from annual leave in Aruba." Nora was slurring but Lexi was able to piece the information together.

She frowned in confusion. "Who's Millicent?"

"She was on the council. You know before the…" She finished the sentence with a finger across the throat.

"I thought Eric was the only one to survive."

"You know what they say—only the good die young." Nora opened her drawer, pulled a bottle of gin out, and took a swig.

Lexi couldn't blame the woman. She had already suspected that the secretary was adding a little pick-me-up to her coffee. "Did no one warn this woman to stay away?"

Nora squinted at her as though the sentence she had delivered was received at a much slower speed. "Nope."

Her eyebrows raised. "Why not?"

The woman burped. "Sheesbish."

"Excuse me?"

The secretary repeated herself with a nod of the head on each word. "She's. A. Bitch."

Lexi nodded. "I thought you said that."

"Where is Millicent now?"

Nora giggled. She leaned forward. "She's on her way up." She giggled again.

The sorcerer had a bad feeling. "What have you done?"

"This controls the elevators." The secretary opened the top drawer of her desk and withdrew a keyring with a little black box set with a moonstone. "She won't get here until I press this."

"Nora, how long has she been in the elevator?"

"Oh…a couple of hours." The woman snorted before she thunked her face heavily onto the desk and began to snore.

"Nora?" Lexi shook her. "Nora."

Her efforts brought no response.

She thought for a moment. With Nora being as stressed as she was, she needed a more reliable conspirator and wondered if this Millicent might do the job.

With a frown, she put a hand on Nora's shoulder and drew the woman's drunken consciousness into her dimensional pocket. She stretched her on her sofa and threw a blanket over her. Next, she focused on the secretary's body and her unhealing scar. She spoke her will and in an instant, stood next to the woman at her desk.

Damn it.

She tried again, then opened her eyes. The world was sideways and she shook her head. She raised her head from the desk and grimaced when she realized she was inside Nora's body.

Lexi had never been this drunk in her life. "Dear God!" She swayed and was moments from throwing up into the woman's drawer but managed a clarity spell which removed most of the effects of the alcohol.

Thank you for that one, Scott.

She glanced at the button and pressed it before she put the gin bottle into the drawer and closed it.

Moments later, the doors to the elevator opened and a distressed-looking woman stumbled out. She stared across the office for a moment, then disappeared.

"Shit. Where did she go?" Lexi sighed. There hadn't been much point to all that effort. She poked around in Nora's desk and flipped through the diary. It looked like everything was in code. She was about to vacate the woman's body when Millicent appeared in front of the desk.

"I've been in that goddam elevator for two hours. Two hours." Her voice was a screech. "I couldn't translocate out and I almost disgraced myself."

"Good heavens. It must be on the fritz. I'll call Maintenance." Lexi tried to sound like Nora when she was being professional.

The woman looked around at the silent offices. "Where is everyone?"

She checked Nora's clock. "It's after ten. Almost everyone has gone home."

"What about Gordon? He never goes home before midnight and I've been trying to contact him for days."

"Ah! There have been some changes at the top. A hostile takeover, I suppose you'd call it." She smoothed Nora's hair. "In fact. It might be wise for you to hop into the elevator and take another vacation."

"A hostile takeover? What nonsense. I want to speak to Gordon."

"I'm afraid he didn't make it."

"Are you saying he's—"

"It was an extremely hostile takeover."

The woman opened her mouth to speak several times but simply closed it again repeatedly. She leaned on Nora's desk and looked a little pale.

Lexi had never seen someone literally clutch their pearls before. She slid the bottom drawer open, retrieved the gin, and offered it to the horrified woman. For a moment, it looked as though Millicent would take it but instead, she frowned and shook her head. The young sorcerer shrugged and put the bottle away.

"What about the rest of the board? Who's leading the council?"

"Millicent, we missed you." Eric spoke loudly from the end of the hallway as he walked beside Azatoth.

Lexi looked at him. His tone hadn't been friendly. She guessed he was saying *we killed everyone else but you weren't here*. She had tried to warn the woman but it was too late now. As he approached, she glanced at the folders in his hands but couldn't see what they were. She risked a glance at Azatoth but the demon's attention seemed to be on the frosty atmosphere between Eric and Millicent. It was clear from her face that she was thinking something that delighted her and probably wouldn't delight the others.

"Eric. What a surprise." Millicent tried to gain some ground and strode to the door of Azatoth's office before the other two reached it. She turned to Azatoth. "Two coffee—" She froze as her mage senses caught up with her panic. Lexi watched the woman twitch in shock as she realized she was addressing a demon.

Eric indicated for her to continue. "After you, Millicent."

"Nora, three coffees please." Azatoth closed the office door without even looking at her secretary. Lexi exhaled.

She raced as best she could in Nora's heels to the little kitchen and sniffed the coffee pot. It would do, she decided and hurried to find three mugs. She poured the drinks and placed them on the tray with sugar and cream, then tottered to the office with the tray and tapped on the door before she let herself in.

Eric and Millicent were both on their feet in front of the desk. Azatoth had her feet on it and a delighted grin on her face. Lexi stepped to the small meeting table and removed the items carefully from the tray while she cast a glance every few seconds at the other three.

Millicent glared at Eric. "The very idea is utterly abhorrent."

"Please, my lady," he beseeched the demon. "If I could bond with anyone else—anyone." He glanced at the angry mage. "Literally."

Azatoth leaned forward. "I've caught up on the gossip I know you two had a relationship back in the day. I'm sure you'll get on famously and we have considerable work to do."

Lexi moved to the door and was about to step through it when the demon glanced up.

"Thank you, *Nora*," she called.

Lexi turned, nodded once, and left the room. She closed the door behind her, sat at the secretary's desk, and gulped. She didn't like the way the demon had said Nora's name. It felt like she could see straight through her disguise. Both relieved and disappointed, she recalled that the wards on the office made eavesdropping impossible and decided it was time to go.

She was about to move the administrator into her own body when the door opened and Azatoth peeked out. The demon gazed at her secretary for a moment with her head tilted before she laughed. "Marvelous. Your antics do amuse me." On that somewhat open-ended statement, she withdrew into the office and closed the door.

Lexi sighed. There was no doubting it. Azatoth knew it was her. She was disappointed in herself and it simply reinforced the fact that it was time to get out of there.

She entered her dimensional pocket and pulled Nora out.

The secretary stood in a panic and looked around. "What happened? What did you do?"

"There's gratitude." She raised an eyebrow. "You were sloshed and I've been covering for you." She pointed at the door. "She's in there with Eric and Millicent."

Nora had the decency to blush. They both glanced up as the executive conference room door opened down the hall. A tall, thin man with ginger hair and beard stepped out and walked toward them.

Nora spoke louder than necessary. "I can take it from here, Lexi."

The man stared openly at the sorcerer. "So, you're the dark mage legacy." He gazed at her face. "The resemblance is uncanny."

She wondered if he was an idiot. "Uncanny? It's fairly standard for identical twins."

His face darkened.

Thankfully, Nora distracted him. "Ian, how can I help you, dear?"

He continued to stare at Lexi and very deliberately licked his lips, then turned to Nora. "We're all set up. Is she in there?"

"She's finishing up, I think. I'll call through when she's ready."

Ian turned to face Lexi and studied the full length of her body before he returned to the conference room.

She couldn't help herself. Before he'd closed the door behind him, she turned Nora and said loudly, "Creepy much?"

When they heard the door click shut, the secretary closed her eyes and sighed. "You don't want to be on his bad side. You truly don't."

"I could take him."

"You think you could take Ian Baskerville? Sweetie, you wouldn't see it coming." The woman jerked as though she realized that she'd said something she shouldn't.

Lexi pretended to have not noticed. She opened her mouth to comment but Nora shooed her away from the desk. "Please, go home."

She headed to the elevator and wondered if she should have simply left the woman drunk at her desk. "Fine, I'm going." She waved her ID at the wall and the doors opened immediately. With a tired frown, she stepped in, turned to the secretary, and called, "But if I spend one second longer in this elevator than I have to, I'll shove that little button—" The elevator doors closed but she felt she'd gotten her point across.

Lexi left the building and wandered down the street to the coffee shop. The door opened as she reached it and a man stood aside to let her in. She smiled politely. "No thanks."

His brow drew down in puzzlement as she'd clearly been about to enter. With a shrug, he exited and walked away and she allowed the door to close behind him. When it clicked closed, she stepped forward and opened it to reveal Dolores' apartment. A glance along the street revealed that the stranger waited to cross the street and watched her with an offended expression on his face.

"Oops!" She entered the apartment and closed the door behind her.

Dolores looked up from a book. "What's wrong, dear?"

"Merely one of those awkward door crossings."

Scott grinned. "I told you last time what you should do. Just say, 'Thank you.' Then walk in and buy me a cinnamon roll. Easy."

Lexi sat at the table and glanced at the little fae woman. "You know, one of these days, Azatoth will want to come to the coffee shop with me, and we'll both end up in your living room."

Dolores slipped a pressed flower between the pages of her book and put it down. "It's all about intent. I want you and only you to walk through the fae door. If you arrive with that creature, you'll enter the coffee shop, trust me."

Scott pushed a large coffee toward Lexi. "How's work?"

She put her head into her hands. "She made me go on another job with her. It was a werewolf and now, it's werechunks. Then we went for waffles."

"Aww! I love waffles." He pouted.

A mental eye-roll wasn't quite as satisfying as the real thing. "Should I call you next time? You can come along with the psychopathic demon and me for post-evisceration treats."

The mage screwed his face up. "Maybe not."

"Something interesting happened, though. A member of the original council arrived—a woman called Millicent. I think Azatoth is forcing her and Eric to bond."

Scott frowned. He had strong feelings about forced bondings. "Why?"

Lexi shrugged. "I have no idea, but that brings the new council to thirteen again." She thought for a moment. "And in other news, she's planned a surprise for me tomorrow, so I doubt I'll be sleeping tonight. Oh, and she wants me to start calling her Az."

"Az." Dolores raised an eyebrow.

"Or Azzy." She drew air quotes.

The fae woman walked to the window and looked out onto the lake. "Maybe she's lonely."

Lexi's face hardened. "She can make nice with Eric and Millicent."

"They're both too easy. They want power." The woman turned to her. "You, on the other hand, are a mystery to her. If she truly has no idea that Alicia's consciousness is still alive, she must wonder why you haven't simply run off and hidden somewhere. I think she's intrigued."

The young sorcerer sipped her coffee. "Speaking of running off and hiding, how's Bryan?"

Dolores shrugged. "I have no idea."

She was frustrated that her sister's husband and mage had chosen now of all times to disappear and go find himself. "You don't? I assumed you knew where he was."

"I'm sure he'll return when he's ready." The fae didn't seem concerned.

Lexi had tried for weeks to find out where Bryan was. She was convinced the woman knew more than she was letting on.

"I think I finally met another member of the cabal tonight—a creepy guy called Ian Baskerville. He had…" The words trailed to a halt at the two horrified faces in front of her. "What?"

Scott looked from Lexi to Dolores. "I thought he was executed years ago."

The woman's mouth settled into a thin line. Finally, she responded. "He was imprisoned in The Hollows for life without hope of parole. I need to contact someone about this."

Tension radiated from Dolores as she paced. "What did he do?" Lexi asked.

Scott looked awkwardly into the corner for a moment. "Mass murder if I remember correctly."

"Fifty-three fae," the woman added. "He ate them. Which, you'll be happy to learn, is now against the Kindred accords thanks to the twelfth amendment."

"There was a time when it wasn't?" She began to experience the horror her friends felt.

Dolores stopped pacing. "It didn't become illegal for humans to eat fae folk until the fifties."

She screwed her face up in disgust and considered it for a moment. "Dolores, be careful who you speak to about this. I don't know how long he's been out of The Hollows but people high up must already know. Making a noise will only put a target on your back." She turned to Scott. "Are you ready to head home?"

The mage nodded and picked his bag up.

Working at Kindred HQ gave Lexi some privileges, and one of them was being able to translocate directly into Las Vegas. She and the mage opened the front door of Dolores' apartment into the diner in Boulder City and she took hold of Scott's shoulder and translocated to the condo.

CHAPTER THREE

Eric rolled his sleeve down. Through their new bond, he felt with relief that Millicent was as humiliated as he was—probably more so given that he'd abandoned her for someone else when they were younger and they were now forced together again all these years later. He could see in his peripheral vision that her cheeks were red.

Relieved that the ritual was over, he turned his gaze to the files he'd deposited on Azatoth's desk.

The demon pressed the intercom button on her desk phone. "Are they ready?"

Nora's voice squawked in response. "Ready and waiting in the conference room."

Millicent moved toward the door, but Eric remained where he was.

His boss raised an eyebrow. "Is there something else I can help you with?"

"The Braxton girl. Is it safe to have her here? You do know she's been snooping around?"

Azatoth smiled. "I know. Don't worry about it."

"She's already tried to kill you once."

"And yet, here I am. She's no match for me. In her current state, I could crush her like a bug. Speaking of Lexi, how is your investigation going? Have you found out anything about the mage who sired her?"

A sheen of sweat prickled at his hairline. Azatoth was known to take failure very badly. "I've hit a wall, I'm afraid. I haven't been able to find a shred of evidence that other dark sorcerers exist anywhere."

Millicent gasped. "Dark sorcerers?"

Eric turned to see her jaw hanging open in shock.

"Eric will catch you up shortly." The demon lifted a folder from the pile. "This is thin."

"It's the mother's file. It confirms what you already know. They suspected some mage got her pregnant and didn't want to face the music, so he wiped her mind."

She opened the folder. "And you people call me a demon." Her gaze moved over the first of two pages and she drew a finger down the page as she read. "A unit in Los Angeles, the Camerons, took her in but she never worked as a legacy or became matched with a mage again, merely looked after her daughters until she died of encephalitis in 1996. That was sloppy—how could they let her die of such a mundane illness? Surely it was within the mage's ability to cure it."

"It would have been but because her cognitive functions had never fully recovered, they missed the usual cues. And, according to the medical report—which is the next folder on the pile—by the time they realized what was wrong with her, the spells that should have worked didn't because—"

Azatoth had turned to the second page. "Because it was caused by an unusual strain of a virus."

Eric looked startled. "Yes. How—"

The demon leaned back and grinned. "Well, well, well." She put the file down, open on a picture of Lexi's mother, and smiled at her two subordinates as she stood. "You have your first mission as a team. Send someone to that unit."

He was confused. "The reports say they knew nothing about where she came from."

Azatoth walked around her desk and stopped at the door. "I don't care where she came from. I want to know exactly where she was found and what her first memory was. She must have told someone. And I want to know where she went. Find out who her friends were, her confidants—are they still alive? If so, send a counselor… No, scratch that. It should be someone from the inner circle…send Francesco. I want every thread of every memory of Elizabeth Cameron harvested before the end of the day. Of particular interest are any trips she made to Las Vegas." The demon walked out of her office, then stopped and turned. "And about the Braxton girl. She's exactly where I need her to be."

Millicent stepped toward Nora. "Get me the overseers office."

Eric stayed the secretary's hand. "The Braxton girl works in the overseer's office. I'll contact Francesco directly."

The mage frowned. "I see. Then let's head to the archives and find out where we're sending him."

She paused before she stepped into the elevator.

He frowned. "Is there a problem?"

"Nothing." She sighed, stepped in, and waved her ID to make the buttons appear before she selected the archives.

The elevator began its descent but Millicent held a hand up and it slowed to a halt. She faced her companion. "They're all gone?"

Eric sighed. "The whole council. I'm surprised you didn't notice your legacy's demise through the link."

"I used a proxy. I wasn't interested in what he was doing when I wasn't around." She tapped a polished fingernail on her cheek. "Is she truly that strong?"

He nodded. "Surely you sensed that."

"What I sensed was off the charts. It confused me. But you're okay with all this?"

"This is happening." He shrugged as if to indicate that what he felt about it was irrelevant. "This is our reality now. What I'd like to do is run, but I can't think of anywhere she wouldn't find me. And I saw what happened to the others."

Millicent's face twisted as she chewed the inside of her cheek. It was a nervous habit he had always thought made her look simultaneously ugly and cute when she was young. "I assume your new charges are under threat from her."

His jaw tightened. "They're already gone."

"Oh, I see. And why is she interested in Alexa Braxton? She's the runaway legacy, isn't she? How is it that she is now working at HQ?"

"I guess you've never seen her. She had a twin sister, Alicia, who is currently serving as our new mistress's vessel. And for some reason, Lexi is now a dark sorcerer." Eric pinched the bridge of his nose. "Which I can't even begin to fathom. Let's get on with this. People who displease Azatoth have a habit of turning up in pieces."

Millicent nodded, waved a hand, and the elevator continued. She turned to her companion. "What is the demon planning?"

He shrugged. "She's searching for a portal called the demon gate which is somewhere in Las Vegas."

The woman's eyes bulged. "She wants to bring hordes of demons here? That doesn't sound survivable."

"She could do that by herself already. Maybe she wants to go back or she has a boyfriend over there. I don't know. Honestly, I simply want to be alive at the end of all this. If I were you, I'd start thinking the same or this will be a very short partnership."

The mage nodded and straightened her suit jacket. She turned to face the elevator doors as they opened. "I'm sorry about your young charges."

Eric raised an eyebrow. Surprisingly, he felt through their bond that she was sincere.

They walked along the hall and Millicent flicked her wrist to make the door to the archives fly open ahead of her. "Devon?"

An elderly man appeared from the stacks. "Miss Millicent. How may I be of service?"

"We need unit records for the Cameron unit in Los Angeles."

"Years?"

Eric took a seat at one of the study tables. "1990 to 1996."

The old man shuffled away and returned surprisingly quickly with the large books loaded onto a cart. "Call if you need me."

As the elderly man left them to their search, Eric pulled the first two books onto the table and slid one of them across to Millicent. They flipped through the unit's records for a few minutes until he looked at the pile of books and sighed. "This will take forever."

She nodded her agreement. "Can you put all the books onto the table please?"

He did as she asked without voicing his reflexive question. She stretched her arms over them and whispered, "Elizabeth."

The books flipped open to the first mention of the woman. They took three books each and checked the entry. After a few seconds on each one, the book went to the next.

A few minutes later, Millicent halted the procedure. "I see numerous mentions of another family member—Susan."

Eric nodded. "I see that too. It seems they were best friends."

Millicent called the old man again. "Susan Cameron. Journals, 1990 to 1996, please."

After the archiver had deposited the requested records with them, Eric picked up the 1990 journal. Like all Kindred journals, it was made up of separate pages that were filled out at the same time as the reports and sent to the archives. The one in his hand jumped to the first mention of Elizabeth. After a few seconds of skimming it, he looked up in surprise. "Did you know Caleb's father was the Grandfather of California?"

Without glancing up, Millicent nodded. "Of course."

His lip twitched. "Did you know Caleb was the leader of the cabal?"

Her eyes bulged. "I thought the cabal was a myth."

"The day you saw me visiting Gordon, he had replaced Caleb at the head of both the cabal and the council. He invited me to join the cabal." Eric enjoyed a brief flash of envy through the bond until he realized that she would be equally able to feel his smugness.

She shrugged. "That was the day I left for Aruba."

"Also the day Azatoth joined us."

The woman sighed. "Great timing for me. Shitty timing for you."

He grimaced. "We're still alive," he muttered and continued to read.

The Grandfather came to visit today. He brought his son along. I don't like him. They told us we're getting a new legacy. She's pregnant and it sounds like she's a simpleton. They'd better not put her in my room.

He skimmed further into the journal.

Liz had the babies today. Two girls and they're beautiful. She's calling them Alexa and Alicia. I'm so excited I'm going to be an aunty.

Eric turned to his new mage. "Have you ever read your journals?"

Millicent looked up. "Good Lord, no. Why would I want to do that? I know I've been counseled and I trust it was with good reason."

She moved her journal closer to the light. "This is interesting —from 1992. *Lexi crushed Jeff's hand today and broke three of his fingers. She's only two years old. I've never seen a kid so strong.* Then later that month, *The Grandfather visited with his revolting son Caleb again and he asked me on a date. It was all I could do to not throw up.*

She looked up "I know how she feels. Caleb was revolting." She turned to the pages and continued to read. *"He's interested in the twins. He thinks his father should take them away and experiment on them. There isn't one member of this family, me included, who wouldn't run him through with a sword if he tried it. If Liz had been here, she'd probably have done it. The Grandfather seemed embarrassed by him and rightly so."*

Half an hour later, they stood and gazed at the same journal.

"Do you think this is it?" Millicent asked.

"It's the only mention of a journey to Las Vegas. 'I'd have preferred to go to the bars on the Strip but Liz had her own agenda.' I wonder where they went." Eric tapped the page. "If this isn't what she wants, it probably doesn't exist."

Millicent dropped her journal onto the desk. "Let's check the staff database for a current location and we can find Francesco."

CHAPTER FOUR

Sam's mouth watered as the pungent aroma of the corpse drifted from the house to his position at the garden gate of the attractive house in Echo Park, Los Angeles. While others might have turned away in revulsion, Sam's gait lengthened to bring him to the front door in a few strides. The security light burst into life and momentarily blinded his already milky white eyes.

His colleague, Krish, had to jog to catch up. A face appeared, distorted by the obscured glass. The door opened and they were dragged inside the unassuming house.

He faced a dangerous-looking uniformed man who studied him with curiosity. The young zombie deliberately kept his gaze away from any identifying insignia on the uniform. As always, he didn't need to know which organization their client worked for and it didn't matter. Another man peeked out from the kitchen at the end of the hallway.

Maybe zombies make him nervous.

Krish closed the door behind him. "I'm Krish and this is Sam."

"You can call me Bill." He directed his attention to Krish, the human of the two. "It's upstairs. How long does it need?" He darted a sidelong glance at Sam.

The smell was stronger now and two distinct smells meant two bodies.

The zombie answered for himself. "It depends on how many. You said there was one. I smell two."

Bill stared at him, then shook his head. "I'm sorry. They said you could speak but I didn't know you'd be so... I've never seen that before."

Sam delivered his educational line to Bill, even though he would probably never see the man again. "My sister and I were reanimated with witch magic, not voodoo." That was the limit of his explanation. He could have added more but there was no point as he was simply there to do a job.

The man glanced at the stairs. "Your job is to clean the guy up. You can leave the woman. I thought there would be two of you."

"My sister's unwell."

Bill's lip twitched. He clearly found the thought of a sick zombie amusing.

"Nothing serious, I hope."

"No. Merely someone she ate." Sam walked past him to the stairs. "I should get this done in around two hours if I'm not disturbed."

The crime scene cleaning zombie headed up the stairs without a backward glance.

He heard Bill's steps behind him and wondered if the guy had the stones to follow him into the room.

The man's body lay on the floor and the back of his head had been crushed. A woman lay dead on the bed. Her eyes had been burned away. Sam looked up to where Bill stood in the open doorway and held the door handle. He was rooted to the spot as they often were, unable to turn away.

Sam felt generous. He decided to help him decide and settled himself next to the head. "I like to start with the eyes." He positioned his fingers as though about to pluck the corpse's eyes out. The door slammed with the man on the other side.

He turned the head. Bill would never know that he'd lied about the eyes. He preferred to start with the brain.

Thirty seconds later, the young zombie straightened in alarm. Something was wrong and he realized with horror that he was getting a vision.

Oh no! This guy was a mage. It's too late now, though, and it's best to let it pass.

He leaned against the bed and the vision came. It was confusing as these things often were and ran backward.

The mage's last feeling was the back of his skull blowing off. It was kind of a relief after the build-up of pressure. His last thought was of a girl he had a crush on when he was thirteen. Before that, he fought for his life, but he was a counselor in his sixties. His name had been Francesco. He'd never felt comfortable in the field and wasn't built for it. Before working at Kindred HQ, he'd spent thirty years working for the Grandfathers of Michigan, counseling unit members after difficult missions.

His memories flickered over something called the cabal. Francesco regretted ever getting involved with it, but Caleb had promised him power beyond his wildest dreams. He recognized the mage who was killing him. He'd sat in meetings with him and nodded greetings in the hallways.

In those few seconds, Sam thought he was experiencing the last moments of one of the victims. He was wrong. A moment later, he experienced what had happened before he was killed. The mage was blackening the woman's eyes so their reflection couldn't be used to identify his face. He watched helplessly knowing Francesco was there to kill her. She sat up when he placed his hands on her head.

Sam's head spun. That part of the vision had flashed through his mind in three seconds but now, the memories came in the correct order and seemed to be the threads of memory Francesco had taken from the woman's mind.

Her name was Susan and she remembered the day the strange woman had joined her unit. She had appeared to be in her twenties and was three months pregnant with no recollection of her name or where she had come from.

They gave her the name Elizabeth. Her memories had been so ruthlessly extracted that she didn't recognize the world around her and she had to relearn almost everything. She had been a wonderful mother to the twin girls but she rarely left the house. Susan recalled the Grandfather visiting because of a strange phenomenon around the girls' legacy abilities.

More memories of Liz flashed past, some faster than others depending on how relevant they had been to Francesco's search.

The woman had become animated one day as they watched a show featuring Las Vegas. She turned to Susan and shook her arm. "I want to go there. Can we go there?"

The two women drove to Las Vegas but Liz wasn't interested in the bright lights or the casinos. She wanted to travel to the outer edges of the city. It was like she'd been looking for something but couldn't identify what it was. They never returned to Las Vegas and within a year, Liz had died. The Grandfather of California returned and arranged for Liz's twin daughters to be taken to different units.

In Francesco's memories again, Sam watched as the mage waited for the woman to open the door. When she did, she smiled and recognized him as a mage. "Susan Cameron? I'm Francesco. We spoke on the phone."

"Please, come in. I haven't been in the field for years but I'm happy to help in any way I can."

The memories went back further. Sam saw Francesco meeting with a man and woman. The man had a scar across his eye which had turned it eerily white—even whiter than his. The woman was thin with a pinched face and dark hair pulled back severely. They asked him to visit Susan, return with memories about Liz and Las Vegas, and to leave no loose ends.

Sam shook his head. The vision was ending and he was aware that only a minute had passed.

He stared in disgust at the mage who had extracted information from the woman, then murdered her. All for a secret she didn't even know was buried in her mind, but he too was murdered before he could tell anyone.

The zombie knew that Bill worked for very scary people. As soon as the uniformed mook had his information, Sam and Krish wouldn't walk out of this house again. He knew he had to act fast. The man was still outside the door. He could smell his stale sweat, even over the odor of the bodies. The zombie moved quietly to the woman's body and got to work removing her brain. When he was done, he stuffed it into the mage's head. It was whole and looked untouched. He turned the woman's head to hide the gaping hole he'd made in the back of it, then grasped the handle and pulled the door open. "He's got sepsis. I can't do it."

Bill blocked his way. "You have to do it. Get on with it."

Sam pointed at the corpse. "His blood's infected. I can't finish the job. You said he was fresh."

"He is fresh. He was only killed an hour ago."

"Then he was already ill. I doubt he'd have lasted a couple of days."

Bill drew a gun out and leveled it at him. "I'm on the clock here. You have to get the job done."

A gun clicked but it wasn't Bill's. Krish stood behind the hulking man. "Do we have a problem here?"

The uniformed man glanced toward the stairs but didn't risk calling his colleague from the kitchen. He held his hand up with the gun dangling from a finger. Krish took it out of his hand.

"I need to check the body," the man protested. "If what he says is true, you can go. But if he's lying, you don't want to find out who I work for."

Ideally, Sam would have preferred to simply kill the guy. He watched as Bill stepped to the body and pushed the head to the side with his foot to expose the cracked skull and the brain within. Bill nodded.

Sam and Krish headed down the stairs.

The other man came out of the kitchen. "What's going on?"

"Let them go. Call the witch. There's more than one way to skin a cat," Bill called from the stairs.

Krish shook his head with a look of disappointment. He dropped the man's gun onto the lawn as they returned to the car.

"What the hell is going on?" he whispered. "If there was sepsis in that body you'd have smelled it from the car."

"Let's get the hell out of here." Sam walked to the passenger side while Krish climbed into the driving seat.

His gaze flickered constantly between Krish securing his seatbelt and the door of the house. His companion started the car as the front door flew open.

"Drive now. *Now*." Sam's urgency was all the motivation Krish needed.

"What the fuck was that about?" the man demanded as they raced to the end of the road and away.

"That was about him discovering I'd pulled the brain out of the woman's head and stuffed it into the man's."

"And why would you do that?"

"Bill intended to kill us. Well, probably only you straight away. Me, he needed for information. Then he would have killed me."

Krish stared at him. "The body was a supe?"

The zombie nodded. "A mage."

His companion's gaze flicked between the road, the rearview mirror, and Sam. "What did you learn from him?"

"I don't think you want to know. If the inside of that room is any indication, knowing will get you killed."

Krish shook his head. "Then don't tell me. What next?"

"We need to pick Adele up and get out of town." He thought of the mage who had killed Francesco. "I might know someone who can help. If anything happens to me, you need to make Adele your first priority."

His companion studied his dashboard for a moment with a frown. "Okay, but I need gas."

Sam bought a copy of the National Enquirer for Adele. His sister loved the trashy magazine and he hoped it might distract her from the situation. At the checkout, he ignored the strange looks the woman was giving him. He'd been told many times that sunglasses at night were so eighties, but she'd freak if she saw his eyes. Quickly, he paid for the gas and the magazine but before he turned away, he caught the smell of something sour through the small window beside her. He glanced at Krish seated in the car, his wide-eyed gaze on him.

He knew he wasn't the kind of guy to bail on a friend without giving him a heads-up. The sidelights on the car flashed briefly. Sam barely nodded.

As the cashier turned to take his receipt from the printer, he signaled his friend to get the hell out of there.

It wouldn't be so easy for him as he was now in possession of information that wasn't sensitive, it was explosive—or maybe apocalyptic was more appropriate. He couldn't let himself get caught and wondered if he could escape out the back. "Is there a bathroom?"

"Through there." The woman pointed.

Sam walked along the hallway. As he reached the rear exit, the smell of Bill's sour sweat hung heavy on the other side of the door.

He heard the buzzer indicate that someone had entered

through the front door. Quickly, he stepped into the bathroom and grimaced at the bars on the windows.

The handle on the back door pressed down as Sam skipped across the hallway to the small office. Again, bars on the window denied him an escape route.

I'm trapped!

exi stepped out of the elevator onto Kindred's executive floor with a tray and three coffees. Nora was at her desk and looked prim and proper as she talked to three young men.

Thank God she looks sober.

"But we booked it and it's on the system. Every second Tuesday morning for the year," a young man whined.

The secretary leaned forward. "Didn't you get the memo? The executive conference room is not available for bookings for the foreseeable future."

The sorcerer glanced along the hall. *I wonder what's happening in there.*

Undeterred by Nora's firm expression, the whiner persisted. "Where are we supposed to find another room?"

The woman removed her glasses and placed them on the desk in front of her. She leaned forward with her elbows on the desk and laced her fingers to give the young man—who took a step back—her full attention. "You are standing in a magical building with over a thousand stories. Look for one."

The three milled around as though expecting her to change her mind. She gave them a final stern glance before she placed her glasses on her face. The motion was dismissive and they chose to move rather than argue.

Nora lifted her desk phone and dialed. "Remove executive floor access for everyone below Management M3 level…no, M4." She replaced the phone and sighed.

Lexi walked to the desk and passed a coffee to her. "How are you feeling today?"

The secretary lowered her face into her hands and looked appropriately ashamed. "Thank you for what you did yesterday, whatever it was. I'm so sorry for being in that condition. It all got too much for me. For the last few weeks, I've been in the habit of taking two slugs of gin with breakfast before coming into work. Yesterday, I simply didn't stop." She sipped her coffee.

"Don't worry about it. I couldn't let her kill you. It would probably have been my job to drag your body away and I don't know where you've put them all." She decided this might be an opportunity to get intel out of the woman. "Well, either my job or that guy who sometimes brings the reports up." She added casually, "What's his name?" It was clumsy and intentionally so.

Nora raised an eyebrow and leaned back with her coffee in hand. "Sebastian. Are you interested?"

Lexi's first instinct was to screw her face up and say, "God, no!" Instead, she allowed a small smile to play across her lips. "Maybe. I've only seen him a couple of times and never had the chance to talk to him. I thought he looked quite cute. Then that grumpy guy started bringing the reports up and that was that." She shrugged and sighed.

"Would you like me to set a date up for the two of you? He works in the accounts department."

She grimaced to cover her delight at having finally gotten something out of the woman. "Eww, seriously? An accountant?"

Nora laughed. "He's not an accountant. I think he's a data analyst."

Lexi screwed her face up. She had everything she needed to find the man. "Nope. No thanks. I'm bored already."

The woman shrugged. "I suppose it's just as well. I'm not sure how you'd get on with dating someone who's met the boss. You're identical to her and I'm sure Sebastian pees himself when he goes in there."

The sorcerer glanced toward Azatoth's office door. "I thought we all did that." She looked at the assistant. "Should I start sending your coffees in the internal mail?"

Nora looked puzzled.

Lexi added, "I don't know what level I am but I doubt it's M4."

"You have executive level E3 clearance so you're fine. Do you even check your wage slips?"

She stared at her in surprise. "I get paid?"

The woman groaned. "Yes. Very well."

"Cool. I might go shopping at the weekend." Lexi looked at the door to Azatoth's office again. "I've never imagined the day-to-day life of a high-level demon walking the earth but I wouldn't have guessed this."

Nora remained silent. Every time she mentioned Azatoth, the woman would purse her lips and say nothing. She wondered if there was any point in bringing her a cup of coffee every morning.

If she doesn't start opening up soon, I'll take away her latte privileges.

A little frustrated, she tried again. "Meetings and data reports. Maybe that's what hell on earth looks like." She shrugged as though she'd come to the end of that train of thought and turned to her companion. "She said she has a surprise lined up for me today. Do you have any idea what that might be?"

The secretary's gaze returned to her screen. "I'm afraid I can't discuss that."

"Come on. One clue is all I'm asking. You'd tell me if I needed to go hide in the fae realms, wouldn't you?"

Nora looked at her with an eyebrow raised. "I think you're about the only person on this planet with a free pass." She looked past Lexi and lowered her voice. "Well, you and—"

"Alexa. Don't you have work to do?" Footsteps sounded in the hallway behind her. Eric approached accompanied by someone in heels that clicked an irritating staccato rhythm on the hard floor.

Lexi allowed the secretary to see her eyes roll dramatically before she turned to the Kindred council member. Millicent walked beside him. It seemed like they'd worked out their differences. "Hey, Millicent. You're not dead."

The woman's eyes bulged. She'd clearly been unprepared for the resemblance but she recovered quickly and bristled. "I don't believe we've met."

The young sorcerer berated herself inwardly. *Damn! That's right. I was cosplaying Nora yesterday.* She wondered frantically how to get out of the hole she seemed to have dug for herself when Nora interrupted.

"Eric, Wu has called eleven times this morning. He asked if you can call him."

Millicent frowned. "Who's that?"

He turned to her. "Francesco's legacy."

Lexi noticed they shared a frown but it didn't seem likely that anyone would explain any further.

Eric checked his watch and took a step toward Azatoth's office.

Nora glanced at him. "She's not in there. She asked me to tell you she'll see you at the eleven am meeting." The secretary picked up a blank ID card from her desk and turned to Lexi. "Show me your ID."

She held it out and Nora tapped it with the card she held. A brief surge of energy moved from one card to the other.

The assistant spoke to her as she turned her screen. "You should hurry for your nine-thirty. The elevator will take you straight there." She glanced at Azatoth's beverage still in the cardboard holder on her desk. "Take that with you."

Lexi realized the woman had given her a heads-up that she was going to meet with the demon. It was the first she had heard about a nine-thirty meeting. She usually spent a few minutes in Azatoth's office before she left to see what was happening in her department and water the plant Scott had given to her.

She hurried to the wall, waved her ID, and the elevator doors appeared immediately and opened.

"Hold the doors." Millicent began to walk quickly to the elevator and Eric followed.

The dark sorcerer took a step back to make space for them, but she knew the woman was merely curious about where she was headed. She looked at Nora who watched her from beyond the two who approached. The woman reached quickly into her drawer and retrieved the little black button. With a wink and a malicious grin, she pressed it and the doors slammed shut an inch from Millicent's nose with such ferocity, it generated a strong gust of wind. The mage's loud squeak receded as the elevator descended.

Lexi wondered how long she would be in the elevator but a moment later, it slowed to a stop and the doors opened. The sign ahead read *Learning and Development*. She paused and hoped she wouldn't have to sit through a Health and Safety induction video.

After a short walk along a hallway, she stepped through the only door. It bore the sign *Training Room* and she stopped at the threshold of an impossibly large room. It reminded her of Phil's giant maze but was empty. Warily, she looked both left and right and noticed walls way off in the distance. She looked ahead and her gaze settled on a desk—one she was sure hadn't been there when she entered.

With a frown, she twisted to face the door but it was gone. When she turned again it was to face a grizzled-looking man who leaned against the desk holding two cups. She looked at her hands. They were positioned as though the cups were still in them. A little confused, she relaxed her arms and looked questioningly at him.

He put the cups on the desk. "You won't need refreshments quite yet, little girl." He sounded European. Somehow the accent made "little girl" sound even more condescending.

Lexi frowned. "Where's Azatoth?"

"That's not your concern. You're here to learn."

"Learn what? And who are you?"

"I'm Sven. But let's talk about you, shall we? You're a dark mage with no concept of what it means. You don't know how to use your powers and don't even have a grasp of what they are."

"And you do?"

He sneered. "Did you think you were the only one?"

She thought about that for a moment. "Honestly, yes." She didn't know if he was telling the truth as he was masking his true nature.

The man opened his mouth as though to respond but leapt toward her and a katana appeared in his hand. When he stepped back, she felt the sting of a cut on her cheek and the warm trickle of blood.

/ CHAPTER SIX

Lexi's blade appeared in her hand as she put the other hand over her cheek and muttered an incantation to heal it. The man glanced at her blade. "I see you're not a complete dud."

She cracked her neck and smirked. "Those days are far behind me."

He lunged without warning and she parried, and the sound of their clashing blades rang out in the large space. They exchanged blows for several minutes and danced around one another.

Beads of sweat appeared at the edges of her hairline but she couldn't keep the grin from her face. She was enjoying this. The man had skills and she hadn't been properly tested in a long time. Sven hadn't even broken a sweat, though, and it annoyed her so she pushed harder.

In response, he began to speed his attacks up and she parried as best she could. Impossibly, he became increasingly faster until his movements were a blur she was unable to follow with her eyes. She fought back using pure instinct until his blade sliced down her arm.

Lexi grimaced at the sting but didn't risk a glance at the wound. She plunged on until he made a deep incision in her opposite shoulder and she stepped back in shock. The blurred man stood immediately and withdrew his sword and she thought it was over. She was wrong.

He thrust a hand out, muttered a word, and he and the room disappeared. She stood alone inside a black bubble and stared at herself reflected in its shiny, liquid-like surface. Acting reflexively, she whipped her blade and attempted to hack through the black wall that encircled her, but it offered no resistance. She tried to step through but it moved with her in every direction and remained a little beyond her reach. Finally, she risked an energy blast, half-afraid that it would bounce back and obliterate her. It sailed through her prison wall.

She growled in frustration, then noticed that the surface seemed closer than it had moments before. The bubble around her was shrinking.

What will happen when this shrinks completely? Will I suffocate?

Within a few seconds, it was close enough to touch. Lexi extended a hand, assuming it would go through the liquid prison as her katana had done. As she pressed against it, the surface wobbled and distorted her reflection. She stared as it drew closer and her reflection looked back in shock.

My reflection.

She spun to look around her. Everything was black and the floor and the bubble enclosed her.

How can I see my reflection if there's no light source? She sighed. *This isn't real.*

With a scowl, she placed her hand onto her unhealing scar and called to Scott's light energy which coursed through her. "Reveal the truth of this bubble."

It was still there and still shrinking. She felt a real sense of danger from it even though she knew it was a glamour of some kind. Unfortunately, she'd never experienced anything like it and it was nothing like a fae glamour or anything Scott had done.

Instinctively, she held her hand out and called her sulfur vial.

It appeared in her palm. The bubble wobbled and vibrated and she didn't even have to voice her command. She merely thought the words. *I've had enough of this.*

The illusion shattered.

She stood in the original room. It was smaller than it had been—the size of a large conference room, she decided.

Her opponent stood with the coffee cups in his hands. "Well done, lass."

Lexi put her katana away. She grasped her shoulder and arm to heal her wounds and thought about her ability to create illusions in other people's minds. Until now, she had associated it with her dark sorcery. "That illusion. Was it in my mind or in the room?"

He looked at the demolished desk. "Does it matter? I didn't anticipate that you'd throw an energy ball at it. If it had been real, you'd probably have blown yourself up."

Not quite trusting that he wouldn't attack her again, she kept the vial in her hand. As she stared at him, her vision blurred. It was like she suddenly saw double. There were two faces in front of her and she saw the face behind Sven's features. "It's you."

He took a sip out of Azatoth's cup and smiled.

The visage of the burly man disappeared and the body of her sister stood before her and held the other coffee cup out.

Lexi took it. "What was all this about?"

The demon answered her question with a question. "Do you think I was alone in wanting to escape those barren realms?"

She frowned, then shrugged. "I hadn't thought about it, honestly. We get demons from time to time—"

Her companion frowned and raised a hand. "Please don't insult me by putting me in the same category as those black, bug-eyed creatures. It's like me calling you an amoeba."

Azatoth paused as though deciding whether to continue. "I came through first so this world is mine and I don't intend to share it with others should they succeed in their efforts to enter this realm." She indicated their surroundings. "I am now the head of the most powerful magical organization here. I have an army at my disposal. But what I don't have is a competent dark mage."

Lexi pretended offense. "I'm standing right here."

"You are untrained. I'm changing that because I value you. I know you won't work with me if I remove Scott, so I'll teach you how to work around his light magic. Your precious bond will still be there but you should focus on using your innate abilities."

She looked away. "So I am the only dark mage."

"As far as I'm aware. I've wasted considerable time searching for others but I now believe you're the only one."

"So you think my father's dead. Do you know who he was?"

Azatoth shrugged. "I know you're the only dark sorcerer in this realm. Who knows? Perhaps he's in another."

Lexi didn't like the idea of the demon searching for her father. "But more than likely dead."

The demon paused for a moment. "Perhaps…probably."

She felt the entity had somehow given something away but couldn't see what it might be.

Azatoth took a sip of coffee. "What were you doing last night with Nora?"

Lexi rolled her eyes. "She was unwell. I tried to cover for her."

Her companion laughed. "Was she drunk again?"

There seemed to be no reason to not ask the question straight out. "You saw through the glamour but no one else did. Why?"

"That's another gift from your friend Scott. I recognized the light sorcery powering your spell. It isn't effective against everything but you're doing okay. Dark magic has seeped out of you almost since we met. You use it more than you realize and merely need to learn to harness it properly. Without a doubt, you have great potential."

She nodded, surprised the demon had answered her question, although she wondered if she was telling the truth.

Azatoth's cell rang, "Speak." She stood and listened for half a minute. "Who do you think started it? This sounds like we have another player in the game." Her gaze flashed to Lexi, then away. "Follow the new trail." She disconnected and began to walk toward the door. "I have another meeting. Who knew that world domination involved so many meetings?" She glanced at the writing on the side of the cup in her hand and turned to the sorcerer as she held it up. "Who's Damon?"

Lexi rolled her eyes. "It was supposed to be a joke. I said demon but the barista misheard."

Her sister's possessor frowned as she seemed to consider what she had said, then stepped out of the room. Her laughter could be heard as she walked down the hallway. She wondered if the demon believed her friendly act. It didn't matter, she decided. She wasn't the only one playing this game. *I value you...yeah, right!*

She thought about the workout she'd had and grinned as she readied herself to leave. When she realized how she felt, she caught herself and frowned.

I shouldn't be smiling but I can't help it. I feel elated at having used my magic successfully to see through Azatoth's glamours.

Encouraged, she smiled again—a much wider smile this time.

More fool Azatoth if she thinks I won't use my abilities against her.

Lexi left the room and waved her ID at the wall. She glanced from the silver unhealing scar on her outstretched arm to the light above her.

Strange...it must be the light; The silver looks a shade darker.

She headed to her office and checked the board. There were no new jobs that required her attention. A report had come in from her old unit, though, and she wondered how her pregnant sister Maggie was getting on as she opened the email app. She thought about the last time she'd seen them and the look of disappointment on all their faces, even little Bobby. She couldn't imagine what she might say to them, so she closed the app and forwarded the report to her team.

When she checked her cell, she saw a text had come from

Scott while she'd been in the training room. *Are you okay? I sensed that you were stressed and hurt.*

Touched by his concern, she tapped a hasty reply. *I was training. Had my ass kicked.*

Lexi leaned back and spun a shuriken between her fingers as she thought.

Sometimes, it's a real inconvenience when someone else knows how you're feeling all the time. That reminds me—Francesco.

She searched the database for him. *Not Found.* She checked the spelling, then tried Fran with an asterisk at the end which returned forty results, none of which were Francesco. It seemed there was no employee by that name.

Nothing," she muttered as she typed. "That's weird."

After a few more fruitless attempts, she walked to the elevator and ascended to the executive level. A powerfully built Asian man paced in front of Nora's desk.

The guy was irate and raised his voice. "What was so secret that he had to go to LA without me? I'm his legacy. I should have been there."

This must be Wu.

Nora looked up. "Not now, Lexi."

The dark sorcerer didn't want to leave. Aside from the fact that she wanted to find out more and that she was fairly certain Nora could handle herself, it didn't hurt to let the woman know she cared. Instead of turning away, she fixed her with a look of concern. "Are you sure you're okay?"

"I'm fine. I'll see you later." The secretary smiled but her tone was final. The man had stopped pacing and seemed to have calmed himself somewhat.

"Okay. You know where I am." Lexi stepped reluctantly into the elevator and descended again. When she reached her desk, she opened her laptop and decided to see where Wu was located in the building. She searched for his name. *Not found? But I saw him a minute ago.*

She had the horrible feeling the man would never be seen again.

This would give her something to tell Scott when she met him later in Dolores's apartment because she'd already decided it would be best to not tell him who was training her.

CHAPTER SEVEN

L exi and Scott arrived at the condo and he frowned.

Scott frowned. "Someone's here."

Her katana appeared in her hand.

"We're in here," Dick said from the living room.

She sniffed as she walked through the house and screwed her face up at a revolting smell. "Good God! What is that? It smells like something die—" She entered the living room and noticed the zombie seated on her couch.

The vampire sighed with relief when she walked into the room. "It's about time you got here. I thought I might have to call you at work."

"Why didn't you?" Lexi shrugged.

"What if the demon answered? I might not know the difference."

That drew a nod of agreement. He had a point. "I hope you haven't been waiting too long." She glanced at a young man seated quietly in the chair.

Dick rolled his eyes dramatically. "Hours. But luckily, I'm the consummate host."

Lexi smiled sweetly. "You could have waited in your condo."

He raised an eyebrow. "I don't think so. Our visitors wanted to speak to you."

Curiously, she looked at the woman with the milky white eyes and flaky skin. "It's Adele, isn't it?"

The girl nodded. "My brother's gone missing. I want you to find him."

She grimaced. "I'm afraid I'm a little stretched at the moment."

"But you help people. And we helped you."

Dick tutted. "You were paid for that. In cash and you got a meal out of it."

Lexi remembered the twin zombies arriving at her motel room in Palm Springs to clean a particularly nasty crime scene. She recalled how enthusiastic they were about their work.

"But we don't know anyone else who will help. We can't risk going to Kindred. They're more likely to kill me than help me." Adele began to cry. As she shook with sobs, a faint haze of dust shook from her skin and settled on the couch.

Lexi looked at Dick. He shrugged, unconcerned. It wasn't his couch.

Scott put a hand on the girl's shoulder. "Lexi's in a tight situation right now but that doesn't mean the rest of us can't take the job." He turned to the sorcerer and indicated Dick with a tilt of his head. "We've been stuck for something to do while we're waiting for news to come from you every day."

A glance at the vampire revealed that his eyes were bulging and she smirked.

She sighed. It took all her willpower to not gag at the zombie's smell. "I've been cooped up in an office all day. Let's sit outside." She turned and walked onto the deck.

Adele was wearing a hat and large sunglasses when she reached the doorway. "You'd be amazed at how often people don't want to be indoors with me. Or maybe you wouldn't."

They all sat except for Dick who returned to the house. In the next moment, the vacuum started. At least he was making himself useful.

Scott whirled his finger to secure their conversation. "How did you know where to find us?" He took his cell phone out to open a file.

The young man straightened. "A mutual friend. Edward."

Lexi smiled and nodded as she recalled the alpha of the Palm Springs pack.

She looked from Adele to the young man. "Tell us."

The zombie looked down so Lexi made eye contact with the man.

"My name is Krish Patel. I'm Adele and Sam's agent."

Scott raised his eyebrows in surprise as his fingers paused on the device. "Agent?"

"Go-between, deal-maker," the man explained. "When someone wants a scene cleaned, they call me and I take the twins to the job and bring them home."

The mage nodded. "But you weren't on the same job this time?"

"Adele had been unwell so Sam and I went alone. It was supposed to be a straight clean-up with only one subject but it looked hinky from the moment we got there."

Lexi interrupted. "Don't all your jobs look hinky? Given the illegal body disposal and everything."

Krish sighed. "Maybe I mean the opposite. There were two uniformed men and it looked more official than we're used to. Anyway, the body had been a mage and they never told us that."

Lexi furrowed her brow in confusion. "I don't understand the significance."

Adele looked up. "With some supernatural creatures, when we eat the brains, we learn things. We get visions." She looked at her hands again.

Krish put his hand over hers. "Sam learned something important from the body. It was clear they must have known about the visions when they hired us."

"Is that not a service you're usually prepared to provide?" Scott asked.

The man shook his head. "On the contrary. We charge more for it—much more—but our clients aren't usually so secretive about it. It seems the mage knew something big. It must have been extremely big because Sam freaked out. Whatever it was, it wasn't intended to go any further. He realized we would both be killed as soon as they got the information."

Lexi narrowed her eyes. "He didn't tell you what this big secret was?"

"He didn't want to put me in danger by telling me. It was thoughtful of him but I don't think it would have made much difference."

Adele gulped and Krish squeezed her hand gently. Lexi looked at him as he gazed at her. She could see he had feelings for the zombie girl.

I don't want to know how that relationship works.

"Sam's a quick thinker. He got us out of there but they soon realized what he'd done and pursued us. We thought we'd lost them, but they caught up with us at a gas station. Sam went in to pay for the gas. I'd filled the tank and climbed into the car when one of them sneaked up beside my window and told me not to move or I'd be dead. While the guy was focused on me, I flicked the lights and Sam gave me the signal to get out of there.

"The guy took my keys and went into the store after him. I pulled out the spare set and floored it while they were distracted looking for Sam. When I'd gone a few miles, I left the car and called a cab, then made it drive me around while I looked for him."

Lexi leaned back to allow Scott to continue the interview.

He made notes. "Did you return to the gas station?"

"Not at that time."

"So you don't know if he got away."

"I saw their car a couple of times, driving slowly around the area. He must have given them the slip at the gas station. Finally, I called Adele and told her to get their stuff together.

"On the way out of town, we stopped at the station. She distracted the guy on the checkout while I looked around. He'd been in the bathroom and the office, but there was no clue as to how he got away."

"We drove past the house on our way out of town but it was on fire." Big tears rolled down Adele's cheeks. "If they took him there—"

"We'll look into it." Scott's voice broke and Lexi looked at him. He was sincerely moved by the girl's distress.

She took the interview over. "Is there a safe way for him to contact you? Do you know of any reason why he hasn't?"

Adele squealed and bounded to her feet.

Limpet leapt onto the table in front of her.

"Limpet, no." Lexi said quickly. "Come over here."

The little demon looked from Adele to Lexi with a puzzled face that seemed to say, *She's already dead so what's the problem?*

After a moment, the creature jumped across the table and onto Lexi's shoulder. He gazed at Adele with his huge eyes.

The sorcerer sighed. He'd adopted no physical cat disguise today but he wore a little charm around his ankle that hid his demon nature under the smell of cat.

Adele sat again slowly. "Sorry. It licked my leg and I wasn't expecting it." She pulled her sunglasses down to see Limpet better with her milky eyes. "It smells like a cat but... What is it?"

"It's a cat-monkey," Dick said from the doorway. "A rare breed."

Krish's eyes narrowed and he stared at the demon. "Rare breed of cat or

rare breed of monkey?"

The vampire pointed indoors. "I think I hear the...thing." He disappeared into the house.

Adele frowned "I haven't had an animal come that close to me since I died."

Lexi didn't think it appropriate to upset the girl further by explaining that the demon had probably been about to take a bite out of her. She felt a swell of pity for the girl.

Limpet jumped onto the table but she sensed that he didn't intend to harm their visitor. Instead, he settled into the girl's lap and curled up.

The zombie stroked the little demon tentatively. He rolled onto his back and offered himself up for tummy rubs.

Mmm. Nice smell.

Sometimes, Lexi was unsure whether she was interpreting his expressions or picking up on his actual thoughts. She knew she had connected with the thinner psychically when he rescued her team from Azatoth but she hadn't heard his thoughts. She decided it was probably her imagination.

Scott had recovered his emotions. "I'll need the address of the house."

Krish took his cell phone out, scrolled quickly, and placed it on the table where the mage could read the screen.

The mage glanced at it and tapped his phone. "Where are you staying?"

"We're at the Aria." Krish took his cell and slid it into his pocket.

"Nice. Your...work must pay well." Scott's device disappeared. "We'll go to the house tomorrow and let you know what we find."

Adele moved Limpet onto the table, stood, and glanced at the flakes of skin she'd left on the chair. "I'm sorry about that. It's how the magic works. When we eat, it stops us from decomposing. I haven't eaten for a couple of days."

Lexi thought about Nora disposing of all the bodies at Kindred HQ. There were probably enough corpses there to bring the girl back to life. She hoped sincerely that she would never stumble across them on one of her late-night wanderings around the building.

The odd pair left the condo and Dick set to work spraying air freshener.

The sorcerer chewed her lip. "Are you sure you want to take this on?"

Scott nodded. "I don't mind looking into it."

"They have multiple ways to reach each other," the vampire said as he joined them. "The fact that Sam hasn't contacted them —honestly, it doesn't seem hopeful."

She agreed with him but didn't voice it.

Dick parked the car and stared hard at Scott.

The mage sighed. "I said I'm sorry."

"It's still relatively early. You could simply hop to the outside of Vegas and wait for a bus."

"A bus?" Scott's jaw dropped.

"Then call Lexi and explain how you went looking for Sam without asking his sister for a personal effect to do a locator spell."

"Let's look around here first." The young man climbed out of the car and stretched. "My back is killing me."

Dick rolled his eyes. "Look, I don't mind hopping into your little magic pocket in a dire emergency but I prefer to travel in this world or through Dolores's lovely fae doors or her charming little apartment."

"I don't understand. We could have been here in half an hour instead of four hours. What's the problem with a dimensional pocket?"

The vampire closed the car door. "I simply don't like it and I don't want to talk about it."

Scott closed his door and glanced at the fire-damaged house. He wandered to a police car parked across the street.

The officer glanced at him but didn't see him as a threat. He dropped his elbow out of the window. "Can I help you, sir?"

Scott smiled. "Sleep."

Instantly, the man slumped and started to snore. His arm hung limply out of the window.

The young mage tucked the arm into the vehicle and walked to where his companion waited for him on the sidewalk.

The vampire stared at the blackened house. He frowned as he turned to the car, then looked at the house again.

"Is there a problem?" Scott guessed what was going through the vampire's mind and managed to hide a smile.

"I didn't think ahead. I'm going into a black, burned building wearing a white shirt. It won't be pretty."

Scott looked into the vehicle. "But your black jacket is in the car—"

Dick's face was a mask of horror. "That's Valentino."

He folded his arms. "Not what people are wearing to crime scenes this season?"

The vampire gave him a withering stare.

"I could rustle you up a t-shirt."

"No, let's get on with it. I'll simply have to be careful." He shooed the mage toward the house.

"Had we traveled inter-dimensionally, you could have left a case in there."

"But we didn't. We traveled like normal people."

"Okay, but neither of us are what might be called normal people."

They walked up to the front door and Dick pulled the crime scene tape out of the way. He let Scott lead the way into the house and they paused to study the damage, which was extensive. The stairs were gone, the ceiling in the kitchen had fallen in, and the sky was visible through the roof at the top of the stairs.

Dick raised an eyebrow. "Was this caused by magic?"

Scott sniffed. "It smells like gasoline."

"Clearly. I meant was it assisted by magic. The damage seems excessive."

The young man shrugged. "Maybe, but I'm not sensing it yet."

The vampire leaned back to look at the second story of the house. The doorway to the first room on the right remained but it was unclear if the room still had a floor. "Do you think it's safe?"

"Probably not." Scott looked around to see there were no mirrors or shiny surfaces. "I'll try to work from here."

He muttered his words and twirled his hand. The black ash whirled in response.

"Scott!" Dick protested.

The mage turned quickly and stared at what had previously been a white shirt. "Oops."

His companion rolled his eyes and sighed. "I'll look around." He headed up the hallway, opened a door on the right, and disappeared through it.

Quickly, the ash reversed past the fire services. Nothing happened for a while until it finally revealed a figure moving around the house. Scott stopped the scene when he was at the top of the stairs and played it forward.

The figure stood at the doorway of the bedroom, stepped forward and back, and held his arms up in a protective gesture. It looked like he had been unable to enter the room because of the flames. He ran down the stairs and froze, staring directly at the young mage. The ash man shook his head and. Scott's heart leaped. Was this remnant trying to communicate with him? He'd never seen such a thing.

He moved to the side to see if the remnant's gaze followed him. When it didn't, he turned and laughed nervously as he discovered the vague shadow of another ash man in the doorway of the house, pointing to the stairs. They'd been looking at each other.

The first man shook his head again and ran out of the building. The ash that made him drifted to the ground.

"Did you find anything?" Dick returned from his exploration.

"It looks like two guys entered the house but couldn't get into the room up there. I'll head upstairs."

"There's no need. It's in the garage."

"What is?"

"The bedroom. The floor collapsed."

"Oh. That'll do." Scott hurried to the garage where he raised the ashes and watched from the doorway as the scene reversed past the emergency services. He saw the ceiling fall in and two corpses tumble along with a blazing bed.

Dick stepped around the whirling ashes into the garage to get a closer look at the bodies. He took his cell phone out and snapped a few pictures, then glanced up. "Can you pause this?"

Scott put a hand up and the ashes hung suspended in the air. He stepped closer to the vampire and followed his gaze.

A figure stood in the doorway of the room above, watching the bodies burn. There wasn't enough ash to distinguish features but he had a hunch who it was.

He flicked a hand and the ash dropped. The figure disappeared. He muttered and raised his hand until the shape of the man reappeared. This time, he was easier to see.

Dick narrowed his eyes. "Isn't that—"

"Sam. I do believe it is."

"He's much clearer now. What did you do?"

Scott moved the scene forward. "I'm not using ash. These flakes are epithelial cells."

The vampire shuddered. "Flakes of dead skin? How revolting."

As they watched, Sam took something from his pocket, threw it into the room, and stepped back.

"If I were a betting man, and I am, I'd say that was a lighter." Dick began to sift through the mess on the floor of the garage.

"Do you think it will still be here?"

"So far, I've seen the mooks and the fire department. I guess the scene is still waiting for a safety assessment before the CSIs move in and comb through it extensively. That's why the cop's outside in the car. This is still an active crime scene."

Scott raised his arms. The lighter flew out of the detritus and Dick snatched it. He squealed and it flew out of his hand. "Son of a bitch! It's silver."

The young mage picked the lighter up. "At least I don't have to go back to Adele for something that belongs to Sam." He thought for a moment. "I think we need to find out where the bodies are."

Dick stared at him. "Why?"

Scott screwed his face up. "We need the mage."

"We do? Why?"

"There are other ways to get answers from a corpse if you have the time and resources. Sam came back to destroy those bodies so others couldn't learn what he knows."

"Oh, for God's sake." Dick marched to the door. "I hate morgues. Why do we keep having to go to morgues?"

The young mage turned to the room and lifted the skin cells again. He watched them rise through the roof and drift away with the wind. "Now, no one else will know it was him."

His companion raised an eyebrow. "Unless they beat us to it."

As they walked out, Scott glanced at the police officer. He was still snoring and they hurried toward his car. The mage prodded the man's arm. "Wake up."

The officer jerked awake, startled.

"Sleeping on the job? Are you shitting me?"

The man spluttered and rubbed his face. "I'm sorry. I—I…"

Scott felt bad for him but continued. "Do you need to be relieved?"

"No, sir. I don't know what happened."

"How long have you been here."

The cop checked the time. "Only a couple of hours."

"Were you here when they took the bodies away?"

"Yes, sir."

"When was that?"

"Yesterday, sir. They went to the County Morgue around mid-afternoon."

"Why so late?"

"Structural damage in the house. The scene safety officer called it."

"Sleep." Scott put a hand on the officer's head as it drooped again. "Forget."

When they climbed into the car, he turned to Dick. "Can you bring the picture up?"

Scott stared at the screen. "That's Sam. I'm sure of it. He was brave to come back here."

The vampire raised an eyebrow. "It seems reckless to me. Sam and his sister appear to be quite flammable."

The mage pointed at the screen. "He was so determined to stop those mooks from getting the mage's body that he came back here knowing they were looking for him and torched the house."

"At least we know he's not dead." Dick raised his palm. "And before you correct me, I know he's dead. I mean he's not dead, dead."

Scott clipped his seatbelt into place. "Unless they caught up with him after he left the house for the second time. In which case, I think he could be dead, dead."

CHAPTER NINE

They drove to the county morgue and parked at the back.

Dick turned to the mage. "How should we play this?"

"Carefully. The chance that no supes work here is zero." He dug into the glove box and pulled a pack of cigarettes out.

They went around to the back of the building and stood near the door. After a few minutes, the door opened and a uniformed man walked out. "What in the hell do you think you're doing?"

Scott hid the cigarette behind his back. "I'm sorry. He's…" He glanced at Dick and almost gasped in shock. The vampire's eyes were red-rimmed.

Dick put a hand up and his voice shook as he spoke. "Please don't blame this guy. I've…I've never identified a body before. I've never even seen…" Two huge tears rolled down his face. "Don't get him into trouble."

"Are you done?" the guard asked.

"He hasn't signed anything. I'm sorry. He was going to throw up," Scott said hastily.

"I'm sorry for your loss, sir. But you're not supposed to be out here." The man held the door open and let them both inside.

Scott glanced at a board with names as he went past—dates and times of arrivals. There were many of them as expected in a city that size.

"What room were you in"

"We were in C."

"Oh. I am sorry for your loss."

"He was my cousin." Dick's voice shook again as he held sobs back.

They opened the door marked C and the security guard continued through the hallway and around the corner.

"I'll make sure he's gone," the vampire whispered.

Scott entered the room where two charred bodies lay on gurneys.

A man wearing a white lab coat looked at him. "What are you doing here?"

"I'm sorry. I have a relative here who needs to identify the bodies."

The man frowned. "Where are your gloves? Get them on." He pointed to a box of disposable nitrile gloves.

Scott walked to the box. "Of course. We'll be out of your hair in no time."

"Yes, you will," the man answered curtly.

"Scott? Scott. Are you okay? Wake up." Dick's voice sounded like it was coming from the far end of a tunnel.

"What happened?" He looked at the vampire.

"You'll have to tell me that. I simply came in and found you unconscious."

He shook the dizziness off. "Where's the guy?"

"You were alone in here." Dick looked at the gurneys. "I assume our mage was on the empty one."

Scott sighed. "I think I met someone from the other team." He pushed to his feet. "He distracted me and must have hit me with a blast when I wasn't looking."

Dick frowned. "Let's get out of here."

They hurried out of the building and to the car.

The mage was disgusted with himself for being ill-prepared. "I was so consumed by the idea that we were the interlopers that it simply didn't occur to me that the guy didn't work there."

"Don't worry about it. Our job is to find Sam. We have the lighter. Hopefully, we can track him with it so we won't have to get any personal effects from Adele." Dick started the car.

Scott remained silent. He felt like a prize idiot.

His companion glanced at him. "How about I take you to a fast-food place where you can eat your weight in carbohydrates."

"Shouldn't we return to Vegas?"

"While we're so close, I'd like to check on my house to see how Jesús is treating it. We can check in with Lexi by phone and get some rest."

"I'm not sure. With Azatoth—"

"You seem to have forgotten that I have a private swimming pool."

Scott perked up. "Okay."

Three hours later, the car rolled through the gates and stopped on the drive.

As they climbed out, a scream issued from inside the house and Dick vanished. Scott translocated to the kitchen as the vampire appeared next to Jesús and spun, looking for danger.

His employee looked up and squealed again. "You almost gave me a heart attack."

Seeing no assailant, his boss returned his gaze. "I almost gave you a heart attack? Why did you scream?"

Jesús pointed at the TV. "She said yes to the dress."

"Are you kidding me right now?"

The man blushed. "I wasn't expecting you home."

"Well, I'm home. And this…" Dick waved vaguely in Scott's direction. "Savage has covered my car in fries and crumbs and shredded lettuce."

"I'll see to it right away, Mr. Levin…Mr. Erwin." Jesús launched out of the chair and ran out of the room before he hurried out the door with the dustbuster.

"He'll be the death of me." Dick froze and looked around.

"What's wrong?" Scott was instantly on guard.

"These walls are a different color."

"They look the same to me."

"Well, they would, but trust me. They're different." He smiled. "I like it."

The mage couldn't see the slightest difference in the walls.

His companion walked to a flip chart easel at the edge of the room, and Scott followed. They stood side by side and looked at two columns of words. One column was headed *William Levin*, the other *Dick Erwin*. They seemed to be describing two different men. William was bored, directionless, and uninspired while Dick was optimistic, had purpose, and had close friends.

Scott wondered if Jesús would be in trouble over it.

Dick lifted some pages to reveal very nice drawings and fabric swatches.

Jesús entered and stood stock still, his eyes wide as he realized that his boss was reading his assessment of him.

The vampire dropped the sheets on the board and nodded. "You have an excellent eye."

Scott wandered to the breakfast bar which was loaded with books on interior design. He looked at the young Mexican man. "Are you enjoying college?"

"Yes, Mr. Scott." Jesús remained standing at the entrance to the room.

Dick stepped across to him and took the dustbuster from his

hands. "Jesús, I would like to apologize. You're no longer my house boy and I shouldn't treat you as such."

"You don't want me to live here?"

"Of course you may continue to live here. But you're my house sitter, not the help. You only need to tidy up after yourself." He looked around. "I like the new paint. It suits Dick Erwin very well."

Jesús grinned. "I'll move these books out of your way."

"Thank you. We'll need the countertop. I'll get the maps." Dick disappeared down the hallway.

Half an hour later, Jesús had left for a date and Scott had a map of the USA open on the counter. He took the lighter out and swung his divining crystal gently over the map.

Dick frowned. "Is there any point to doing this? If he's on the run and hasn't even contacted his sister, what are the chances he'd be unshielded?"

Scott shrugged. "That's what I thought." He moved toward Washington State, then across and down through Idaho and Nevada. When he moved over Arizona, the crystal stopped moving.

He looked up at the other man. "Arizona."

"Arizona coming up." The vampire ran a finger across the maps in an old box. He stopped and withdrew the correct one.

Scott folded the USA map and handed it to him.

Dick stared at the proffered map. "What's this?"

"It's the USA map. I need the Arizona map."

The vampire narrowed his eyes. "You're not allowed to fold the maps. You're clearly not qualified." He handed him the Arizona map and reopened the first one to fold it correctly.

After a few seconds, the gem stopped near Phoenix.

"He's on the I-10. Here, let me turn this over." Dick flipped the map to reveal a map of Phoenix. They switched to Google and found that Sam's location matched a motel just outside of Phoenix.

Scott checked again a few minutes later and the crystal stopped at the same place. "He's not moving."

Dick folded the map carefully and returned it to the box.

The mage looked at the time. "What's that—about three hours away? If we start now—"

"No. We're not going immediately."

"Why not?"

"I'm not driving all the way to Phoenix only to find he's traveled back to LA. Let's give it an hour, then check the maps again to be sure he's still there."

"That's a good idea."

"Also because you'll want to stop for burgers and donuts and chips every five minutes," Dick added. "I'll make you something to eat before we leave. In the meantime, you can take a quick dip. I see you sneaking peeks at the pool."

Scott grinned.

"There's swimwear in the guest bedroom, first on the left." The vampire turned to the refrigerator.

The young mage headed down the hallway and into the room on the left. He opened the dresser and found a collection of swimsuits and swimming briefs. With a frown, he held the briefs up. They were tiny and he checked the label to make sure they weren't intended for ladies, then held them up again. "These are minuscule."

Dick shouted from the kitchen, "You could always skinny dip. I won't judge you."

He kicked himself mentally for not leaving a pair of swimming shorts in his dimensional pocket.

After a moment's deliberation, he put the briefs on and took a robe from a hook on the bedroom door. He walked out to find two sandwiches waiting for him. "That smells great."

"It's a Cuban. Ham, roasted pork, Swiss cheese, mustard, and dill served on Cuban bread. Jesús loves them. Take it to the pool.

I'm going to my room to call Albin." Dick took a can of soda from the refrigerator and put it next to the food for him.

Scott swam ten lengths of the pool, then climbed out and ate his meal. He swam another ten lengths before he pulled the robe on and sat in the sun until the vampire returned with a cup in hand.

His companion sat on the lounger next to him. "I know how Sam escaped from the gas station. According to the news, a gas station attendant collapsed after opening the safe at the end of her shift and a dead body fell out of it. When she came to, the body was gone."

"That was clever." Scott looked at him. "Can I ask you a question?"

"Yes, vampires do go to the toilet."

Scott laughed. "I've known you long enough to know the answer to that one. Do you have urges to drink people's blood?"

Dick answered with a question of his own. "What's your favorite meat?"

He thought about it for a moment. "Chicken...or pork. No, lamb."

The vampire took his cell phone out and tapped the screen a few times. He held it out to him. It showed a picture of a fluffy little lamb. "Does looking at this picture make you hungry?"

"No."

"If you went to a petting zoo and saw this baby lamb there, would you want to rip its legs off, drizzle them in olive oil, and throw them in the oven?"

"I get your point. I merely...didn't know that."

Dick raised an eyebrow. "Is that not what they taught you at Kindred school?"

He shrugged, more than a little embarrassed.

"I'm not saying there aren't vampires who get carried away with it all. You met Lorenzo and I dare say you've met a few others who were problematic. If they are like that, they're either young and without supervision or complete assholes."

"Like Lorenzo," Scott said thoughtfully.

"Exactly. Let's get ready to hit the road."

He groaned. "How about if I meet you there"

Dick looked shocked. "You wouldn't abandon a buddy on a road trip."

The mage dropped his shoulders and climbed off the sun lounger to prepare for more hours in the car.

CHAPTER TEN

Scott and Dick made good time along the I-10. The mage had secured the crystal to the rear-view mirror but instead of swinging wildly at the end of its chain, it swung forward and remained there, moving slightly to the left or right depending on how the road curved. A few minutes from the hotel, it jumped, clicked against the windscreen, and dropped limply.

The vampire's head jerked to the side. "What the hell was that?"

He frowned. "I don't know." He removed it from the mirror and took the lighter out. "Maybe I need to charge it again."

The mage held the two items together in his hands while he muttered under his breath.

Dick pulled into the hotel parking lot.

Scott climbed out and let the crystal drop to the end of its chain. It pointed across the street from the hotel. He squinted into the distance. "What's over there?"

"I'm guessing nothing." The vampire glanced at the crystal. "What's it doing now?"

It turned slowly in an arc, taut on the end of the chain.

The mage gazed at it in bewilderment. "This has never happened to me before."

"Don't feel bad. I'm sure it happens to all mages at least once."

Scott looked at his companion, who met his gaze with a smirk. He returned his focus to the crystal and shook it as though it might reset itself. It now pointed south. "The truck parking lot?"

"Well, shit!" Dick sighed.

The mage glanced at his friend. The vampire was looking up and Scott followed his gaze. A small plane flew off into the distance. "At least I didn't lose my mojo. Well, we're four hours from Vegas."

"That's it? You want to go home? Scott, we're intrepid investigators. Why was he here? Where has he gone? We need answers."

"Okay. Can we eat first?"

"Good grief. You're like a garbage disposal unit that never shuts off. Let's ask at the hotel first, then the airport. Then, if you're good, food."

They headed into the hotel and to the check-in desk. Dick took a wallet out and flashed it at the woman behind the desk. "We're looking for a young man who would have stayed for a night or two and checked out today."

"May I see your badge more closely?"

Scott stepped forward and smiled sheepishly. "You caught us. It won't help. We're from LA and don't have jurisdiction here. Sorry for trying to pull the wool over your eyes. It's been a long drive."

The woman smiled smugly and looked proud of herself for having caught them lying. "What does he look like?"

"Very pale skin—" he began.

She held a hand up. "I know the one. I didn't want to give him a room at all. I don't approve of his type but you can't turn the business down."

Scott stared at her in surprise. "You know what he is?"

"Of course. I dated a goth in high school. He needed a good wash too. I don't know how that woman could stand it."

"He had a woman with him?"

"They arrived in one car—one of those Herbie cars with eyelashes." She gave a dramatic eye-roll. "She stayed a couple of hours and drove off alone. He asked me to call a cab to take him to the airport."

She checked the screen. "Mr. Brooks."

"Right, yeah. Goths. He's calling himself Mr. Brooks." Scott rolled his eyes.

The woman checked the screen. "Yes. Max Brooks. What did he do?"

Dick frowned. "We can't disclose that. But, out of interest, are all your staff members accounted for?"

The woman's jaw dropped. "I…think so."

"Would you like us to take a look inside the room?"

Wordlessly, the woman handed them a key card.

"Thank you." The vampire took the card. "Which room?"

"Fourteen."

The two men walked away from the office.

Scott grinned. "Well, you can't say he doesn't have a sense of humor."

Dick narrowed his eyes. "Why?"

"Max Brooks wrote a Zombie Survival Guide."

"There's a survival guide for zombies?"

"Never mind." He pointed at the room and opened the door.

The vampire waved a hand in front of his nose. "It does smell bad in here, even for a zombie."

Scott went into the bathroom and pulled a bag from the wastepaper basket. "He's been eating raw liver."

"That explains some of the smell." Dick checked the basket in the bedroom. "This is interesting."

The mage stepped out of the bathroom to see his companion tipping rubbish onto the tabletop. "Burnt offerings. Literally." He poked through the burned twigs and leaves, pinched some ash between his fingers, and sniffed it. "What do you think?"

Dick shrugged. "We can assume his friend was a witch. I haven't a clue what they were doing, though. Let's scoop this into the bag and take it to Vegas. Perhaps Albin's witch friend could tell us what they were up to."

Scott scraped everything into the liner and they took it with them.

After returning the keycard, they returned to the car and headed to the little airport. They drove directly to a plane with a man up a ladder, working in an open panel. Dick called, "Excuse me."

The man turned and smiled. "How can I help you?" He offered his hand to Dick, then Scott. "If you need to fly out somewhere, I can't take you until tomorrow. I gotta head out to Henderson in an hour."

"A friend of ours flew out of here about an hour ago. Can you tell me where he went?"

"Oh yeah, the freakishly pale guy. I'm sorry, the office has closed."

"Could it be opened again?" The vampire retrieved his wallet and held up two hundred-dollar bills "For the inconvenience."

The man took the money. "Nope."

They stared at him.

The man chuckled. "I don't think the office will help. Your friend paid cash. He might not be going where the official records say he's going." He pulled his wallet out, stashed the money, and withdrew a business card. "Call me in the morning before eight."

Dick raised an eyebrow. "Did you say you're going to Henderson? Are you taking someone?"

"It's an early morning pick-up so I'm staying over. Do you want to grab a lift?"

"That would knock several hours from our journey. Thank

you. We'll meet you here in an hour." Dick jerked his head toward Scott. "I have to feed him regularly or he whines."

The young mage rolled his eyes but he didn't disagree.

A few minutes later, they parked outside a McDonald's around the corner from the motel.

Scott decided he was hungry enough for a few McRibs. He walked toward the restaurant, but Dick put a hand on his arm.

The vampire grinned. "I think you might prefer donuts." He pointed through the parking lot to a VW Beetle with eyelashes over the headlights. It was parked near the Dunkin' Donuts coffee house.

He gave the vampire a lopsided grin. "Donuts it is."

As he approached, he looked through the glass walls. Only a few patrons were inside. They went to the counter and looked at the menu. "A frozen donut dunkaccino, please."

The young girl smiled. "Sure, and for you?"

"That is for me. And three Boston Cremes. Also for me." He smiled.

She looked at Dick who put a hand up. "He's eating for both of us."

Scott paid and while they waited for his order, they looked around. An older woman smiled at them. Dick smiled courteously but it wasn't the witch. He certainly didn't get the vibe of a witch or the driver of a car with eyelashes.

The server's perky voice disturbed his focus. "Here you go."

He studied the order and stared at the pink and white drink.

Scott stared at it too before he looked at the picture "Where are the sprinkles?"

"Sorry. I wasn't sure if… Sorry." She snatched the cup and added the multicolored sprinkles.

The mage headed directly to a young woman with red hair and a deep-pink aura. "Excuse me, I'm sorry to bother you. Can we talk to you for a minute?"

She looked at the two of them, then at Scott's drink. "Sure."

He shuffled along the bench so Dick could sit. The mage took a long slurp of the drink, then helicoptered his finger.

"I'm Scott and this is Dick. We're working for Adele, Sam's sister. She's trying to find him."

The woman stared at him without comment.

He tried again. "I know there are people who want to do him harm, but we're not with those people." Scott shoved a donut into his mouth and took a big bite.

She smirked. "Yeah, I'm getting that. But I can't help you."

Dick reached for his wallet. "Please. If you could simply—"

"I'm not refusing to tell you where he is. I'm saying I can't. We parted a short while ago after I gave him a cloaking charm. He's off the grid."

The vampire sighed. "Shit. Did he say anything about what he's doing?"

"He was looking for someone but he wouldn't tell me who it is. He said it would be best that I don't know anything. He looked spooked and I believed him."

Scott nodded. "Thank you for your help and for trusting us."

She smiled. "I have a knack for seeing the good in people. I hope you can help Sam. He's a good guy too."

They sat on the plane and stared out of the window.

The vampire sighed. "I can't wait to get back."

"You're missing Albin." Scott smiled. "This looks serious."

"I'm missing him sorely. I think it is serious but he's an incubus so who can tell?" He looked at Scott. "You haven't even been on one date in all the time I've known you. Unless you count that fae girl."

Scott responded with a mental eye-roll. "Are you talking about the one who assaulted me and turned me into a drone?"

"That's the one."

"I don't think that counts as a date. And I don't have time for that nonsense."

Dick tilted his head. "That's exactly what Lexi says."

"She's right. We don't live the kind of life that's safe for others. You made a good choice with Albin. He can protect himself but I wouldn't like to get some poor girl killed simply because I bought her dinner."

"Warren's gone." Dick held his whisky flask up. "And good riddance to him."

"But Azatoth's here. I don't want to spend all my time worrying that someone else isn't safe."

"You mean someone in addition to Lexi?"

Scott sighed. "If Azatoth decides she doesn't want her around anymore, she could simply rip her apart."

"Do you think Alicia would allow that?"

He leaned forward. What he was about to say was something he'd often thought about but hadn't dared to articulate to Lexi. "There's been no indication that Alicia's still in there aside from that one time. It must have taken all her strength to stop the demon. That could have been the end of her."

Dick nodded. "I've had the same thought. But I don't think Azatoth will harm Lexi. She needs her for something and as long as Lexi plays along, we might find out what that is."

"I wonder what she's up to?" Scott leaned back and looked at Las Vegas below them. "All this waiting is unnerving."

Dick agreed. "You are not wrong."

He looked at the vampire. "Is Dolores keeping Bryan out of the way? That's what Lexi thinks."

"I couldn't possibly say." Dick kept his gaze focused on the window.

"Okay. Do you think the demon could have plans to attack Fae? Has she been there?"

"I don't see why not, but I haven't heard anything that

suggests she's been there. I'm very sure Dolores would have told us if a higher-level demon was tearing it up in Fae."

The young mage felt troubled. "I don't understand why there hasn't been a response. It's like the whole supernatural world has simply rolled over for her."

"I'm not sure the whole supernatural world knows exactly what's going on. After that original wobble which we all felt when she woke up, she's been almost exclusively busy inside Kindred but not so much outside of it." Dick pulled his flask out and took a sip of bourbon.

"I wonder why she hates Kindred so much."

"It's probably not personal. My guess is it was merely a bold strategic move. Kindred is the most powerful organization on the planet. Now, she runs it."

The pilot's voice came over the address system. "Please make sure your seats are in the upright position and your tray is stored away safely."

Dick shouted to the front. "You could simply have said that and we'd have heard it."

"Now where's the fun in that?" the pilot responded.

The vampire retrieved his cell phone and turned it on. He looked up with a puzzled expression. "I thought Albin was going to stay at my place but he's back at his apartment."

Scott's cell pinged. "The magical wards over Vegas have gone down again."

Dick's shoulders sagged. "But it's not fair. I wanted to see my boyfriend."

"We should go to update Adele anyway."

When they arrived at the Aria it was late and Krish was waiting in the opulent lobby. Scott noted that his hand was bandaged. "Is everything okay?"

With a wry smile, the man shrugged it off. "It's nothing."

The moment they stepped into the seclusion of the elevator,

Krish turned and looked into their eyes with worry etched on his face. "Did you find him?"

"No," Scott answered, "but we have news."

Krish closed his eyes and breathed deeply. "Is it bad? If it's bad, tell me first so I can prepare her."

Dick shook his head. "It's not bad. We merely haven't caught up with him yet."

The young man exhaled slowly. "Thank God. It would have broken her."

They entered a suite and Adele stood from the couch. She'd spread a sheet across it, obviously concerned about her flaky skin. Her gaze went straight to her friend and relief flooded her face.

"We haven't seen him but he's definitely still alive…or whatever." Scott paused and wondered if he'd been insensitive.

Dick interrupted. "Scott, he's as alive as I am."

The mage looked at him, then at Adele. "Anyway, we went to the house. It seems that while they were out looking for Sam, he doubled back and set the house alight."

Krish's jaw dropped. "He did that?"

He nodded. "We tried to get to the mage's body to see if we could learn anything new but someone else got to it first. We were able to follow Sam's trail as far as Phoenix but he flew out from there. We don't know his destination yet. I'll try another locator spell but there might be no point. A witch drove him to a motel outside Phoenix and gave him a cloaking spell."

"We might be able to track his flight," Dick interjected, "but he paid the pilot in cash. Do you know where he would have got that kind of money?"

"We have stashes all over the place," Krish said quickly. "Do you want me to call around to see if he's contacted anyone else?"

Scott shook his head. "I don't think it's a good idea to draw that kind of attention to yourself. It's possible people are looking for you or maybe already watching you to see if you can lead them to him."

"We're covered. Your friend Albin arranged for us to be shielded."

The mage nodded.

"What next?" Adele asked.

"It's late. We'll start again tomorrow."

"Did you hear about the wards?" Dick asked.

Adele sat and covered her face. "Oh, we know about the wards all right."

Krish grimaced. "Albin was here when they went down. He had to lock himself in the bathroom to get away from Adele. I picked her up and carried her into the bedroom."

Scott looked at the bandaged hand again. "Oh. You won't…erm?"

"No, we're not contagious," Adele muttered from behind her hands. "But he had to muzzle me. How humiliating."

Dick looked around. "Is Albin still in there? He didn't go outside, did he?"

Krish shook his head. "He called your friend Dolores. Because the wards are down, she was able to get him home safely. In fact, we thought he was still in the bathroom until he called to let us know he'd left. That's some potent level mojo he has."

The vampire nodded. "Tell me about it." He looked puzzled for a moment and raced across the room. "That's strange. My speed and senses should be affected by the hotel's wards. Why aren't they active?"

Scott shrugged. "Maybe it's simply taking time to kick in."

He agreed to update Adele the next day and the two of them left.

In the lobby, the young mage asked. "Back to the condos?"

Dick sighed. "I might go sit outside Albin's apartment until the wards are up." He turned to Scott. "What if they never go up? Is that it—the end of us?"

Scott put a hand on his friend's shoulder. "Love always finds a way."

"That's nice. Very poetic."

"I think I stole it from Jurassic Park."

"That was life always finds a way." Dick patted his hand. "But thank you for the sentiment. I'll walk along the Strip for a while."

The young man watched as his friend walked out of the hotel with uncharacteristically stooped shoulders.

CHAPTER ELEVEN

L exi raced around the house getting everything she needed for work while Scott sat at the table reading the newspaper. She was aware of him watching her.

Finally, he put his cup down. "You're buzzed. What's going on?"

"Nothing. I'm simply getting ready for work." With an attempt at carelessness, she avoided his eyes. She knew he'd feel her excitement but there was nothing she could do to hide it.

He persisted. "Have you found Bryan?"

"No." She latched onto the excuse. "But I plan to look for clues in Dolores's apartment. I think he could even be there. You know how weird that place is. Rooms that suddenly appear and disappear."

The mage looked horrified. "Do you know what she'll do to you if she finds out? We'll pick up the pieces for months."

She redirected the topic to him. "What are you doing today?"

"Continuing the search for Sam. We need to call the pilot who flew him away yesterday and we need to go out and buy maps. I'll try some listening spells and search for people using specific words."

Lexi smirked. "Like pale and flakey?"

He nodded and looked at his watch. "I've tried calling Dick a couple of times but he's not picking up. I'll try knocking on his door. We should get moving." He stood, walked to the door, and opened it. "Oh. There you are."

Lexi joined him in the entrance. Dick was pulling his door key out. He must have been out all night. His hair was messed and his jacket looked scruffy, but he had a smile on his face.

The vampire held his arms wide. "My people. My family. How are you on this fine morning?

She grinned. "Did you have a good night?"

"Almost completely excellent. But I came across some rowdy young vampires in the supe bar so I left, then this happened." He opened his jacket to reveal drops of blood on his white shirt. "Some idiot tried to mug me."

Scott stared at the blood. "What did you do to him?"

"Nothing. That's my blood. I tried not to retaliate but he landed a good blow on my nose. I spun him around, gave him a wedgie, and disappeared before he could look back." He turned to the mage. "If you can give me a couple of hours for a shower and a nap, I'll be ready to go." He opened his jacket and took the pilot's business card from his inside pocket. "In the meantime, perhaps you could chase this guy up. See if we can get my money's worth of information." He walked to his front door and stepped inside.

Scott and Lexi returned to the house.

He closed the door. "I'm glad he had a good time, apart from the idiots at the end of the night. He was sad about not seeing Albin last night."

Lexi went to collect her purse. Her cell phone beeped and she checked it to find a message from Nora saying that Azatoth was rescheduling her training session for the afternoon. She slumped.

"What's wrong?" Scott asked from behind her.

She couldn't hide her disappointment. "I should have had a meeting this morning but it was rescheduled."

He raised an eyebrow. "You're taking your Kindred job seriously."

"I have to keep my eye on the ball. Somewhere in that building, there's a roomful of body parts belonging to people who didn't see it coming." She leaned against the counter. "There's something else, though. All the jobs that come to my team are righteous. I expected to find Kindred doing horrible things to the supernatural communities, but I'm left wondering if the organization as a whole is as bad as I thought it was. Maybe it was only a few rotten eggs." She shrugged. "Anyway, I'm not in a hurry to go out now. Do you want me to help with the maps?"

Scott stared at her in surprise. "Don't forget the most rotten egg of all is now at the head of that organization."

She didn't want to talk about Azatoth. "If you don't want my help, that's fine."

"No…yes. If you don't mind keeping me company." He didn't get any further as she grasped his arm and translocated. He stared at Dick's Palm Springs living room. "How did you do that?"

Lexi blushed. "What?"

"In one jump. I've never seen anything like it."

"I don't know." She shrugged and glanced around. "But it's quicker, though, so…"

"Lexi?"

The two of them turned to find Jesús in shiny gold boxer shorts with a baseball bat. "What are you doing sneaking around in the middle of the night? I could have killed you."

"It's just gone seven-thirty am. And how were you planning to kill us?"

Jesús shrugged and put the bat down. "Sorry. I'm jumpy. Some weirdo was hanging around the other day and it put me on edge."

Scott frowned "Did you tell Dick?"

"No. I didn't want him to think I can't look after his property and the guy left anyway."

"We've come for the box of maps."

"Oh, right. Well, it's still there on the countertop. Lock up after yourselves." The young man yawned, picked the bat up, and plodded down the hallway.

Back at the condo, Scott swept the morning's newspaper and a pile of take-out menus onto the floor, opened the map of the USA, and spread it across the table.

Lexi stared at the crumpled newspaper and menus. "Why did you do that?"

He grinned. "I don't know. I always wanted to do it."

She rolled her eyes so hard it almost gave her eye-strain.

Lord, give me strength.

Scott held Sam's lighter along with his crystal. He muttered and swung the gem but nothing happened. "I guess I'd better call the pilot."

The dark sorcerer poured coffee while he spoke on the phone out on the deck.

"Seriously? Okay, that's great. Thanks for your help." He disconnected and entered the kitchen. "He was flown to Chihuahua, Mexico."

She folded the US map and selected one that covered the whole of North America.

The mage picked the crystal and lighter up. The gem pointed immediately to the middle of Mexico. "Chihuahua. But I didn't expect that to work. The witch said he's supposed to be shielded."

"You said it was a charm. He wouldn't be the first idiot to remove his charm to take a shower." Lexi shrugged. "I need to get to work. Call Adele and ask her who Sam might know there. Then see if you can print some city maps to get a more precise location. I'll see you tonight."

He retrieved his phone as she translocated directly to the lobby of Kindred HQ in New York. She'd been doing so in one jump for a couple of weeks and thought she probably should have mentioned it to Scott.

Her conscience agreed as she walked down the street to the coffee shop and opened the door. She stepped inside and froze for a moment. That was unusual. She should have entered Dolores's apartment.

"Are you simply going to stand there?"

The hairs on the back of Lexi's neck stood up and she turned to face Azatoth. "Hi. I was getting the coffees but Nora said you were busy with another meeting so I didn't know whether I should get two or three."

The demon narrowed her eyes. "I don't need your life story. I simply want my coffee."

Lexi smiled widely and walked to the counter. "Do you want a cinnamon roll with it?"

"Why not?" Azatoth smiled with Lexi's sister's face.

She simultaneously felt dread, horror, hope, and then, at the thought of continuing her training, excitement.

As they walked to the office, Azatoth asked, "Do you have any interesting cases?"

"No. A coven of witches in Iowa was caught growing seven hectares of weed and glamouring it to look like corn."

"Let me know if anything comes in that looks like it could be fun. I might see if I can make time in my schedule."

Lexi cringed inwardly. "I'll check the board when I get in."

"Either way, I'll see you this afternoon for training." They stood at the elevator and the demon took two of the drinks and pastries out of her hands.

She waited for the next elevator and headed up to her office. When she walked through the main office, she was aware as always of the little jump everyone evidenced when they saw her face. Relief that it was her and not Azatoth followed quickly and finally, resentment flared as she entered her corner office. She rolled her eyes mentally as she closed the door.

Yeah, I'm so lucky to have a corner office. Never mind having lost my sister to the demon. Small-minded idiots.

She walked to her plant on the filing cabinet beside the floor-to-ceiling window, took the little jug, and watered it. That done, she looked at the board to see what jobs were scheduled for the day. The words *Las Vegas* immediately drew her attention. It hadn't been picked up by the Las Vegas unit yet. She opened her laptop and scrolled to see what had happened in her current home city.

Hmm! A man has been found dead in an alley. Supernatural involvement suspected. Lexi remembered how Braxton didn't like it when head office marched in and took a case over. *I'll give them a half-hour to accept or reject, then I'll take over.*

As she scribbled the details from the screen, her cell phone beeped. Scott had messaged her.

Adele says no friends or contacts that she knows of in Chihuahua.

Lexi texted her response. *I might be heading to Vegas soon to investigate a murder. Want to tag along?*

The response was immediate. *I'm waiting for Dick to come over, then I'm probably heading to Mexico.*

She tapped the screen. *Suit yourself.* She stepped out of the office and waited for her colleagues to look up. "The Vegas unit is still working on the problem with the wards so I'll investigate the homicide on the Strip."

No one answered.

"No donuts for you," she muttered.

CHAPTER TWELVE

When Dick walked through the door, Scott was seated at the kitchen table, laying out the maps of the city of Chihuahua he'd printed.

He glanced at the vampire in jeans and a t-shirt and did a double-take.

Dick looked down at himself. "What? I'm trying a new look."

"It's a good look." He nodded and turned to the maps. "I'm thinking that if I find Sam, you could hop over to the Aria and we'll get the two of them on a call." He dropped the crystal on its chain and muttered his locator spell. He waved it over the map with no reaction.

His companion shrugged. "Maybe he's in the countryside outside the city."

"Or he's wearing his charm again." Scott scooped the sheets up and replaced them with others showing more of the area. He suspended the crystal over the sheets. "Nothing. Okay. Let's do the whole of Mexico." He rifled through the pile of maps to find the North American one again but Dick was faster. "You've lost your map-folding privileges, remember?" The vampire noticed a handwritten note on the front of the map. "Hey, this is mine." He looked around and saw his map box on the counter.

"Oh, right. We borrowed them this morning and were almost brained by a fledgling interior designer with a baseball bat." He thought for a moment. "That reminds me. He mentioned some weirdo had been hanging around a couple of days ago, but I think he scared the guy off. Or rather he thinks he scared the guy off."

"He never mentioned it, but we do get fans and weirdos occasionally. A famous movie star once lived in that house." Dick picked invisible fluff from his pristine t-shirt.

Scott's eyebrows raise. "Really? Who?"

The vampire sighed. "Me, you idiot." He opened the map and spread it flat.

"Oh right, of course." He laughed and turned to the map.

The mage swung the crystal but there was no sign of Sam. "Do you think it's worth going to Chihuahua to look around?"

Dick shrugged. "Only if you're bored. The town's not huge but it's not small either. Personally, I think it would be a colossal waste of time. If he's taken his charm off once, he might do it again. It's probably a better use of your time to check the map every five or ten minutes from here, then race there if he surfaces."

Scott nodded. "I think I can narrow down roughly where he was yesterday so I might take a look."

"Either way, I won't go so I'll update the clients." Dick headed to the door.

Alone in the kitchen, the young mage shook his head. He retrieved his bag and translocated to Mexico.

He appeared on a plot of land with nothing on it but a parking lot and a church. "Well, that narrows my search."

Once he'd gained his bearings, he pulled his cell phone out and called Lexi.

She answered after the first ring. "Hi. How's it going?"

"I've arrived in Chihuahua."

"He sure gets around for a dead guy."

Scott looked around as he spoke. "What are you doing?"

"I'm heading down the street from the office. Nothing to report. I tried to drop in to visit Dolores this morning but she wouldn't let me in."

He laughed. "Maybe she has the condo bugged and she knows what you're up to."

"Well, I'll try again so I guess I'll find out."

"Maybe think about it before you do something rash. I trust Dolores. If she's hiding Bryan from us, it's probably for good reason."

"Okay. I'm at the coffee shop. I'll speak to you later. Good luck."

Before she disconnected, Scott asked, "Hey, do you have any idea why Dick is suddenly against the idea of dimensional pockets?"

She was quiet for a moment. "Not a clue."

Scott frowned. He had the idea there was something she wasn't saying and for some reason, he couldn't get much of a read on her emotions through their bond. "Okay. I'll see you later." He disconnected before he could ask the questions that clamored for answers.

As he walked toward the church, a loud crack split the silence. It was the familiar sound of magic snapping in the air. He ran toward the building and peeked through the open door. Two men were trapped behind the pulpit while a mage launched another streak of lightning into it. Their flimsy cover blew apart and the men scrambled to the rear of the altar. Scott didn't discern any form of magical or supernatural aura from them.

One of the guys peeked out from behind the altar. He had a dark red burn on the side of his face and pressed buttons frantically on his cell phone.

Neither side of this fight involved a zombie, but while it might not be any of his business, it was one-sided and poked at his natural instinct for fairness. Still, he felt hesitant to enter the fray as he didn't know who anyone was or how it had started. In the next moment, the mage turned slightly and Scott had a view of the attacker's face. It was the man who'd knocked him out at the LA County Morgue.

Suddenly, he had skin in the game.

The man hadn't noticed him and Scott smiled, relishing the opportunity to get some payback. He blasted the mage with an energy ball and hurled him against the wall.

The magical rolled into the pews. His head appeared and he looked at Scott. "Shit." He glanced at the men with a sour look on his face, then disappeared.

Scott ducked quickly into the vestibule and prepared for the mage to reappear behind him but it didn't happen. He glanced at the men and was about to step out to see if they were okay when a couple appeared. It was the former grandfather of Colorado, Eric, with a female mage.

Hastily, he stepped into the alcove and frowned. Exactly how many people were looking for Sam? He'd assumed it was only the mooks and himself.

Eric offered a hand to the man with the burned face and helped him to his feet. "Is he here?"

"There was no sign of him, but this mage showed up and attacked us."

"Did you recognize him? Could it have been the man who killed Francesco?"

The other man turned and Scott recognized him from the ash spell at the house. *Dammit. I helped the mooks who were going to kill Sam.*

One shook his head. "I don't know. I didn't get a good look at either of them. Didn't you see him when you blasted him from the doorway?"

Scott stepped back.

"That wasn't us. We've only just arrived."

It's time to get out of here.

The woman appeared directly in front of Scott but luckily with her back to him. He translocated out and returned home.

CHAPTER THIRTEEN

L exi watched the crime scene. She'd been there for nearly forty minutes. The location was buzzing with cops, which made it awkward for her. The uniforms had already arrived and there were quite a few of them, so she had to hang back among the gawkers, hoping to locate a Kindred-friendly uniform. When the ME's truck pulled up, she began to get concerned that she wouldn't get a good look at the scene. She cursed her decision to go to Palm Springs with Scott in the morning instead of heading straight to work.

Irritated, she stepped up to the crime scene tape at the entrance to the alley. She craned her neck to get a glimpse of a body bag being lifted onto a gurney. It was surprising that the body was still there in the blistering heat of a morning in Las Vegas.

A large, uniformed man came to stand in front of her. "What do you think you're doing?"

She leveled her gaze on him. "I'm trying to see what's going on but I can't see through you."

A rushed voice called, "Sorry. She's with me."

Lexi turned to see who had spoken. It was Sebastian, the guy she'd been all over Kindred headquarters trying to find. He was a mess and she wasn't surprised. Everyone who visited the executive level at Kindred HQ had the same disheveled appearance. He flashed an FBI badge.

"Why didn't you say that?" The man rolled his eyes as he lifted the tape for them.

She considered making a glib response but remembered she was at the scene of a murder.

Sebastian took a pair of latex gloves out and passed another pair and overshoes to her.

Lexi muttered, "I've been searching for a data analyst called Sebastian and here you are playing cop."

"Not here." He scrutinized her quickly. "Where's your ID?"

She shrugged. "I don't have one."

"Everything was sent to your office. I know that because the paperwork came through my office."

"Ah. Yeah, my colleagues don't like me very much. They probably shredded everything."

He smirked. "Maybe it's your face."

There wasn't much she could say to that. He was probably right.

The body was in the bag and ready to be zipped closed. A woman looked at Sebastian. "You're late."

"Sorry, I was waiting for a new colleague who doesn't seem to know where she's supposed to be."

They both looked at Lexi. She opened her mouth and closed it again.

"I can give you roughly thirty seconds. Make them count." She gave Lexi a supercilious smile and redirected the others with paperwork.

The sorcerer stepped to the other side of the body. "I've been here for almost an hour."

"But if one of us gets into trouble with Martha, I'd rather it be you." Sebastian turned the victim's head to the side. "Look at the pallor. He's been drained."

She nodded and studied the wound. "Vamp." She glanced at her scribbled notes. "It seems he was a lawyer. The list of suspects will be long." She went through his pockets. The only thing that hadn't already been removed was a receipt for the pharmacy next to the alley and she slid it into her pocket. "I heard there were a few boisterous vamps in the supe bar last night. It might be worth a visit." She took a quick picture of the victim using her cell phone.

The uniforms returned so they moved out of the alley.

Lexi ducked her head under the tape. "Let's go for coffee. You can tell me why you don't want the management to know—" She turned to face him but he'd vanished. Startled, she turned a full circle.

Son of a bitch!

She began to walk toward the supe bar but paused when her cell phone beeped. It was Azatoth. The demon was ready to begin the training session.

Immediately, she felt a thrill and hated herself for it. She translocated to the office, opened the file, and entered her conclusion that the victim had been drained by a vampire.

She stepped out to the main office. "Has anyone seen my badge and ID?"

No one bothered to even make eye-contact.

"I believe they were sent here."

No response was forthcoming.

"Fine. I have a meeting with Azatoth. Maybe she can help me look for them."

Heads started to rise. One of the women smiled. "I'll chase them up for you."

"Thank you. That's so helpful." She smirked and headed to Learning and Development.

She walked into the training room to find it empty and

checked her cell phone, but there had been no further communications from the demon. When an awareness touched the edge of her consciousness, she realized she wasn't alone.

Lexi studied the room, first with her physical vision and then with her mind. She narrowed her eyes as she stared directly into the seemingly empty corner. "Are we starting or what?"

The air rippled and Azatoth stepped forward. "Well done."

"What am I learning today?"

"How would you like your wounds to heal themselves without any effort on your part?"

"I can already heal myself."

"You heal yourself consciously using magic. You don't need to do that."

She smiled uncertainly. "I don't understand."

"Or would you be interested in never requiring sustenance? No food or water. I can show you how to exist without either."

"For how long?"

"Indefinitely."

Lexi wondered if Azatoth was making fun of her.

"Never mind. Let's try this." The demon stepped closer to her and put a hand on her shoulder.

The young sorcerer looked around. For a moment, everything was gray. In the next moment, they stood in a small cave and the air seemed a little acrid. "Another glamour?"

Her companion smirked. "Not this time. We're in a demon dimension. I forget which one but I can travel to it quite easily. Your only way back is through that door."

Lexi turned around to see a large metal door in the cave wall. "Is there a trick to—" She turned but was suddenly alone.

Cautiously, she stepped close to the door and held her palm up to it. Before she was able to touch it, a magical resistance pressed back and brought a sickly feeling with it. She stepped away and turned her back to it. After a moment, she shook her head and approached again, but she couldn't escape a feeling of dread that came over her the closer she got to it.

It was as though whatever was behind the door wasn't what Azatoth had said. She walked away again and sat on a rock. The sensation both confused and irritated her and after a long, deep breath, she stood, intending to approach again. Despite her determination, she sat again quickly and had to acknowledge that she didn't even want to go near it. Everything inside her screamed that the other side of that door held fearful horrors.

Instead, she looked around the cave. She could see the opening and it wasn't far. A short walk brought her to the edge where her magical energy levels climbed from the presence of sulfur, but the air became more acrid. She didn't move any farther, concerned that the lack of good air out there might kill her. Other than that, there wasn't much to see, merely miles of scrubland.

So, this is a demon realm. I thought it would be scarier.

Lexi walked back to the rock and turned to face the door again. It wasn't there.

"What?" She spun quickly. "Where?" She looked toward the entrance to adjust her bearings and in her peripheral vision, she could see the door in the same place it had been before. It was as though it didn't want to be noticed.

Is that it? Is the door itself trying to put me off looking at it?

If it was, it was working. The more she wanted to see it, the less she was able to.

She'd have given good money to have Limpet with her. Any other exit would be preferable.

Finally, she faced where she knew the door was, ignored the feeling of revulsion, and closed her eyes. She walked directly to where the door should be with her hand up and palm out and stopped when she touched the door. Her next inhalation told her she was in the training room. She opened her eyes to Azatoth looking at her with a completely feral stare of satisfaction and smug achievement. In a moment, the look was gone. "Well done. I thought it would take you a week at least."

Lexi's jaw dropped. "You'd have left me there a week?"

"I did offer to teach you how to live without sustenance."

"I thought you were joking." She followed the demon out of the room. "What was the point of that exercise?"

"You can't practice magic you've never felt. That door was created hundreds of years ago by dark sorcerers. Caleb was never able to get past it."

She raised an eyebrow. "How long did you leave him there for?"

Azatoth stepped into the elevator. "No more than a day at a time." She turned and barred Lexi's entrance, making it clear that she was to take the next one.

"You're saying Caleb couldn't live without sustenance?"

"There were many things Caleb couldn't do." She gave the young sorcerer a finger wave as the doors closed.

Lexi retrieved her ID to call the elevator. "Why the hell am I waiting for an elevator anyway?" She translocated to her department.

When she appeared, a couple of team members smirked and looked down. It was clear they'd been talking about her. She narrowed her eyes and wondered what was so amusing. Ignoring them, she entered her office and looked at an internal envelope on her desk. She opened it and withdrew a Kindred Vari ID, currently appearing as FBI, a badge, and business cards.

Surprise, surprise. My credentials turned up.

She glanced at the board. The case in Las Vegas had been handed to Chris, another investigator. He was one of the smirking assholes outside.

Her head held high, she marched out of her office and straight to him. "What's the problem with the Vegas job?"

He leaned forward, placed an elbow on his desk, and twirled a pen through his fingers. "You came to a hasty conclusion and you were wrong. The job was moved to me because I have years of experience, even if I don't have a big corner office." He clicked his pen and continued to make notes.

She didn't move. "What hasty conclusion?"

"It wasn't a vampire, which you'd have known if you'd bothered to interview the guy's colleagues."

"Bullshit. I've been working in the field since I was sixteen. I know what a vampire kill looks like." She stormed into her office and closed the door, logged into the system, and put the job back in her name. For good measure, she locked the others out of it.

Fuck today. I'm going for coffee. She teleported to the lobby and left the building.

CHAPTER FOURTEEN

Lexi approached the coffee house and drew a calming breath. She put her hand on the door and pushed. This time, she stood in the entrance of Dolores's apartment. She stepped in and closed the door behind her. "Thank God. I was worried after this morning."

The fae looked up from a notebook and smiled. "Sorry dear. I'd have let you in this morning but you had a demon with you."

"I didn't know she was there until I'd stepped into the coffee house. On the bright side, I got a cinnamon roll."

Dolores put her notebook down. "Did you get one for me too?"

"No, but that was hours ago. I'd have eaten yours by now anyway." Lexi grinned.

The woman clicked her pen and put it down. "What's happening?"

"Az is playing nice, although my team doesn't seem to know a vampire kill when they see one."

Dolores's raised an eyebrow. "Az. You're using the psychopathic demon's nickname. How adorable."

Lexi's cheeks warmed. "She insists. I don't care what she calls herself. Anyway, Scott's still looking for Sam and Dick's pining away because he can't see Albin."

The fae tilted her head. "Why don't they meet at Phil's?"

She stared at her in surprise. "I don't know. I expect it didn't occur to them. Given that you're connected, maybe you could get them a table for tonight."

Dolores frowned. "I think I'm running out of favors at Phil's."

"Could you try?" She fluttered her eyelashes at the fae woman. "For Dick? He's so sad."

"Oh, all right." Dolores pulled her cell phone out.

"I'll be a minute." Lexi headed to the bathroom. She walked down the short hallway which ended with a wall and put her hand on it. It simply felt like a wall. She stepped into the bathroom and locked the door behind her. Carefully, she felt along the walls but nothing seemed unusual. She didn't have the first clue how to find a hidden fae room that might or might not even be there.

She sighed, flushed the toilet, washed her hands, and stepped out and walked down the hall.

Dolores looked at her with an eyebrow raised. "I have to be honest, that's taken me quite by surprise."

Lexi froze like a deer in the headlights. "Erm… What?"

"They've had a cancellation. Dick and Albin are in for seven thirty."

"Hey, that's great. I'll let him know." She sat at the table, took her cell phone out, and tapped a text. Her gaze flicked to Dolores's notepad. Unfortunately, she could see writing but couldn't work out what it was. She looked at the woman. "Any chance of coffee?"

"Of course." The fae turned and headed into the kitchen.

Lexi walked around the table and leaned on the counter.

Dolores pulled a mug down and poured the coffee, then added cream and sugar. She passed it to her. "What will Scott do next about finding Sam?"

"We'll catch up later." Lexi turned, took a sip, and glanced at the notepad which had one word written on it. *Rabbits.*

Her brows drew into a frown. "Are you getting pets?"

Dolores looked at her with a puzzled look, then saw the notepad. "Good heavens, no. That's the Wi-Fi password."

The sorcerer looked around. "I didn't know you had Wi-Fi."

With a smile, the fae gathered her notebook and pen. "I'm a fairy of the technology age, dear. What's next for you?"

"I have to get back onto the vamp attack in Vegas." She took another gulp of her coffee. Her phone beeped and she checked it. "Speaking of which, another murder victim has been found on the Strip." She finished her beverage. "I need to get to this one fast. It was difficult with the uniforms around earlier." She stood hastily. "I'll catch up with Scott and let you know how it's going with Sam." She opened the door and stepped out at the condo. "At least there's one good thing about the wards being down. You can drop me at the door."

She said goodbye, closed the door, and walked into the house. "Scott? Are you there?"

There was no answer so she translocated directly to the scene. Two cops stood at the entrance to the gardens outside the MGM Park Casino and Hotel. They were both shifters and she saw their gazes linger on the scar on her arm. One of the cops broke away and walked with her to the body. The victim was a woman in her twenties. She was dressed smartly but the body was found with no shoes.

The cop watched as she looked around. "We haven't found the shoes. This is a weird one."

She stepped closer to the woman's body and checked the neck. "Vamp bite and drained. What's weird about it?"

He frowned. "She wasn't here an hour ago."

Lexi judged the distance from the street. They weren't close enough for the body to have been pushed out of a car. She looked up.

The cop stared at her. "She doesn't look like she was dropped from a plane."

She blushed, then chewed her lip and touched the woman's cheek. It was still warm. "Made to look like a vamp attack, then?"

A lanyard hung around the woman's neck and she tugged it out with her pen. "Gemma Cole. She works at one of the stores in Crystals."

Lexi used her cell phone to snap a few shots of the wound, her face, her ID, and her bare feet. "Okay, you can call the uniforms now."

She headed to the store, flashed her new ID, and asked to speak to the manager.

"I'm sorry, she's not in today. Can anyone else help?"

"When did you last see Gemma Cole?"

"She's on lunch. She's due back in about ten minutes."

The sorcerer raised an eyebrow. "She was here this morning?" She tried to keep the incredulity out of her voice.

"Yes. She left for lunch about half an hour ago." The woman's eyes lit up. "What did she do?"

Irritated, she ignored the question. "Thank you." She left and walked to the pharmacy where the first victim had been found. She noticed a damaged security camera on the side of the building.

Lexi took out the receipt from the store. The lawyer had purchased a packet of antacids and a sandwich at seven am.

He was alive after daybreak. No wonder those assholes in the office were laughing at me.

Her cell beeped with a message from Dick.

Thank you, thank you, thank you.

Lexi was momentarily confused, then remembered the dinner booking.

She called Scott. "Where are you?"

"At the condo."

"Stay there." She disconnected and translocated to the condo. "How did it go in Mexico?"

He was ironing a t-shirt. "Interesting. It seems the mooks from the house in LA work for Eric, and the guy who blasted me at the morgue was there, only he seems to be on a different team. I have no idea what's going on." He looked up and frowned at her worried expression. "What's happening with you?"

"We have a problem. We've had two vampire kills on the Strip."

Scott raised an eyebrow. "If you think it's only two, you haven't been paying attention to those trashy vampires at the supe bar. They aren't very careful—"

"These two were both drained during the day."

He froze. "Do you mean they were found drained during the day?"

"No. One was last seen at seven am leaving work and the other was last seen alive an hour ago."

The mage looked horrified. "But that's impossible."

Lexi stared pointedly at him and answered carefully. "I wouldn't say impossible."

His brows raised when he caught the meaning of her statement. "It can't have been Dick."

"Except that he came home with blood on his shirt."

Scott shook his head. "I still don't think he would."

"Have you heard of any other day-walking vampires?"

"No. But…" He seemed to be thinking.

"What?"

The young mage sighed. "This could be a problem if others jump to the same conclusion."

She frowned. "What others?"

"Yesterday, Dick mentioned that he walked past a shifter he knew from the supe bar in the middle of the day. The guy called out to him but he kept walking." Scott looked at the t-shirt he was ironing. "I guess that's why he's suddenly started dressing differently."

"A disguise?" Lexi frowned. "Do you know where he is now?"

"I have no idea. What does Kindred say about the murders?"

"Oh, that's hilarious. Before I found out it was happening in daylight, they were certain it wasn't a vampire and I insisted it was."

Scott shook his head. "It might be time for Dick to get out of town—or the country. Look, are you certain it was a vampire kill?"

Lexi took her cell phone out and showed him the pictures.

The mage looked through them. "Shit." He nodded and put the device on the ironing board. "We have to tell him. If there are people out there who know he's out in the daylight, your next job could be to hunt him."

She wasn't sure if that was the best course of action and couldn't get his strange behavior that morning out of her head. He had seemed euphoric. And there was the blood.

"Don't say anything yet. It sounds like he's already being discreet. Give me some time to work the case."

Scott didn't look happy. "I don't feel okay about this. He's our friend and I don't think for a moment he's running around murdering people in broad daylight."

Lexi folded her arms. "You're very trusting for someone who had to heal me after I was stabbed by a possessed little old lady from Palm Springs."

He looked thoughtful. "Do you think he might be possessed?"

"It's unlikely, but the fact is we don't know what we're dealing with here. What if it's him and he's not in his right mind? He could have been spelled by a witch."

Scott's eyes widened. "Or Azatoth. Or a dark fae."

"My point exactly. So for now, let's keep an eye on him."

The front door opened. "Keep an eye on who?" Dick pushed

inside with what might well have been a dozen shopping bags from designer stores.

"Marcel. When you're out at the restaurant tonight."

"Lexi, you're an angel." He held the bags up. "Look! My self-pity shopping turned into happy shopping."

He dropped the bags on the couch.

Lexi noticed the name of the store her victim had worked in. She wondered if he had visited it before or after the girl died, but she couldn't think of a subtle way to ask that wouldn't raise his suspicions.

She walked into the kitchen and sniffed the coffee in the pot. With a grimace, she poured it down the sink and refilled the machine. When she returned to the living room, Dick was holding her cell phone.

He turned the screen and showed her the picture of the girl's face. Fortunately, it didn't show the wound. "I've seen her—alive, I mean."

The young sorcerer raised an eyebrow. "She works in one of the stores at Crystals."

"Yes. I saw her only this morning. What happened to her?"

"We don't know yet."

Before she could stop him, he scrolled through the images. "Why did you take a picture of her feet?"

Thank God it's not the picture of the bite. "Her shoes were missing."

Dick sighed. "She was wearing Red Manolo Blahniks if that's any help."

Lexi took the device. "You noticed what shoes she wore?"

"Yes. Her colleagues wore designs from their store. The manager in Tiffany & Co wears Gucci and you wear...I don't know, Walmart probably. I notice these things."

She rolled her eyes at the insult and looked at her feet. In all honesty, she hadn't a clue where she'd bought her boots. They had steel toecaps and she'd selected them for their damage-causing potential.

The vampire continued, "I think she must have bought them second-hand, though."

"Why do you think that?"

"The products in those stores come with heavy price tags but the sales staff don't earn much. They probably get a discount on their store's brand but I remember thinking she couldn't possibly earn enough to buy those shoes unless they were second-hand."

"Maybe she comes from money."

"No. She's had those same shoes on every time I've been in there for the last month." Dick shrugged. "I need to choose what I'm wearing tonight. I'm still waiting to hear from Albin. He's been on a Zoom conference call all day. I have to be sure we don't clash." He picked his bags up and headed to his condo.

Scott folded his t-shirt. He looked at Lexi. "He doesn't—"

Lexi shook her head.

He stopped speaking and twirled his finger. "He doesn't look guilty to me."

Lexi thought for a few seconds. "I'll run interference until we can discover what's going on here. And the best way to do that is to probably give the job back to the smug prick who wanted it."

A few minutes later, Scott's phone beeped and he checked the screen. "Dick's asking if we want the table at Phil's tonight. It seems Albin's meetings will run late."

She narrowed her eyes. "What about keeping an eye on him?"

Scott looked at his friend. "Please say yes, please say yes, please say yes." He pulled a handkerchief from his bag and polished his little seeing ball to a gleam. "We can keep a watch on him with this." He muttered a spell, opened the door, and sent the ball onto the roof.

Lexi looked at the handkerchief. "Dick's, I presume?"

He sighed. "Yes. The idea was to find him if he's ever kidnapped but I guess it works for spying on your friends too."

She could see this situation wasn't sitting well with him. "We're looking after him. What if he's doing this and isn't even aware of it? Can you imagine how he'd feel if he knew we could have stopped him and didn't?"

The mage nodded. He hadn't thought of it that way. With a sigh, he removed the speech cloaking spell.

The young sorcerer frowned. "Oh, nuts."

"What's wrong?"

"I don't think I have anything to wear tonight."

"You've got the dress Dick bought you and that nice outfit you stole from that girl who wound up in the pool." Scott grinned.

Lexi rolled her eyes. "I'm heading to the Strip. If you see Dick, tell him I've gone to Walmart for something fancy."

The vampire shouted through the wall. "I heard that."

His two young friends smiled briefly at each other.

CHAPTER FIFTEEN

The two young people stood at the desk in Phil's Cornerdown Kitchen. Scott was as formal as he could endure in beige chinos and a black polo shirt. Lexi had found a black dress she didn't hate. She would never have admitted it to anyone, but she quite liked to dress up and she felt she needed to decompress.

Cassidy sighed as she checked Dick and Albin's names on the list. "I'm sorry Albin couldn't make it but it's good the table's being used. Come along."

They followed the young fae woman through the restaurant. When they had passed the last few tables and kept walking, Scott turned to Lexi and frowned.

She shrugged.

They continued down a little hallway with intimate little rooms and tables for two and were guided into the last one.

The lighting was muted and came mostly from a candle in the middle of the table. After Cassidy had left, the two young people gazed around the room.

Lexi looked at a painting on the wall—a Greek scene with a

naked woman in the arms of a bull-headed creature. "Well, this is…"

Scott grinned. "Nice. I know."

She had intended to end the statement with uncomfortable.

Phil walked past and stopped. He looked into the little room. "I'm sorry to see Dick couldn't make it. He and Albin must be having a difficult time of it."

The mage nodded but neither of the young people spoke.

The minotaur looked at Lexi and tilted his head. "Good choice." He looked at Scott, laughed, and walked away.

She frowned. "What were you thinking of eating?"

"I wasn't thinking of food at all. I was thinking about Sam."

"You better hope he doesn't bring you a zombie head. How's it going with the case?"

"I'll keep looking tomorrow. It'll be like searching for a needle in a haystack."

The waiter brought a cold bottle of beer for her and a tall milkshake for Scott.

Her gaze followed the waiter as he walked away. She watched him pass another man carrying a cage. As the other man came closer, she saw that the cage contained four rabbits.

She spoke to Scott as she made eye contact with one of the white, fluffy little creatures in passing. "Did you know Dolores's apartment has Wi-Fi?"

"No. I've never seen a router."

Lexi smirked. "That's because she hasn't got Wi-Fi." She stood. "I'll be back in a minute."

His face screwed up in confusion.

She stepped out of the little room and followed the man with the cage along the hallway. He turned left into the corridor that led to Phil's office. She stood at the corner and peeked out to see he had stopped at the office door, knocked, and entered. With a smile, she returned to the table.

A few minutes later, Phil passed them again. "Dinner should only be a few more minutes." He looked at Lexi and narrowed his eyes.

Scott held his chocolate milkshake up. "This is lovely. It's so creamy."

"It's Minotaura milk. I'll tell her you like it. She'll be pleased." He walked away.

The mage paled and shuddered.

"Are you okay?"

"I threw up in my mouth a little."

Two minutes later the food arrived—a huge pile of ribs in sticky sauce with twice-cooked chunky fries for Scott and chicken curry with rice for Lexi.

He grinned with sauce around his mouth. "I wonder how he does it. This is exactly what I wanted and I didn't even know it."

Lexi didn't answer. She'd heard, but she was thinking.

"Earth to Lexi."

She stared at him and leaned forward. "I need a distraction."

The mage frowned. "What kind of distraction?"

"A big one." She thought for a moment, then smiled. "You know what? Never mind. I've got this." She translocated to Dick's condo. The vampire lay on the couch with his eyes closed and earphones on. She could hear classical music issuing from them.

Limpet looked at her and yawned.

She squatted and crooked her finger. The thinner demon jumped into her arms. She put him onto her shoulder and returned to the foyer of the restaurant. There was no way to avoid going through the revealing spell.

Cassidy looked up. "You'd better keep an eye on him. Phil will hit the roof if he runs amok again."

"Will do." She made her way through the restaurant to the table.

Scott's jaw dropped. "I don't think it's wise to bring him here."

"He won't kill any pixies, will you, Limpet?"

The demon blinked his giant eyes at her.

She grinned at him. "Maybe play with them a little."

Limpet sniffed the air and he darted away.

Scott watched him go with a slack jaw. "I feel like this was a very bad idea and I can't fathom why you would do it."

As they finished their food, the chorus of tiny screams started and Phil thundered past their table.

Lexi stood and handed a napkin to Scott with a smile. "Wipe your face. You eat like a toddler." She stepped out of the room and walked toward Phil's office. Hearing steps behind her, she turned to her friend. "Where are you going?"

"With you. You seem to have forgotten lately that we're partners."

"We are. And your job is to make sure Phil doesn't kill Limpet."

The mage stopped. He almost turned back but continued to follow her. "He won't kill him."

She walked through the open door into Phil's office.

Surprise, surprise. No rabbits.

"Could you at least tell me why we're about to be murdered by a giant minotaur?"

Rather than answer, she stared at the wall behind Phil's desk. She didn't even know if this would work.

Scott continued. "Well? What now?"

"Now we find out if Bryan is where I think he is." She didn't want to admit that what she was planning might leave him standing alone in Phil's office.

Holding her palms out and closing her eyes, she stepped toward the wall. She felt the magic of the portal pushing back. It felt different. While it wasn't trying to make her turn away, there was another difference. This had been created with a different kind of magic.

She persisted and tried to remember what she had done to get through the portal in the demon dimension. After a moment, she recalled that she had automatically seemed to harmonize with the frequency of the energy coming off the door which had, of course, been a portal. This one seemed to take more effort to put herself into synchronicity but as she stood and followed the magical trail, she heard Scott take in a sharp breath. She opened her eyes and watched as the door revealed itself and the handle appeared. "I did it!"

"How?" He sounded suspicious.

"I've been getting extra training at work."

"From who?"

Lexi looked at her feet.

The mage kept his voice low but he was furious. "Are you fucking kidding me? You're taking magic lessons from that demon?"

Her face reddened.

"When did you learn this trick?"

"Today as a matter of fact."

"What if she knows where Bryan is? What if this is a trick to get to him through you?"

"It's a coincidence. I'll explain later." Lexi grasped the door-knob and opened the door to the maze. It looked different. She looked up and could see a beautiful night sky above the maze and she turned back to Scott. "Are you coming or not?"

"I'm not letting you go on your own as you seem to have taken leave of your senses lately."

They stepped through. Lexi kept the doorknob in her hand and pulled the door closed. She led the way down the steps but stopped to look behind at the door and steps disappearing and the maze opening in all directions around them.

Scott gazed around, fascinated. "Holy shit. It's everywhere."

Lexi threw a vial of sulfur onto the wall where they were

entering the maze and continued down the stairs. "Keep away from the walls. That green stuff has poisoned thorns."

"Great. Which direction?"

The sorcerer produced her dark metal ball and threw it into the air. "Let's see if we can cut out some of the hard work." She closed her eyes to focus on her connection with the orb.

"That's odd," her companion muttered.

She opened her eyes. Scott was looking upward and she followed his gaze to the moon.

"What?"

"That looks like our moon but it shouldn't be a full moon right now."

"Maybe it's simply a spell for ambiance." She had already guessed why it was there. In fact, the full moon had confirmed the suspicions the rabbits had already given her.

A blood-curdling howl issued from somewhere within the maze.

Scott's jaw dropped. "Bryan has shifted. He's a wolf."

"Which explains the moon and the rabbits." She smiled with satisfaction.

"So you didn't already know the rabbits were for Bryan? What led you here?"

"Merely putting two and two together. The important thing is that I was right."

"Is it? Because I feel like the important thing is that we're in here with a werewolf."

Lexi rolled her eyes. "Would you prefer to hide inside my dimensional pocket?"

The wolf howled again. It was louder this time.

Scott was fuming. "We have to talk about this."

She closed her eyes again and the ball resumed its search. After a few minutes, she sighed. "Where the hell is he?"

"Probably stalking us," the mage muttered.

She spun to face him "Could you help?"

"I thought you had this all planned."

"What in the name of all that is holy made you think that?"

He muttered and waved an arm.

A green haze appeared around them. "Ew, what's that?"

"It's the wolf's pheromones made visible. How does it look now from up there?"

Lexi closed her eyes. "He's been almost everywhere but I see one area that's a very bright green." She grasped Scott's arm and translocated them across the maze. They appeared at the end of a long passage. The wolf was at the other end with his back to them, about to disappear around the corner. He froze and turned to face them. With a snarl, he surged forward.

She grabbed Scott again and translocated into Bryan's dimensional pocket. Except it wasn't. Instead of the closet with a mirrored door at the end, they were in a den of leaves and dirt.

Puzzled, she shook her head. "I don't understand."

Scott thought about it. "I hope you weren't expecting to find a human version of Bryan in here."

"Well, that was the idea."

The mage stepped forward and reached into the dark branches at the other end where the mirror would have been. The growth moved away and two more steps took them into the large hall of memories.

Her gaze went immediately to the screens. The wolf was running through the maze at an incredible speed.

Lexi shouted, "Bryan."

Once again, the wolf ground to a halt.

"Bryan, it's Lexi. Can you shift back?"

The wolf howled and bolted through the corridors of the maze again.

Over the next half hour, she kept trying to communicate with him but the man was completely overtaken by the wolf.

She snatched a sheet of paper and pinned it onto the most recent board.

Bryan, I need you to get in touch with me. Lexi.

That done, she translocated them to the bright yellow vial and picked it up on the way up the steps. Retrieving the ball from the air, she sighed. "I can't believe what a bust that was."

She put the doorknob into the door and opened it. They walked into the office to find Phil and Dolores waiting for them.

CHAPTER SIXTEEN

Dolores rounded on Lexi. "What the hell do you think you're doing? Do you realize the danger you've put Bryan in? And Phil too."

"I needed to speak to Bryan and you've been hiding him from me."

The fae put her hand over her face. "I've been hiding him from Azatoth."

Lexi pointed at the door. "Why do you have him in there? Azatoth isn't even interested in him anymore."

"What on earth gave you that idea?"

"It was one of my conditions of working for her. She said she'd leave Bryan and Scott alone."

Dolores and Phil exchanged a look.

"What?"

The woman sighed. "He's been a wolf for weeks. It stops Azatoth's psychic attacks and makes it impossible to get a fix on Bryan's location."

"I don't understand. Azatoth's been trying to attack him? All this time?"

"Bryan's been under constant psychic attacks for weeks."

She was horrified. "Why didn't you tell me?"

"You're not supposed to know where he is. If you accused Azatoth of attacking him, it would reveal that you know his whereabouts. I didn't want to put you at any more risk than you already are. It's bad enough that you're working at that place every day."

"We agreed we needed someone on the inside."

Dolores shook her head. "I'm not certain it's even worth it anymore. I thought there might be a chance we'd discover what she's up to but she seems to be keeping you well on the outside. You've barely even seen her." Lexi flicked her gaze to Scott. He said nothing, keeping her secret, but the news about Bryan changed everything. She could no longer put her selfish needs before others. "That's not entirely true."

The woman stared at her and waited in silence.

"She's been training me," the dark sorcerer continued and her cheeks heated.

Dolores turned her gaze to Scott. "You knew this?"

"Scott didn't know," Lexi interrupted. "But she somehow seems to know much more about dark sorcery than anyone else."

Phil stood and made the room seem suddenly tiny. "What exactly has she taught you?"

"How to see through glamours." She shifted her gaze involuntarily to him. "How to get through a portal."

He frowned, which surprised her. She didn't think his face could possibly frown any further. "She must know Bryan is here."

She shook her head. "No, I don't think she does. I noticed Dolores had made a note about rabbits and the next thing, I see a cage of rabbits go past our table."

The fae sighed. "My fault, then. I'm sorry, Phil."

"It wasn't anyone's fault." Lexi felt bad enough herself and didn't need anyone else to take the blame.

A high-pitched whine came from the corner of the room. Lexi noticed Limpet in a little cage looking at her. His huge ears hung down and he held onto a pixie brain. She felt wretched as her eyes filled with tears. "I'm sorry, little guy."

She turned to Phil. "I'll pay for any damage."

He raised an eyebrow. "There wasn't any. He merely ran around making the pixies scream. Surprisingly, didn't eat any of them." The minotaur opened the cage.

The little thinner demon dropped the brain and scampered out. He scrambled up to cling to her shoulder and lay his head in her neck.

There was a knock at the door but surprisingly, it wasn't the office door. It was the door to the maze.

Phil opened it and Bryan stepped through looking disheveled.

Lexi noticed that the roof of the maze had returned and the moon was gone.

Dolores checked her watch. "You have five minutes. We'll have to move him."

The sorcerer gave Bryan a hug.

He looked tired but his only thought was of Alicia. "How is she? Is she still in there?"

She put a hand on his arm. "I need you to help me find out. I've noticed the demon can't seem to access Alicia's dimensional pocket. I think if she's anywhere, she's there."

His face contorted. "I didn't even think of that. I cut off the connection to my magic so Azatoth couldn't use it. What if she's been trying to contact me and I simply put up a wall between us?"

Lexi took his hand. "We'll find out. Scott once pulled me physically out of a difficult situation by taking me into his dimensional pocket. Could you pull Alicia through into yours?"

Scott shook his head. "I don't think that's a good idea. If she's in there and she exits into another dimensional pocket, she might not be able to get back in. She could be lost forever."

Bryan rubbed his rough, bearded face. "I think I can get through into her pocket."

"Can you get me in there?"

"I can open the way from mine. I didn't break the link irreparably. I couldn't bring myself to do that." He looked at Dolores. "Do we have time?"

"This could be risky. If Azatoth senses where you are—"

"It's worth it," Bryan interjected. "I have to try."

Lexi turned to Phil. "Can we do it from here?"

He nodded.

"I'm coming. I'll stay on Bryan's side in case you need my help." Scott didn't look like he would take no for an answer. Bryan nodded.

Lexi and Scott went into his dimensional pocket. They found him in the hall at the bottom of the stairs. As they walked down to meet him, a door that hadn't previously been there stood to their left. He put a hand on the door and looked at Lexi. After a deep breath, he opened it and he and Lexi stepped through into Alicia's bedroom in her old family home. The room wasn't identical, however. Everything was smaller.

Bryan looked around. "Ali?" He walked across the room to open the bedroom door.

"Don't open it." Alicia's head came up from the other side of the bed. "This is all there is now. I made it as small as I could so she can't find me." She stood and ran to Bryan.

Lexi was shocked. Her sister was the strongest legacy she'd ever known but in there, she was diminished and terrified.

"The things she's done, Bryan." She glanced at a small TV in the corner.

She realized she must have seen what Azatoth did to her parents.

Alicia looked at her sister but instead of love, there was anger. "You seem friendly with her. Bringing her coffee every morning. Always excited for your training sessions."

"I'm trying to get you free of her." Again, she felt embarrassed.

She knew she'd let herself down by putting her training ahead of finding out what the demon was planning.

Her sister pointed a finger at her. "You should have killed her when I gave you the chance. Why didn't you kill her?"

"I'm not giving up on you." She looked at the TV. "Have you seen or heard any of the meetings she goes to?"

"I try not to look at what's going on out there, but I've seen her in discussions with the cabal, talking about something called the demon gate in Las Vegas. I think it's a portal."

Lexi narrowed her eyes. "A demon gate?"

"They've been disabling the wards to try to find a gate that leads to the same dimension the demon originally came from, but something's blocking them. She said that only a shadow mage can open it."

Lexi shook her head. "That term again—shadow mage. It's not a huge leap to assume it's another name for a dark sorcerer, but who uses it? It's not in any of the books I've read."

"That's right. She means you. When she's with the cabal, she refers to you as 'that pathetic excuse for a shadow mage.'"

She raised an eyebrow.

Alicia shrugged. "Her words, not mine. She tried to detach herself from my body to take yours over but she couldn't get herself free of me. She was furious."

Lexi was shocked. "She what? When did she try to do that?"

"When you had the sword and you were supposed to kill her, she was choking you, trying to make you weak so you'd be easier to possess. It didn't work."

"You stopped her."

"I stopped her from strangling you. I had nothing to do with keeping her bound to my body. She thinks Caleb did something wrong when he prepared my body to be the vessel."

Now, the dark sorcerer was confused. "But the demon was living in Caleb's head. Why doesn't she know how he did the spell?"

"Azatoth was projecting from the other side of the veil. She wasn't present like she is now."

"I wonder if Caleb messed it up deliberately." She looked from her sister to Bryan. "That spell could be the answer to getting rid of her. If she's looking for it, we need to get to it first."

"You're safe at the moment. That's why everyone has orders to keep you sweet. She can't kill you because right now, you're the only one who can open that gate for her."

"Right now?" She didn't like the sound of that.

"She's had the cabal going through every document in the archive to find Caleb's spell. I think she's been looking for something else too. She keeps complaining that the records don't go back far enough."

Outside the mind link in the dimensional pockets, Dolores put her hand on Lexi's shoulder. "Wrap this up."

She turned to her sister. "We have to go. Dolores is keeping Bryan safe."

"I know. That monster is furious that she can't find him. She thinks his magic might be the key to getting her out of my body and into you. I'm not so sure."

Lexi nodded. "And don't call me sis again. She noticed that."

"That wasn't me. It was her manipulating you. You need to watch yourself. When you're training, your magical energy goes dark. She's trying to make you give up Scott's magic. I don't know why."

She hugged her sister.

Alicia whispered. "If you get another chance, you have to kill her. I'm not important."

Lexi looked into her sister's eyes. She couldn't agree to that.

Bryan kissed his wife. "Stay strong. I love you." He turned and left.

"Stay safe. Both of you," Alicia called.

He closed the door and the three of them stood and watched as it faded away. In the next moment, they were fully back in

Phil's office. Bryan nodded once and ran into the maze. As Phil closed the door, Lexi's last view was the moon-filled sky returning.

She smiled a malicious smile. "It looks like we have someone way more on the inside than I am. We need to find a way to leverage that without risking either of them."

Dolores nodded. "I'll see you both tomorrow." She looked at Phil. "We'll talk later."

Lexi watched as the fae left quickly.

Why is she in such a hurry?

Phil led the young people back through the restaurant but veered down a different hallway. "You're leaving through the back door this time," the minotaur explained.

As they walked through the bar, she noticed the mural on the wall.

There will be no breaking and entering by order of the management. Breaking and entering will result in expulsion to a dumpster realm. How you get home from there is your problem.

She'd barely given the words a thought when Phil opened a door and pushed Lexi, Scott, and Limpet through it.

CHAPTER SEVENTEEN

Lexi was falling.

She looked at Phil's satisfied face where he smiled at them from a door in the sky. He shouted, "You're good with portals. Try this one," pulled the door closed, and disappeared. Limpet had crawled around her and hung onto her face with his hands grasping her ears. It was useful to have something covering her ears because all she could hear was Scott screaming. They landed all too soon.

It wasn't ground beneath them as such. It was soft and squishy and it smelled extremely bad.

Limpet opened one giant eye and lifted his head. He squealed and barreled through the garbage like a kid on a snow day, rolling around.

Lexi straightened and looked at Scott, who seemed like he wanted to cry.

"Are you hurt?"

"I have…" He sniffed. "Something in my hair. And everywhere else."

She gazed around and stared at Limpet. He seemed to be building a den out of potato peelings and eggshells.

"I'm sorry. You didn't deserve this." She tried to push to her feet but her hands sank into the stinking trash. "How the hell can we get out of here?"

"Can't you make a portal?"

"I only know how to open portals, not make them."

A whistle sounded and Lexi looked around. Limpet hadn't been building a den. Instead, he'd made a wall out of the stinking garbage to create a portal.

The two friends crawled toward it on their arms and knees and tried to spread their weight across the trash as much as possible to avoid sinking into it. They reached Limpet's portal. She went through first, Scott followed, and the little demon appeared with a huge grin on his face but looked back as the portal closed. He seemed sad to leave the dumpster realm.

They had crawled out of a wall at the bottom of a long stone stairway.

Lexi looked around. "It looks like Earth. Where are we?"

Scott took his cell phone out. "Edinburgh, Scotland."

She sighed. "Cool. I'd like to visit here again when I don't stink."

"It sounds like a plan." He looked at her. "You have some…" He pointed at her hair. "Never mind. How are we—"

Lexi caught his arm and translocated. It was nighttime and cold. She looked at him. "Oh. Where are we now?"

He checked his phone. "Nova Scotia."

She scowled. "Seriously? I was aiming for Vegas."

"I guess we're lucky we didn't end up in the middle of the Atlantic Ocean, then."

"Let me try again."

"Maybe you should—"

They arrived in the condo.

Dick stood from the couch. "Where the hell have you been?"

She fainted. The last thing she was aware of was being caught by the vampire.

Lexi was aware of voices around her and pain on the back of her head.

Dick spoke softly. "I don't know what the hell I'm going to do. We can't meet for dinner for the rest of our lives and I have no idea how much magic is required to keep me from attacking him."

"You attacked someone? Lexi sat up.

"We'll think of something," Scott muttered.

Dick rolled his eyes. "Of course not. I'm talking about Albin and the wards."

Lexi grimaced and felt a lump on the back of her head. "What happened?"

The vampire looked at her. "You passed out."

"Okay, I remember starting to faint and you caught me."

"But you stink," he explained, "so I dropped you." He noticed her face fall. "Sorry. It was a knee-jerk reaction to the smell."

Scott passed her a glass of water.

When she reached out for it, she could see the energy in her unhealing scar was bright silver.

"You exhausted yourself," the mage explained. "I did what I could but I don't have any sulfur. Maybe you should give me one of those little vials to keep for you so you can fill up with your fuel of choice."

"Thank you. You did the right thing." She nodded and drank the water. "I desperately need a shower."

Dick stared at Limpet. "So does he."

The demon narrowed his eyes at him.

"You'll be welcome to join Marcel in my home when you've had a bath. That goes for you too, Lexi." The vampire stood and looked at the mage. "What's the plan for tomorrow?"

"I'll keep looking for Sam. You're welcome to—"

"No, thank you. I have some errands to run." Dick left quickly.

Lexi looked pointedly at Scott who took the hint and made it safe for them to talk.

She glanced toward the roof. "Is your seeing ball up there?"

"Yes, it's back up. I took it down after I got out of the shower and checked it. He didn't leave his condo until he came round here after you took Limpet. Marcel started howling when he discovered him gone."

She nodded as she thought it through. "That's good. With us across the country, we need to make sure he's accounted for. If there's another murder, it would be great to scratch him off the list."

Scott raised an eyebrow. "The list of one?"

"Yes, that list." She stood and pointed at Limpet. "Come on you. Bath time."

The little demon glowered at her.

She gave him a lopsided grin. "You don't fool anyone. I know you swim in the sink when no one's there. You need to clean your hair out of the plughole if you want to keep that kind of thing secret." She looked at the state of her new clothes and shook her head. "And what exactly is the point of a dumpster realm?" she demanded as she stormed up the stairs.

CHAPTER EIGHTEEN

Lexi walked into the office. She wasn't looking forward to what she had to do.

Chris gazed slowly at her after she had stood at his desk for five seconds. "Can I help you?"

She wanted to ram a fist into his smug face. "I have an apology to make."

He leaned back in the way office assholes the world over did, lounged in his chair, and spread his legs as though his boys were so big they needed the extra space. "Go on."

It took effort to hold her snide comment back and she worked her jaw for a moment until she had herself back under control. "I acted hastily yesterday. You were right. I'll send the job to you on the system." She turned to walk away.

"So where is it?"

She swiveled on a heel to look at him. "What?"

He folded his arms. "The apology. There wasn't one."

Oh, you noticed that did you, Big Balls?

Lexi was aware that the others were watching. She smiled. "I apologize."

Chris smirked. "That wasn't so hard, was it?"

The fact that this guy was still in one piece was a testimony to how well she was working on her abilities.

She had almost reached her office door when he called after her.

"That was nice of you but it wasn't necessary. The post mortem results came back. You were right. Somehow, it was a vampire. Keep the job. You can find out how it happened. I've linked the two murders together on the system. Happy hunting."

Lexi didn't turn. She thought that if she looked at the little prick again, she'd probably obliterate him. Instead, she stepped into her office which was spelled for privacy, closed the door, and screamed. She looked for something to throw. Her gaze settled on the plant Scott had given her and she translocated to the condo. Unfortunately, the mage had already left.

She thought for a few seconds, then knocked on Dick's door before she opened it. "It's me," she called.

"Come in if you've showered since I last saw you."

"Funny." She entered the living room, where Dick was spraying starch on his shirt collar. "I didn't know people still used that."

"What can I say? I'm an old-fashioned guy. How are you feeling?"

"I'm not having a great day. I need to borrow Limpet."

He frowned. "For how long? I need to go out and I don't like leaving Marcel alone."

"Would an hour be okay?"

Dick smiled. "That works for me."

Lexi jerked her head at the little demon. He climbed onto her shoulder.

She looked at him. *I need you to be a cat.*

He jumped down and shook himself until he resembled a black cat. He purred and rubbed against her leg.

Marcel sniffed the cat demon, then licked his face.

Lexi smiled at the two of them. She glanced at Dick. "What are you doing today?"

"I'm returning a jacket I bought yesterday. It's honestly not me."

"I thought that was the point of the new clothes."

"I mean it's not new me."

"Good luck with that." She badly wanted to tell him about the vampire kills but she forced herself to keep her mouth shut.

Instead, she picked Limpet up and translocated to the scene where Gemma's body had been found.

She stroked the cat. "I'm looking for portals. I can find where a portal is but I can't tell if one has been here sometime in the past. Can you?"

The demon cat went straight to where the body had been. He sniffed and licked the ground.

"Dude, gross." She stared at the cat. "Portals?"

Limpet spent a few minutes wandering around the area, then returned to sit at her feet.

"Nothing, huh? Let's try the other scene." They appeared in the alley where the first drained victim had been found. The thinner demon scooted around but returned to her feet in seconds.

"I'll take that as a no. Come on, then. Let's get you back so Dick can go out and do what I sincerely hope isn't murdering people."

Limpet's gaze seemed to communicate that the vampire was more fun to be around than she was.

Once she'd returned to the office, Lexi scowled at the board. She hated unresolved cases. Both sites had been searched with Limpet and they had found no signs of portals or residual magic. She couldn't sense fae, wolves, or demons aside from the one that had accompanied her.

Her cell phone beeped and she glanced at the screen. It was Azatoth. *Are we doing this or what?*

Her feet flew off the desk. "Shit."

She was late for a training session. Startled into action, she tried to translocate to the training room but appeared in the lobby. It seemed there were places in the building she simply couldn't jump to.

Irritated now, she tapped a response as she walked to the elevators. *On way.*

Moments later, she burst through the door. "Sorry I'm late. Crappy case."

Azatoth smiled. "It's fine, I've…" She paused. "Well, don't you smell all fresh as a daisy."

Lexi was puzzled. "Thank you?"

"You have all that lovely white magic coursing through you."

She realized what the demon was getting at. "Oh that. I had a—"

The demon interrupted her brusquely. "Many of the things I'm trying to teach you won't work as long as your magic is so heavily polluted by your little mage friend. You're wasting my time and yours." She walked closer to Lexi and put a hand on her shoulder. As she leaned forward to speak into her ear, the young sorcerer felt an excruciating pain in her stomach. She looked down hastily. The demon's fingers had turned into long talons which were sticking into her. As she dropped to her knees, she watched the blood-soaked talons slide out.

Azatoth continued to speak. "Your body could already be healing itself. Instead, you have to use your magic on it. But if you passed out, you'd simply die. I'll leave you to mull that over." She headed to the door. "Don't be late again." In the next moment, she was gone.

Lexi held her hand over the bleeding wound. She healed it using a spell Scott had taught her and remained alone in the room for another half an hour before she could stand. Ruefully, she assessed the damage to the top she wore. It now had five distinct holes and was covered in blood. She considered how careless she'd become around the demon.

After using a glamor to hide the mess, she stood. It was time to start getting answers.

She headed to the executive offices and found Nora. "Do you want to get coffee?"

"Yes, absolutely." They ducked into the little staff kitchen.

The frazzled administrator took two cups down and heaped sugar into Lexi's. "Don't tell me you're having a bad day too."

She exhaled an irritated sigh. "You could say that. What's up with you?"

"She came back in a foul mood. Luckily, she went straight into a meeting with Eric and Millicent and will hopefully take it out on them. Now that's a couple of bodies I wouldn't mind hauling away. Why is your day so bad?"

Lexi picked the jug up and poured coffee into both cups. "She stabbed me in the gut."

Nora lowered her head into her hands. "Holy Mother of God."

The sorcerer hadn't intended to say what she had. She'd wanted to steer the conversation elsewhere and so tried again. "She's mad because I haven't been able to solve a case I'm working on. I can't find any records on the system that fit the situation. Do we have a library or something?"

The secretary grinned at her. "We have the largest archive on the supernatural in existence. It's downstairs in the basement."

Lexi held the door open. "Oh, cool. Do I have to search it myself or is there a helpful little elf who can bring the records up for me?"

Nora led the way to her desk. "You can put in a request and someone will search the topic for you, or you can go down there yourself and dig through the files." She glanced at a wheeled trolley piled with books and folders. "I still haven't returned the last pile she asked for."

Lexi looked at it too. She wondered what the demon had been

reading. "I'll go down and have a look, thanks." She pointedly didn't look at the trolley again and drained her cup. "Did you say there's someone down there who will help me?

"Yes. Devon the curator. He's not an elf, though. I hope that won't spoil your day."

"No. I think being stabbed will still win that prize. I merely wanted to be sure before I offered to wheel that down for you. I don't want to get stuck with shelving it. It appears my generosity does know bounds." She smiled and shrugged.

The woman looked at the cart, then at Azatoth's office door. "No, that's fine. I should do it myself." She looked at her watch.

"Cool. I'd better get a move on." She started to walk to the elevator.

"I…um…"

Lexi smiled inwardly as she turned to Nora. "Huh?"

"Would you mind taking the files back for me? That would be very kind of you."

"No problem." She saluted.

The sorcerer stepped into the elevator and waved her ID. The buttons appeared and she pressed the one marked *B*.

She stepped out of the elevator into a hallway with flickering lights and noisy pipes running the length of the hallway.

It's plain creepy down here.

She followed the sign to the archives and stopped outside the room to peer at the door battered with marks at the same height as the trolley. She didn't want to draw too much attention by shoving in so instead, she flicked her finger and the door opened silently.

The space was huge. Reading tables were scattered among the aisles but only a couple were occupied. She approached the front desk but there was no sign of anyone working there. She looked across the desktop at a strange cylindrical box with eight brass bands encircling it. It didn't seem to be fully there. Cautiously, she poked it and her finger went straight through.

Weird.

Lexi rolled the cart to a table that gave her a vantage point to view the entrance and wedged the cart under the table and out of sight.

Quickly, she pulled out a pile of documents and flicked through them. Reports of age-old Kindred jobs and yellowed maps passed through her hands. She glanced briefly at each page and made sure they were recorded on the memory drives in her dimensional pocket.

After an hour, she'd gone through everything. Nothing referred to shadow mages and no maps had an X marking a spot. She rolled the cart to the main desk and left it there. It was time to start going through the shelves for a few reference books to use as her alibi for being down there.

The reference section was easy to navigate. She selected a book on glamours, one on cold cases, and one on vampires. Her cover was taken care of.

As she wandered deeper into the stacks, she heard shuffling and followed the sound as it became louder.

She found an elderly man standing on a rolling ladder slotting books into a high shelf.

"You must be Devon."

He turned and the ladder vibrated as he shook at the sight of her. He dropped the book he'd been holding as he stared at her face.

Lexi caught the book. "I'm not her."

He didn't stop shaking. "Oh. I see. It's you."

She squinted up at him. "Have we met?"

A shushing sound issued from somewhere close to them. He looked around, then at her and lowered his voice. "No. I've heard of you. You're the dark sorcerer, aren't you?"

She opened her arms. "Tada! The one and only."

Someone shushed her again.

"Oh! Shush yourself." She lowered her voice anyway. "While

we're on that subject, if you have anything on the topic of dark sorcerers—like an idiot's guide—that would be great."

"I've combed the whole library. If I'd found anything, I can assure you I'd have handed it straight over."

"I don't doubt it." She narrowed her eyes. It sounded like the demon had already been looking for information on her. She ran a finger across a row of leather-bound books. "Is this everything? The whole history of Kindred?"

He climbed down the ladder. She was impressed. He must have been in his eighties but he was still fairly spry.

When he reached the floor, he retrieved the book he'd dropped, placed it on the ladder, and spoke quietly. "This is all that's left. There was a fire. We lost many of our historical documents."

"How does an organization like Kindred lose so much of its history to something so mundane as a fire?"

"It was completely ablaze before anyone was aware of it. We can battle most things but not time." The man chuckled softly.

Lexi failed to see what was funny but she smiled politely. "Do you get many visitors down here?"

He gazed around the archive. "A few. I spend most of my time here with ghosts of the past." He turned to her and smiled. "They don't like my filing system."

She smiled and decided she liked this gentle old man. "You could tell them to do it themselves if they don't like it."

"Good God, no. They've only recently stopped doing that."

Puzzled, she simply looked at him in silence. She wasn't sure if the man was joking or not. "How long have you worked here?" she asked after a long moment.

"I've worked in the archives for sixty years."

"Did you get injured in the field?" Lexi remembered herself. "I'm sorry if that's too personal."

"No, not at all. It started as a short stint while I looked for a match, but it was a good fit. I never liked the idea of hunting goblins. I was always more of an academic than a magical Errol Flynn."

Lexi grinned at the reference. "You like the old movies. I have a friend who would love you."

They walked to the front desk and Devon asked her to tap her ID badge onto each of the books she wanted.

She gestured to the trolley. "I brought these back for Nora."

"I'll return them for you." He paused and looked at her as though he wanted to say something. Instead, the old man turned away but his gaze lingered on a painting on the wall before he looked elsewhere.

Lexi glanced at the desk. "What's this box?"

"Oh, I keep it around to amuse the youngsters. If you catch it just right, you can spin the brass wheels. Then, if you can line the eight numbers up correctly, it becomes solid and the box can be opened."

"Has anyone ever opened it?"

"Never. There are forty thousand, three hundred and twenty possible combinations."

She laughed. "They're simply not curious enough."

"I don't believe anyone's that curious. No, I think it will only be opened by someone who has the combination to hand."

"Do you know the combination?"

"I did once but I seem to have forgotten it." He smiled wistfully.

Lexi glanced at the wall. The painting didn't seem to be anything special. She looked at the old man. "Thank you." She smiled at him and headed to her office.

The young sorcerer checked the time. Although she wanted to visit Dolores, after the previous evening's antics, she wasn't sure the fae would want to see her. She sent a text to her first.

Am I welcome to drop by or will you shrink and squish me?

At the thought of how angry and embarrassed Dolores had

appeared in Phil's office, Lexi cringed. She wondered if she was still on the team.

The fae responded quickly. *Of course you're welcome, dear. Come along.*

She exhaled a slow breath of relief.

Dolores put a plate of cinnamon rolls onto the table. "The coffee shop is virtually my landlord. It's only polite to support their business."

Lexi smiled and stared at her coffee cup. "I'm so sorry—"

The woman put a hand up. "I should have handled it differently. It's all water under the bridge now. What did you learn from Alicia?"

"Azatoth is behind the problem with the wards in Las Vegas. It seems there's some kind of gate that leads to the demon realm she came from, but they can't find it. The only reason she hasn't killed me is because she needs me to open it."

The fae woman sat. "I'm surprised she hasn't tried to possess you instead of your sister."

"Oh. It seems she has tried but can't get out of Alicia's body." Lexi looked at Dolores. "You know, you don't look very surprised by all this."

"I think I've reached the point where nothing surprises me anymore." The fae stared into space with a thoughtful look. "Those wards—we never did get to the bottom of the problem. I think I'll have to catch up with an old friend for a chat. He's well-placed to bring it to the Seelie Court. I'll call you if I learn anything."

"Okay." Lexi picked a cinnamon roll up and stepped out into the hallway of her condo.

CHAPTER NINETEEN

Azatoth thought about Lexi's training session with a smile on her face. She gazed at the vial containing the young sorcerer's blood. The girl had made it easy for her. She stepped across the hallway into the conference room. "Is everything ready?"

"Yes, my lady." Eric nodded briskly.

A makeshift altar had been placed in the center of the room. The demon snarled on the inside.

These mages love their rituals.

She glanced around the room at the ridiculous number of lit candles. "Is someone planning to summon a demon? You know I'm already here, right?"

A dark-haired young man approached her and smiled obsequiously as he moved closer. "Would you like me to remove them, my lady?"

"No, leave them. They're here now. Let's not waste any more time." She turned. "Eric, I thought you said everything was ready."

He hurried closer. "My lady?"

"The star of the show appears to have a case of stage fright." The demon looked pointedly at the empty altar.

"I think she's making herself pretty or something." He rolled his eyes.

"I'm here." Millicent stepped into the room wearing a long black satin wrap-around gown which plunged dramatically to the naval.

Azatoth's eyes bulged. "I don't remember saying this was a formal occasion."

The woman blushed. "I-I—"

"Never mind. You're here now. Up you get." The demon patted the altar.

Millicent paused and stared at the makeshift structure. "I think it's a little too high for me to climb while maintaining my dignity."

"That ship sailed a long time ago," Eric snarked quietly.

She gave him a withering look.

Azatoth looked at the two of them. "You children carry on. Meanwhile, the shadow mage's blood will become dry and useless." She shook the vial of Lexi's blood to make her point.

Millicent scrambled onto the altar and lay down. She looked from Azatoth to Eric. "Now?"

Azatoth rolled her eyes. "Yes, now."

The woman raised her arm and muttered. The other twelve mages raised their arms and sent pulses of white energy into the center of the room.

The demon glanced at Eric. "Make sure she doesn't break the connection."

He smiled at Millicent and wound his arm sensually around hers to keep her hand in the air connected by magic to the other mages.

Within a blink, Azatoth's eyes reverted to their black and yellow from pure excitement.

"How will you transfer the blood to me? Am I to drink it?" Millicent's voice sounded uncertain.

The demon gave her a malicious grin. "Not quite." She raised her hand and smiled as talons grew from her blood-covered fingers.

Immediately, the woman tried to jerk her arm down but Eric's hold on her tightened.

Azatoth met Millicent's horrified stare as she punched her fingers into the woman's stomach, exactly as she had done to Lexi.

The mage screamed.

***

The cabal formed small groups and talked quietly among themselves. The demon sat at the head of the table and stared at Millicent's unmoving form still on the altar.

Eric drew a chair up. "How long should this take?"

"An hour maybe. I don't know for sure." The demon turned her gaze to him. "You're matched to her. How do you feel?"

"No different." Eric rolled his sleeve up and the magic in his scar was still white. "And if it doesn't work?"

Azatoth spun a little shuriken through her fingers. "I can always get more blood. Lexi can afford to lose a few more pints without any lasting damage."

He raised an eyebrow. "Do you care whether there's lasting damage?"

"I won't after she's opened that portal for me. Why? Did you want her for something?"

"I was fond of young Warren. I'd like to have a long, long chat with Miss Braxton about what happened to him."

Millicent drew a sharp breath and clutched her stomach. The wound had healed and she sat. "Did it work?"

The others in the room stopped speaking and everyone turned to look at her, then Eric.

The legacy held his arm out and the unhealing scar became a brighter white as he drew magic from his match. He sighed. "No."

The woman climbed off the altar. "All that for nothing."

Azatoth stood. "It wasn't for nothing, Millicent. We know it doesn't work so we learned something today." She clapped sharply and addressed the room. "Every day's a school day. Am I right?"

Millicent flounced out of the room.

Ian Baskerville stepped to where the demon stood with Eric. "Should it have worked? Did you find something in the archives that suggested it?"

Azatoth shrugged. "No. I merely thought it was worth a try and it was timed nicely with a motivational speech I gave the girl earlier."

CHAPTER TWENTY

Lexi spooned spaghetti noodles and meatballs in a spicy sauce into two bowls as Scott appeared in the kitchen.

The mage sniffed. "What's this?"

"Dinner. Put that on the table." She handed him a plate piled high with slices of garlic bread.

"Yeah, but it's usually me cooking it." He sniffed the garlic bread suspiciously as he walked through to the dining table.

She followed with the dinner plates. "A girl can only eat so much ramen."

When he saw the table set with cutlery, drinks, and a dish of grated parmesan, he narrowed his eyes. "What's this for?"

Lexi placed the dishes. "I've been an idiot. This is my apology. Along with me saying sorry. You shouldn't have been dropped into that pile of garbage."

They sat and he immediately tucked in. "This is good. I'd dive into that crap without hesitation if it meant you made this again."

She laughed. "You won't have to go to those extremes. How did your day go?"

"It was a bust. I spent an utterly pointless day bouncing from one location to the next every time I picked up someone using the words zombie or flaky."

He gave her a lopsided grin. "How was your day?"

Lexi shrugged. "I haven't killed the plant yet. I had an interesting chat with the curator of the Kindred archive, and Azatoth stabbed me in the stomach." She shoved a meatball into her mouth."

Scott's jaw hung open.

"I'm fine," she added quickly. "It hurt but I don't think it had the desired effect."

He put his fork down. "What do you think the desired effect was?"

"Motivation to do as I'm told. And I think she wants me to believe she could kill me at any moment. Eat your food."

The mage looked at his plate. His hand grasped the fork so tightly it looked like it would break. The lightbulb above them began to grow brighter. "What do you plan to do?"

"I'll do my best to look very, very motivated. Please don't break the lightbulbs."

He glanced up and took a breath. "You need to get out of there. I think we should all move to that maze. It's beginning to look extremely attractive right now."

Lexi gestured vaguely with her fork. "I'm getting close to a breakthrough of some kind. I think Azatoth has been looking for something specific in the archives. I'll befriend the curator to see if I can find out exactly what she's looking for."

Scott looked skeptical. "Are you sure faking friendship is the way to go?"

"I'm not faking friendship. He seems like a nice little old guy, but I honestly don't have much time to become best buds. I have to hurry it along as best I can."

The mage shook his head. "How long have you been trying to become besties with Nora? That doesn't seem to have worked."

His lip twitched as he picked his fork up and stabbed a meatball. "Maybe people simply don't like you."

Lexi gave him the one-eyebrow death-stare combo.

He shrugged. "Just saying. You're an acquired taste."

They both smiled and leaned back to look around the room.

Finally, she sighed. "We can't keep putting it off."

Scott shrugged. "Are you sure? I think we're doing a great job so far."

She picked her glass up. "Bring it down. We'll use the dresser mirror in my bedroom."

A large sip finished her wine and she started to clear the table.

Her companion opened the door and held his hand out, and the metal ball with its mirror-shine finish dropped into it.

He locked the front door and headed upstairs.

Lexi joined him a couple of minutes later and sat beside him on the bed in front of the mirror.

The mage twirled his finger in the air and spun the view in the mirror at a speed so fast she couldn't see what was happening.

It began to play out the day. Nothing of interest happened for a while so Scott increased the speed of the playback. Finally, Dick left the house.

Lexi sighed. "He's not carrying anything. He must have forgotten the jacket he was supposed to take back to the store."

They both knew it was a bad sign. Dick had lied to them.

The vampire climbed into his car and the little ball followed him to a part of town that Lexi wasn't familiar with. He went into an apartment building and the door closed before the ball could follow but they watched through the glass as he entered the stairwell. The ball hovered higher and higher as he climbed the stairs.

The little spy orb stopped outside the hallway window. Dick exited the stairwell next to a sign that read *Twelve* and walked along the corridor. He reached a door and pushed it to enter an apartment. The ball began to move along the outside of the building but then retreated to hover at the hallway a few minutes later. Dick left the room and looked agitated. He descended the stairs, left the building, and drove to the condo.

Scott looked at Lexi. "What do you think?"

"We'll have to go there." Lexi stood.

"Hang on." He rolled the view forward until it confirmed that the vampire hadn't left the house again before he had called the ball back.

The mage took a map out and traced Dick's journey. "I think it's here." He put a hand on Lexi's shoulder and they translocated to it.

She looked at the *Twelve* written on the wall. They were on the right floor and hurried to the door. It was closed but not locked. She pushed it with her foot.

The body of a man lay on the floor. They stepped in and closed the door behind them. She checked the body. "He's been drained. Shit."

Scott gazed around the room. "No mirrors, no shiny surfaces, and the drapes are closed. I could take an eyeball. I hate doing that."

Disheartened, she shook her head. "What's the point? We know Dick was in here."

The elevator in the hallway pinged and they looked urgently at each other.

"Let's get out of here," she whispered.

They translocated across the street.

Scott took his cell phone out. "I'm calling Dolores. There must be an explanation for this. I can't believe Dick did this."

Lexi opened her mouth to answer but he held a hand up. "Hi. Do you have a few minutes to talk? We have a problem."

The fae's reply was audible to them both. "I'm sorry, Scott. I'm right in the middle of something. Can I call you back?"

"Sure." He disconnected.

"Are you sure there was nothing reflective in there? No chrome chair legs or a vase or something?"

"I didn't notice anything. We'd better double-check because we're now a part of that room's history, simply by walking in there."

"What if the elevator noise was someone going to the apartment?"

"I'll hop up there but remain unseen." He disappeared but returned a moment later. "The body's gone."

"What?" Lexi translocated to the room and Scott appeared beside her.

Where a drained corpse had previously sprawled on the floor, there was nothing.

They looked harder for evidence of anything remotely shiny but it proved fruitless. Even the door handles were satin-finished wooden balls. They left and appeared across the street again.

Scott turned to Lexi. "What now?"

"Let's wait a couple of minutes to see if anyone leaves the building with a rolled-up rug or a body-sized suitcase."

They waited a few minutes but when no one left the building, they returned to the condo.

"What will you do about Azatoth."

"Maybe I should do a few dark sorcery spells to darken the energy."

"There's no need for that." Scott extended his hand out. When she took it, she could feel him withdrawing his white magic. They both gazed at her unhealing scar as it turned darker.

She felt his increasing discomfort through their bond. "That's enough." She pulled away. The magic in her arm was noticeably darker. "Hopefully, she'll keep her stabby fingers to herself tomorrow."

CHAPTER TWENTY-ONE

Lexi arrived at Azatoth's office the next morning with coffee as usual. She placed a cup on Nora's desk.

The secretary smiled. "Thank you. I look forward to these."

"Is that Lexi?" Azatoth called from inside the office.

The sorcerer sighed, removed her jacket, and went in. She placed a coffee onto the demon's desk and made sure her arm was visible. Annoyingly, Azatoth didn't seem to notice.

The entity in her sister's body stood and walked to the window to gaze out at the city. "I understand you've been working on the vampire murders in Vegas. How is that coming along?"

Lexi was immediately suspicious. The demon rarely paid attention to what she was working on unless it involved ripping some poor creature apart.

"It's early days." She sipped her coffee and looked out, wondering what was going through the demon's mind.

Azatoth turned to her and smiled. She returned to her chair and sat. "Gossip coming from your department says it's a daylight-walking vampire. What do you think?"

"I think that's highly unlikely. I'm looking for other explanations. My current thinking is that it might be some kind of animal attack."

The demon laughed. "Isn't that a lie Kindred usually tell the regular folk out there?"

She shrugged. "Statistically, at some point, there has to be an animal attack. Why not now?"

Azatoth took a sip of her coffee and ran her finger around the top edge of the lid. She looked at Lexi. "And you're sticking with that, are you?"

"Sure, why not?" She could see where this conversation was going and she didn't like it.

"Because you and I both know a daylight-walking vampire is living right next door to you." The demon grinned but lost the smug face when Lexi didn't react.

There was no use in denying it. Azatoth knew everything Alicia knew. "I don't believe for a minute that it was Dick."

"Are you so sure of him? I heard you've been following him. I think you're doing the right thing. Trusting a vampire seems rather foolish to me."

The dark sorcerer felt deeply unsettled. The only people who should know she and Scott were concerned about Dick were she and Scott. "He's saved my life more times in the short time I've known him than I can count." She forced herself to still with the reminder that she wasn't speaking to someone who could be swayed by emotional outbursts. "If there is one daylight-walking vampire, there could be others. I won't make the assumption that Dick's perpetrating these crimes merely because he's the easy option. Of course, we're keeping an eye on him."

Azatoth raised an eyebrow. "We? You're not bringing your freelance mage into Kindred business are you?"

She allowed herself a mental eye-roll. The demon seemed determined to trip her up. Irritated, she realized that was probably the whole point of this exercise.

The demon leaned back and sipped her coffee. "Purely out of

interest, do your overseer colleagues know that Dick's *Walkin' on Sunshine?*"

"No, and you know that. Let's cut to the chase. What's this about?"

Azatoth looked at her. She didn't seem angry or annoyed, but there was something behind the calm exterior that said, "I want to tear you apart." She smiled at Lexi. "Nothing. I'm merely bored."

"Would you like me to give the investigation to someone else? If you don't trust me, that is." She knew she was pushing it.

"Of course not. I have every faith in your ability to do your job. I'd merely ask you to keep an eye on the big picture."

Lexi shook her head. She looked at her coffee cup and sighed. "I don't even know what that means." She grimaced at a dull ache in her head. The demon was giving her a headache.

Azatoth checked the time. "I'll let you get back to work then and maybe see you later." She glanced at the dark swirling energy in Lexi's unhealing scar. "You look ready to take your training more seriously."

She stepped out and closed the door behind her.

Nora looked up and her eyes bulged. "What happened? Are you okay?"

The dark sorcerer shook her head. "I'm fine."

"You're bleeding." Nora found a tissue and dabbed Lexi's head. When she brought the tissue away, there was blood on it.

Lexi frowned and gave Nora a lopsided grin. "I thought she was giving me a headache. It appears she was."

She returned to her office and called Scott the moment she was inside. "We'll have to speak to Dick about the attacks. Azatoth has all but threatened to out him to the rest of Kindred."

He sighed. "I suppose we shouldn't be surprised. Could she be behind the attacks?"

"It seems a little low-key for her, but I guess she could be fucking with us. We'll talk to Dick. I'm coming home." She disconnected.

When she arrived, Scott stood at the living room window. "Are you turning into one of those people who spies obsessively on their neighbors?

The mage turned to look at her. "Dick left his condo about fifteen minutes ago."

"Did he say where he was going?"

"No. I sent my seeing ball after him."

She nodded. "Where is he now?"

"I'll get the map out." He took a step into the kitchen.

Lexi checked the time. "Call him."

Scott's cell phone appeared in his hand and he connected and put it on speaker.

"Hello." Dick's answer was sing-song but higher than usual.

"Hi, where are you?"

"Busy. I'll call you later." The vampire disconnected.

The mage looked seriously at Lexi. "That was his nothing's wrong but something's very wrong voice. I'll get the map."

Lexi stayed him with a hand on his arm. "Don't bother. We can translocate to the ball."

They appeared at Dick's location and found him rubbing the back of his head while he stood over a man on a park bench who was bleeding from the neck

The vampire turned. "I thought it would be you." He held the seeing ball. "Have you lost something?"

She stared at the bleeding man and gestured to Scott to heal him. "Dick, what's going on?"

The vampire held his fingers an inch apart. "I was this close. I almost caught him but when I stopped around that corner to check the map, this device flew into the back of my head and almost knocked me out." He showed them the ball before he threw it to the mage.

Lexi looked around. "Almost caught who?"

"I'm still trying to find out. I was one step behind last time."

The victim stood and walked away.

Scott joined them. "He's fine. He won't remember anything."

"He what? You counseled him? But—" Dick sighed. "Goddammit! I was about to get a description."

She folded her arms. "Okay, spill."

"I've been having dreams. They started a couple of weeks ago. You'll recall I told you some time ago that I haven't dreamed since the day-walking began. At first, I had vague dreams of walking up and down the Strip, partying, shopping, and drinking, but they were only flashes. A few days ago, I had a more unpleasant dream about a man in an alley. It was so real it freaked me out, but I thought it was only a dream.

"Then I heard a man was found drained. The next time it happened was while I was napping in the afternoon. It was that woman from Crystals and I was attacking her in broad daylight. It was disturbing and horribly realistic, but I'd seen her only that morning at the store so it was understandable that she might appear in a dream, even one so macabre."

Lexi nodded. She could see he was distraught. "Go on."

"When I saw the photograph of her on your cell, I began to fear that I was going out and committing these murders. I spoke to a friend at the bar. He said a psychic connection can happen between vampires who become very close. But as you know, I'm not in a relationship with a vampire. I worried for a moment that it might be Albin, but with the wards down, he'd be torn to pieces if he stepped out of his apartment. Anyway, Hamish recommended a witch I could reach out to for a spell to track my movements. I didn't think I was blacking out and murdering people, but it wouldn't be the strangest shit we've seen.

"I followed her instructions and dropped a spot of blood on the map, then I went to iron my shirts. When I checked again, there were two distinct spots of blood, one at the condo and one across town.

"I drove across town half-convinced I'd find a doppelgänger. I reached the building—an apartment block. I didn't know which apartment so I started in the stairwell but I could smell the blood almost immediately. I found an apartment with the door open and a body inside. It was drained. I'd been awake the whole time so I knew it wasn't me.

Scott shrugged. "Why didn't you simply follow the trail on the map?"

"The spell had a one-time use limit. Once I reached the first location, it stopped working. I had to return to the witch for another one. Her prices were extortionate."

Lexi rolled her eyes in disbelief. "Why didn't you come to us?"

"I wanted to deal with it. You're busy with Azatoth and Scott's hopping around trying to find Sam. Anyway, I tried the new spell and it sent me here. I got here as fast as I could but I was too late."

"Not too late. This guy was able to walk away, unlike the last one who seemed to disappear all by himself." She shook her head. "I can't believe you've been trying to work this alone. The least you could do was ask Dolores for help."

"I did. She got rid of the last body for me. How are you involved in all this?"

"Kindred's looking for a day-walking vampire and Azatoth's threatening to out you." Lexi was pleased that she had avoided admitting to Dick that they'd been following him.

"So did this follow me from the condo?" He held the ball up.

Shit.

Scott nodded. "Yes. We thought you'd been possessed or something."

"You've been following me." The vampire stared at the two of them. "You thought it was me."

The young mage laughed a little sheepishly. "Dude, you thought it was you."

Dick rolled his eyes. "I suppose that's a fair point."

Lexi turned to Scott. "Is there anything we can do to help him track this other day-walking, doppelgänger vampire or whatever it is?

He thought for a moment. "The spell using Dick's blood seemed to work." He turned to their friend and grinned. "Come on then. Little prick."

The vampire raised an eyebrow. He poked a hole in his thumb with a fang and held his hand out. "Show me one of your tiny balls."

Lexi did a mental eye-roll.

Dick dropped blood onto the metal seeing ball and Scott sent it searching.

The orb elevated, then circled Dick repeatedly. He looked up. "Bravo."

The mage cloaked the vampire and the ball drifted through the park. They followed it for a couple of blocks and onto the University of Nevada campus. It finally stopped in front of a student accommodation block and hovered at the top floor.

"He's targeting students now. I'll kill him." Dick raced into the building at vamp speed while Lexi and Scott stepped in, looked at the stairwell, and translocated to the third story. They appeared as Dick stepped back to kick the door in.

A girl's voice came from inside. "We can't keep doing this, Ruby."

Dick's designer shoe hit the door which exploded inward. He entered with a murderous look on his face.

Two girls—who looked barely out of their teens—leapt to their feet and tried to dart past the three of them. The speed at which they met Scott's shield made one of them bounce back over the couch, and the other simply sprawled on the floor, out cold.

The conscious girl stood and stared at Dick. She gave him an awkward wave. "Hi, Dad."

His jaw dropped. "You have to be fucking kidding me."

Lexi's eyes bulged. "Dad?" She looked from the girl to her friend on the floor.

"These are the airheads who hexed me to get my blood at the vamp bar." The vampire pinched the bridge of his nose.

Scott nodded. "That explains why your blood worked for the spell."

The dark sorcerer looked at the student at her feet and tapped her with a foot. "I know you're awake. Get up."

The girl sat and gave Lexi the evil eye before she stood and moved to sit at the table. Seeing them together, Lexi saw the similarity "You're sisters?"

They nodded.

Lexi leaned on the table. "You've murdered three people—"

The one who'd give her the evil eye sighed dramatically. "They were accidents."

Scott shook his head. "They didn't look like accidents."

The dark sorcerer continued, "Assaulted a fourth and forced a vampire to sire you against his will." Her katana was in her hand.

"Wait." Dick stepped in front of her. "Can we talk about this?"

She raised an eyebrow. "Fine." They stepped into the hallway. "Okay. I'll start. These girls are a problem. Not only that, they're a problem that leads directly to your front door which is next door to my front door."

"Look, I never asked for this but whether I like it or not, they're my responsibility."

"Did you miss the part where I told you Azatoth is threatening to—"

Dick interrupted before she could finish. "I'll take them away somewhere and spend a few years teaching them manners."

Lexi looked at Scott who nodded in agreement with the plan. "Who's watching the girls?"

He stepped into the apartment. "Oh!"

The sorcerer closed her eyes. One of her eyelids began to twitch. She walked into the apartment and stood next to Scott where he gazed at the open window. "I'll guess your shield only covered the apartment door."

"Sorry."

She shook her head. "They'll have to be dealt with and destroyed. We can't have day-walking vampires rampaging through the city. And we certainly don't want the company to find them and examine their blood too closely."

"Look at this." Dick held a framed photograph. It showed the girls smiling and posing with their equally happy parents.

Lexi turned to where he stood next to a pile of boxes. The room was filled with them, some labeled *Rosa Jenkins* and others labeled *Ruby Jenkins*. "They were either moving in or moving out."

The vampire continued to dig in the box. He pulled a newspaper clipping out. "It looks like their parents died a few months ago."

Scott removed a piece of paper from a cork noticeboard and held it up. "Eviction notice."

Dick was still staring at the picture. "So their parents died and they couldn't afford to continue their college education."

Lexi ripped a piece of paper from a notebook. She took a pen and wrote. *I can find you anywhere, anytime. No more "accidents." Dick will come to your apartment tomorrow to begin training you. Be here or your lives are forfeit.*" She taped the note to the ball and showed it to the vampire. "Agreed?"

He nodded.

"Blood."

He pierced his thumb again and dribbled blood on the ball.

Scott muttered and dropped the orb out of the window. It glided away with the note flapping behind it.

They headed to the door. Dick looked around the apartment and sighed.

Lexi followed his gaze. A pair of red shoes lay discarded on the floor. "Gemma's?"

The vampire nodded. He sifted through the study books scattered around the table. "Politics, Ethics, Law, Cyber Security… they had their whole lives ahead of them. They'll never have the chance to be mothers. To be frozen in time like this…"

She put a hand on his arm and waited for him to turn his gaze to her. "Suck it up, Pops. Not every woman wants kids."

He nodded his agreement. "True, but every woman should have the time to discover what she wants."

As they left the apartment, he looked at the splintered door. "Oh dear. I'll have to send a man to repair this."

Lexi gave him a lopsided grin. "A breathing, gift basket of blood, delivered directly to the door."

He frowned. "I didn't think of that."

"I've got it." Scott waved a hand and muttered an incantation. The splinters flew into place.

The vampire inspected it. "I can still see where it was broken."

Scott started down the stairs without looking back. "You're welcome to see if you can do a better job."

Dick followed. "I'm just saying. Maybe Lexi should have tried."

The mage grunted and the vampire's lip twitched.

Back at the condo, the three of them sat at the deck.

Lexi turned to Dick. "Where will you take them? And for how long?"

"I don't know. I'll see how it goes. It took me years to adjust but I'd been turned against my will. These two…it seems they knew what they were getting themselves into. Perhaps they'll mature faster."

A flicker drew their attention. Scott had called his seeing ball. It still had the note attached. He opened his hand and it drifted down. The mage pulled the note from the ball, looked at it, and chuckled. He slid it across the table.

They'd drawn a penis on it.

Dick leaned forward and glanced at the note. "Or it might take years."

Lexi facepalmed. "I need to close this case. How the hell can I manage that?"

Scott frowned. "And I still need to find Sam."

CHAPTER TWENTY-TWO

Dick knocked on the door. He stepped back to ensure his friends would get the full effect of his smart gray three-piece-suit.

Lexi opened the door and made a slow and thorough scrutiny. "Are you modeling for D&G now?"

He lowered his sunglasses a fraction of an inch to make eye contact. "You've heard of Dolce & Gabbana? Wonders will never cease."

She smirked. "I meant Donny & Graham, the pest control people off Tropicana."

The vampire pushed the sunglasses back up. "I walk into it every time." He swept past her into the house.

Scott entered from the deck. "Hey, Dick, looking fly."

"Thank God. Someone with class. Hello, Scott, how are you?"

"I'm good. What happened to the ripped jeans and t-shirt?"

"I'm going to see the girls and want to make a good impression." He struck a pose.

Lexi laughed. "The girls who left you for dead in a dumpster? What if they plan to do it again?"

"You only broke my neck and threw me in a dumpster once so

I'm filled with hope." He put his cooler bag on the counter. "Anyway, that's why I'm taking Scott. He'll ensure there are no more hex bags."

"I will?" The young mage shrugged. "Okay."

Lexi raised an eyebrow at the vampire. "Am I not invited?"

Dick removed the sunglasses completely and narrowed his eyes at her. "Of course you are. I think the girls could learn from you." He waited for a moment. "You're the living embodiment of a cautionary tale."

"Ouch!" She laughed. "No thanks. I'm heading to the archives."

Dick smirked. "So keen. Are you hoping Azatoth will make you Employee of the Month?"

She sighed. "I'm still looking for a plausible way to close this case without giving her an excuse to turn you into a raisin."

"I'm all for that. May the odds be ever in your favor. Come along, Scott. Don't forget the cooler bag." Dick swept back out of the house with Scott following.

As they traveled to the residence halls, the young mage turned to him. "Have you told Albin you're leaving?"

"We spoke last night. He understands."

"Yeah, but it sucks. We shouldn't have to break the team up."

The vampire glanced at his friend. "Thank you, Scott. That means a lot."

Scott climbed out of the car. "I'm only saying maybe we should have sent the seeing ball to be sure they're here."

"Ye of little faith, Scott. I'm confident they're here." Dick led the way to the third story of the residence building. He knocked.

They waited in silence.

Finally, the vampire glanced at his companion, cleared his throat, and knocked again.

"I could simply—" Scott started,

"Someone's coming." Dick managed to not sound relieved.

The door opened. A young woman in jeans and a t-shirt gave them a contrite smile. "Come on in."

Scott put a hand on Dick's shoulder. "I'll go first." He looked around the door and muttered a few words. After he'd scanned the room, he nodded to his companion. "There's only one hex bag in here."

They all looked at one of the packing boxes which glowed. It was the bottom box of a pile.

The sisters stared at it and at the same time, both said, "It's in the Instant Pot."

One girl thumped the other's arm. "That was the pile you checked."

"You're the one who put it in there."

The books that had been scattered around the apartment were nowhere to be seen.

Dick raised an eyebrow and wondered whether, if they had known where the hex bag was, they would have tried to attack him again.

"I don't believe you got my name on either of the two occasions we previously met. Dick Erwin. This is my colleague Scott —he's a mage. A sorcerer. That is to say he practices magic."

The angrier of the two girls rolled her eyes. "We know what a mage is."

"May we sit?" he asked.

She indicated the table but remained standing. After a moment, she walked to a set of shelves and began to shove Funko Pop dolls aggressively into a box.

The other sister sat across from the two visitors.

The vampire looked at each of them in turn. "I've introduced myself to you and it's customary—"

The seated girl answered. "I'm Rosa and this is Ruby."

Scott smiled at her. "Are you twins?"

She nodded.

Dick turned to the sister packing the box. "Ruby, tell me about yourself." When she stared at him, he tried again. "What are you studying?"

The girl sighed. "I'm not studying anything anymore."

"What were you studying?" Scott asked.

"Criminal Justice."

Waves of hostility rolled off her. Ruby was an angry young woman.

The vampire turned to Rosa. "And you?"

"Computer Science."

Between the two of them, Rosa undoubtedly had the better temperament. He directed his next question to her. "How old are you?"

"Twenty-one."

"At least you waited until you were adults." He shook his head.

Dick leaned back and stared at each of them in turn. "Some vampires never learn to control themselves. They're usually the ones who die fairly quickly—either at the hands of the authorities or other vampires who don't want the attention. I should have been one of those and it took me several years to control myself. You aren't like that. You turned intentionally and deliberately. You both seem very much in control of yourselves." He flicked a glance at Ruby. "Mostly." He turned to Rosa. "I don't think you killed those people out of bloodlust. What are you up to?"

The girls shared a look but remained silent.

He tried again. "Let's start with the lawyer. Who was he to you?"

"He was—" Rosa began but a look from Ruby silenced her.

"Here's the thing. I've chosen to give you an opportunity to learn how to behave like upstanding members of society. If you choose to not accept that opportunity, you're a liability and Lexi will have to return and believe me, you don't want that." He rubbed the back of his neck absently.

Rosa spoke again. "He was our family lawyer and let our uncle steal our college fund after Mom and Dad died."

"I see. And that's why you're leaving college."

"We don't have the money for our last year." Rosa looked at her hands. "I tried to compel the college administrator to let us stay but it seems that shit doesn't work."

Dick smoothed an eyebrow. "I'm afraid you'll be terribly disappointed if your entire research of the supernatural world is based on Netflix."

Ruby's shoulders sagged and she sighed. "I told you it was a waste of time."

"And Gemma? Why kill her and steal her shoes?"

Ruby threw the box in her hand down. "They were our mother's shoes. She saved for a year for them. Uncle Frank let that bitch walk in and take what she wanted. She took Mom's jewelry too—pieces that should have come to us and even her wedding ring."

"So you turned yourselves into vampires to exact revenge? Did you have any plans for afterward? What did you plan to do with the next few hundred years?"

The angry twin shrugged and returned to packing. "I guess that was the choice. Too much life or no life at all."

"The man in the apartment…" Scott asked. "Was he also part of the scheme to steal from you?"

Ruby took the box to the pile and added it, making sure it was secure. "He was Uncle Frank's lawyer. We found out they were all in it together."

"And the man in the park? I'll guess that was Uncle Frank." Dick waited for Rosa to shrug, a gesture that was one of confirmation. "Why didn't you kill him?"

Scott nodded in sympathy. "When it came to it, you couldn't kill him because he was family?"

Ruby sneered. "Oh, we could kill him all right. But it was too creepy sucking on my uncle's neck. That was plain nasty. We decided to rip his head off instead, but we heard someone coming so we ran." She joined them at the table and sat next to her sister.

Dick unzipped the bag and pulled out two blood bags. "I assume you know what these are."

They nodded.

He passed the bags to the girls with straws. "This is how you will consume blood. It can be a little difficult to get used to but it's that or—"

"Lexi's sword. We get it." Ruby pierced the bag with the straw and took a sip. She screwed her face up. "That's disgusting. I can't."

Dick thought about it. "How about a little incentive? If you can keep a low profile and refrain from murdering people, I will pay the remainder of your college fees and you can keep this accommodation."

Both young vampires looked suspiciously at him.

"Why would you do that?" Ruby asked,

"Whether I like it or not, you're my responsibility. You seem like bright girls. I'm willing to give it a try if you are."

Both girls drank the blood without another word.

Rosa shuddered but finished it. Ruby stared directly at Scott as she drank. Dick could feel the mage's discomfort.

"Why can't we feed off people?" Rosa put the empty pouch on the table. "Like, willing ones? A couple of vamps fed off us when we were in the bar one time."

Dick put the empty pouch into his bag. "You have to get used to this first and feeding off strangers is a bad habit to get into."

Ruby put her empty pouch directly into the bag. "Do you know why we're different? Why can we walk in the sun?"

Scott leaned forward to look at Ruby. "Have you told anyone about that?"

"No. Well, yes, but they laughed at us."

The vampire looked at one girl, then the other. "This is important. You can't tell anyone about that. As far as we're aware, we're the only ones who can do it. If you tell anyone, it will get us all killed."

Rosa looked confused. "Why would it get us killed?"

"One reason is that other vampires will be jealous. They would torture you for answers and that would lead them straight to me, and I don't want to die."

Both the young vampires nodded fervently.

He leaned forward. "Right. It's time to tell you about Kindred."

An hour later, Rosa walked them to the door.

Dick turned to face her. "You know where I am if you need me. You have my number, Scott's number, and Lexi's number."

Rosa snorted. "I don't think we'll call her anytime soon."

He nodded. "It's true you didn't hit it off to begin with, but she is the most loyal, dependable, capable person I've ever known. If she's on your side, she'd give her life for you. If not...well, don't kill any more people. And try to keep your sister's temper under control."

"I can hear you," Ruby called.

"I know," Dick muttered. He had one last thought. "Text your uncle's address to me."

The vampire and his friend headed down the stairway and out to the front of the building.

Scott was quiet as they walked to the car but when they climbed in, he turned to Dick. "Is that it? They murdered three people. You don't think they should be punished?"

"They will be punished. Right now, they're feeling like they had justice on their side and maybe they did. But it will catch up with them eventually, and remorse or the avoidance of it can lead a person down as dark a path as vengeance." Dick looked at the building. "Perhaps having a new family in their lives will help them. I understand if you think differently. I could still take them away and enroll them in another college." He started the car. "Their punishment could be redoing the first two years of study."

The mage grimaced. "Redoing college? I intended to suggest beheading them, but you always have to go one step further."

CHAPTER TWENTY-THREE

Lexi stepped into the archives, where Devon was seated at the main desk. "Hi. It's me—the non-demonic one."

The old man glanced up and grumbled, "Isn't that something the demonic one would say?"

She paused. "Hmm… I think you've got me there."

"How can I help you, Miss Braxton?"

In response, she held up a deli bag and a bottle of Gatorade. "I brought you lunch because I want to manipulate you into being my best friend but time's a little tight so…" She shrugged.

He looked at her over his glasses. "You want to know how to be a curator's best friend?"

Lexi put the bag onto his desk. "Yes please. That would probably shave a few weeks off the whole process."

Devon picked the bag up. "Don't bring food into his archives." He pointed at the wall.

She glanced at the painting on the wall, then noticed the sign above it which read *No Food Or Drink To Be Consumed In The Archive*. "Oh, sorry." When she turned back, the bag was gone.

"And don't give him Gatorade—ever. That stuff is disgusting." Devon looked at the bottle in his hand and shuddered. He placed it on the desk. "So, young lady. Why do you want to be my best friend?"

Lexi leaned her elbows on his desk. "I have so many questions and no one else seems to know the answers."

"Are you still looking for *An Idiot's Guide to Being a Dark Sorcerer*?"

"Yes, and *How to Yank a Demon out of your Sister*. And if you have a copy of *Things That Look Like Vampire Kills but Aren't*, that would be great."

"Anything that might have existed in your first two categories would have gone in the fire. But as for your third request, I might have something."

Her eyes widened. "You're kidding."

"I never kid, Miss Braxton. Why don't you help an old man put some books away? You never know. You might make a friend."

"I think I might have made one already."

As they wandered through the stacks, Devon half-pushed and half-leaned on his trolley.

She decided it might be best to make conversation as they walked. "Are you married?"

"I am. Wanda isn't with us anymore, but I'm still a faithful husband so don't you be getting any ideas."

"I promise I'll keep my hands to myself. Children?"

"Yes, and grandchildren and great-grandchildren."

"Why haven't you retired?"

"It's not time for me to retire. I'll know when the time's right. Until then, I take the books out and I put them back—unless I have a kind assistant who can get up there and put this away for me." He picked up a large black book.

She took it and climbed the ladder. "Where does it go? Just anywhere?"

A shocked inhalation close to Lexi's ear made her almost drop the book.

Her gasp was as shocked as she spun and looked around. "There are ghosts in here, aren't there?"

"It's the next shelf up. To the left of the brown one."

Lexi slotted the book in and climbed down.

Devon stretched to the pile and picked up a paperback. She could have sworn it hadn't been there a minute before.

"If you're ever looking to relax with some fiction, this is worth a read." He handed the book to her.

"*The Fifth Ward*. I'll remember that. Where does it go?"

"Over here."

"The shelf directly next to your hand?"

"Are you being smart with me, young lady?"

"Nope. I'll pop that away for you. Right there." She slid the book into the space she was convinced he'd probably taken it from a moment before.

Lexi scanned the fiction shelves. "Why is there a fiction section in the archives?"

"Sometimes, facts are hidden in works of fiction."

She pointed to a random book. "What is this book about?"

"It's part of a series that suggests vampires and were-creatures are made from alien DNA."

"Is that a fact?" She stared at him in disbelief.

"I always thought it was bat-scat crazy but who knows?" He shook his head as they walked away. "The stuff they come up with."

Lexi continued with her questions as they worked. "Haven't you ever wanted to do anything else?"

"I do important work here." The old man looked into the middle distance and smiled. "I achieved the most important goal of my career forty years ago and hardly a soul will ever know." He smiled like he'd make a joke. She didn't get it.

When she opened her mouth to ask, he continued as if he hadn't noticed.

"I hear you ran away from Kindred."

She was momentarily surprised but then realized the curator would be best placed to know everything. "You heard right. I ingested vampire blood and as a result, discovered that Kindred had kidnapped a child, put him in my unit, and tried to counsel me into believing he was my brother."

"Was he a potential mage by any chance?"

The young sorcerer looked at him with sharp interest. "Yes."

"It happens often. When they're identified, it's best to get them safely into the organization before the dark fae find them. There's quite a market for young mages."

Her jaw dropped. "I didn't know that."

They stopped next to a rack of box files. Devon stepped out of the way so she could take the large file from the cart. As she bent over and wrapped her arms around it, he put his lanyard around her neck.

He winked at her. "This should speed things up."

When she stood upright, the box file seemed to tug upward. She climbed the ladder and the box pulled toward a shelf and as it moved closer, the other boxes made space for it.

"Hey, that's cheating." She shelved it and descended quickly.

"No more than translocating or having a dimensional pocket."

Lexi pouted. "But I assumed you knew exactly where everything in here goes."

"Young lady, I'm eighty-two. I don't even know what I know anymore."

She kept the lanyard around her neck but Devon put the next few books away without magic. "I was right. You do know where they go."

He pulled the ladder into a new position.

"I can do it." She picked the next book up.

"I'll do this one." He went up the ladder and put the book away, then stretched farther along and partially pulled a book out. "This is one you'll want if you're ever stuck in a difficult situation."

She looked at the print on the spine and grinned. *"Roget's Thesaurus.* You crack me up."

When she glanced down for the next book in the cart, she realized it wasn't a book. It was a metal contraption. "What's this."

Devon frowned. "Something that shouldn't ever have been removed from here."

They walked to the corner and stood in front of a stack of shelves. He indicated that he wanted his ID card. She passed the lanyard to him and he waved it across the shelves, then stood back as they moved aside to reveal a hidden room.

Lexi followed him in. The room lit up and she felt a chill. The display cases held a collection of medieval torture devices.

"These items aren't supposed to leave this room but since we've been under new management…" He didn't have to finish.

He opened a display case and returned the object to its position beside a label that read *Pear of Anguish.* He closed the case, waved his ID across the label, and nodded with satisfaction at the soft click when the case locked. "No one should be able to remove this without my approval. And I don't approve."

Lexi looked away. She didn't want to know how it was supposed to be used and despite her inner reluctance, she wandered through the horrible exhibit. Every other display case and exhibit seemed accounted for except one she found at the end of the room. She approached the low, empty plinth. "What's supposed to go here?"

Devon joined her and looked deeply troubled. "An Iron Maiden. It was here yesterday." He frowned and muttered, "I hope it's not that."

"Not what?"

The old man began to walk to the exit. "Nothing."

Lexi followed him quickly. "Should we mention it to someone? It might have been stolen and put on eBay?"

Devon dropped the lanyard around his neck. He paused and

tilted his head slightly like he was listening for something. "It's still in the building."

When they left the room, she noticed a small alcove with a desk and chair. The desk had a vice attached and an electric tool rested in a cradle next to it. "What's this?"

"It's my engraving equipment. I engraved all the brass plaques on the shelves you see in the library. It's my little hobby."

He paused and fixed her with a bland smile. "Let's go find your vampire's get-out-of-jail-free card."

"I didn't say it was for a specific vampire. I merely don't want to spend time walking around Vegas searching for a day-walking vampire. That's ridiculous, isn't it?"

Devon nodded. "Of course. Whoever heard of such a thing." He sounded very much like he was playing along.

Lexi was beginning to think that he might know almost everything about everything.

Instead of continuing to search the stacks, he led her to his computer. The screen activated and he scrolled deftly through various folders. "Here we are. A Chupacabra was caught and killed in Utah yesterday. Their hunting ground is a roughly two-hundred-mile radius of their den. I think we've found your culprit." He scrolled through the screen of recent unsolved crimes. "Is this your file?"

She glanced at the screen and nodded.

He clicked a few buttons. "I've pinned it to the Chupe file and send it to Utah."

"What if it comes back as unconnected to the Chupacabra?"

The old man opened the drawer in his desk and pulled out the deli bag. "It won't." He bit into the sandwich, then put it down. "You're quite useful to have around. Show me your ID."

Lexi held out the plastic card on her lanyard. He tapped it with his own and she felt the pulse of magic. "There you go. Now you're my official helper."

"I don't want the job I've got," she said and rolled her eyes, "and here you are giving me more work." She smiled.

He chuckled as she left.

A few moments later, she stepped out of the building with a plan to grab lunch from either the coffeeshop or Dolores' apartment. Her phone buzzed with a message from Scott. She leaned against the building and tapped a quick reply, then put her phone away. When she looked at the building, she noticed a metal plaque she hadn't seen before. It was the Kindred logo—the letter K—and beneath it was a statement that the building had been there since 1985. She continued toward the coffee shop, then stopped and walked back to read the plaque again.

How did Devon work here for sixty years if the building has only been here for forty years? There must be another archive.

"Are you lost?"

Lexi turned quickly and resisted a groan when she saw Millicent staring at her with a smug expression.

Shit!

"I've only been here a few weeks. I merely wondered what the regulars think this building is."

"They're encouraged to not think about it at all. The dry cleaner on the left of our building thinks he's next door to the attorney's office on the right side of us."

She hadn't expected an answer from the woman and tried to direct the conversation away from the plaque. "My office is on the seven hundred and twenty-first level. I went down the stairwell last week and I was at lobby level after three flights of stairs."

"I've heard you enjoy exploring the building."

Lexi decided to intentionally miss the barb. She smiled. "I'm heading to the coffee shop if you'd like to join me."

Millicent laughed softly and briefly. "Be careful where you stick your nose, Lexi. You won't be untouchable forever." The woman looked at the plaque. "Hmm." With no further comment, she entered the building.

Shit! Shit! Shit!

The young sorcerer continued toward the coffee shop but stopped halfway down the street. She returned to the building and hurried to the archives. Although she walked through the stacks and called his name, the old man was nowhere to be found.

In the elevator, Lexi pressed the button for the executive floor and stepped out cautiously. Nora's workstation was shut down and the lamp had been turned off. Azatoth's door was ajar and the office appeared empty. It didn't seem like a good idea to be caught snooping by any of the scary individuals up there, however, so she turned to the elevator but felt a wave of heavy and intense magic emanating from the conference room. She turned toward it, unsure whether she should risk being caught there. After a brief moment, she walked toward the room and stopped just outside.

It took only a few seconds to realize the futility of standing outside a room protected from snooping by magic and she returned to the elevator. Before she reached it, the doors slid open and a security guard stepped out with a young man.

Her cell phone appeared in her hand and she did her best to look engrossed in the screen. She glanced up and frowned. "This level is supposed to be restricted."

The guard scowled. "I'm sorry. He said it was urgent."

"I was told this file can't go to the overseer's office. It has to be given directly to the council." The young man indicated a file in his hand.

"Oh, it's that one. Finally." Lexi put her hand out and the young man passed the file over hesitantly.

He stared at her.

"Are you waiting for a tip?"

"No...I—"

She looked at the guard and jerked her head toward the lift.

"Come on. It's done." The man guided the courier into the elevator.

Lexi wanted to poke through the file immediately and was about to translocate to her office when the conference room door opened.

Someone was having a conversation near the door but she couldn't quite hear what was said.

She waved her card at the elevator and the door opened immediately. Quickly, she stepped in and held the door open with the tip of her boot.

People were coming out of the meeting. She needed to move.

Her view to Azatoth's office was unobstructed and she watched as the demon approached her office door while speaking to Eric. "It wasn't nearly strong enough. I want to know what's blocking us. Find out."

Lexi didn't wait for the doors to close. She translocated to the condo and opened the file.

Dick's head appeared around the edge of the door. He was seated on the deck. "You're bringing work home now? Such dedication."

"This is interesting." She retrieved a beer and joined them on the deck. "They haven't found Sam yet but they've discovered that Krish and Adele are at the Aria."

The vampire looked at the file in her hands. "I thought they were shielded."

She flicked a page over. "They are, but Krish used the ATM." She tutted. "We'll have to warn them. This isn't official." She passed the file to Scott. "It's the cabal—or the council as they call themselves these days. I've delayed their next move by taking the file but I don't think we can wait for Sam to suddenly appear. We need to find him before they do."

"They know he's not in Mexico, but I doubt they know any more than we do about his whereabouts." Scott picked his cell phone up to call Adele.

CHAPTER TWENTY-FOUR

Lexi stepped out of the elevator into the subterranean world of flickering lights and long echoing hallways. One of the pipes running the length of the passage made a knocking sound. She stopped walking and followed the pipe with her gaze. It ran back along the hallway and disappeared through the wall. She shifted the large tome into her other hand so she could check the time.

I should be able to talk to Devon and get to the training room in time to see Azatoth.

She couldn't believe she hadn't seen it before. Every morning when she walked in and out of the building to see Dolores or go to the coffee shop, she passed a plaque on the front of the building with 1985 written on it. The office block had been built forty years earlier, but Devon had worked in the archives for sixty years. She had to find out where the old archive was. The information that both she and the demon had been looking for could be there. She decided she wouldn't take no for an answer this time. That man knew something and she intended to find out what it was.

The door opened before she reached it and Azatoth stepped

out. The demon smiled so widely it unnerved her. "Why Lexi, what brings you down here?"

Lexi held the book up. "I'm returning this."

"Well…" The demon waved a hand in front of her face to indicate a bad smell. "You might want to wait five minutes." She continued down the hall.

The young sorcerer had a bad feeling as she pushed the door to the archives open. There was considerable blood and the old man's body parts were strewn everywhere. She stared at the chunks of gore and let the door fall closed. For a moment, she couldn't even speak, but she finally regained her voice.

"What? Why?" She turned, expecting to see Azatoth near the elevator, but she was directly behind her, her eyes black and yellow.

"Is there a problem?" The demon smiled as she asked her question politely like a passive-aggressive doctor's receptionist.

Lexi felt a chill. Something had changed. She could feel the danger rolling off her and knew she had to be careful. By sheer force of will, she wound her emotions back from horror and outrage and tried again with mild inconvenience. She indicated the book in her hands. "I don't know where this goes."

"Well, you have more than enough time to find out because I can't make our training session today. I have somewhere else to go." The demon turned and walked along the hallway, humming tunelessly.

The sorcerer turned to the archive door, took a steadying breath, and entered. She gazed again at the curator's body parts and looked away while she fought the nausea. Abruptly, she dropped the book on the floor and translocated to the condo.

Scott had his cell phone in his hand. "I felt you losing it. I was about to call. What's wrong?"

She stepped close to him, grasped his t-shirt, and sobbed into it.

He said nothing and simply put his hand onto the back of her head and stroked her hair.

Between sobs, she told Scott what had happened. "She got to Devon before I did and tore him apart. He was merely a kind little old man and didn't deserve that."

"And with him gone, so has our last lead." Dick stood at the door. "Sorry, I heard from next door. Thin walls."

Lexi wiped her face. "I need to know where Azatoth is. Devon told her something—a location I think. I have to know where it is." She held a hand out and her shiny black seeing ball appeared. She gave it to Scott. "Get this to Dolores. Tell her it needs to go into Alicia's dimensional pocket immediately. We need to see what Alicia can see."

The mage disappeared.

"Dick, I need a body bag. I'm not leaving him there for Nora to throw onto a pile with the rest of them."

The vampire returned with the bag. As he handed it over, he glanced at her lanyard and raised an eyebrow. "That's interesting."

She twisted the ID to look at it. Under *Overseer's Office* it now read *Head Curator*. "He made me his assistant a couple of days ago. I guess I was the only one." Her jaw worked as she fought another flood of tears. "He had grandchildren."

Dick didn't seem to like the look of anger and resolve in her face. "Do you have a plan or will you simply blunder in and get yourself killed?"

"I know exactly what to do." Her voice was thick and rough. "But I don't want to do it." She took the ID card in her hand. "I wonder…" She translocated to the HQ but instead of aiming for her office or the lobby, she thought of the archive and appeared beside Devon's desk.

Cautiously, she glanced around but somehow felt the space was uninhabited. As she closed her eyes and took deep breaths, information came unbidden to her mind. She knew how many books and files were checked out of the archive and where they were. Turning to the door behind her, she sealed it with a spell before she gathered the body parts and unidentifiable lumps of flesh and organs. As she worked, she became aware of a collective sadness in the room. She raised her face to the ghosts of curators past. "I know."

When she had finished, a freakish jigsaw of a man lay in the body bag. She started to hyperventilate as bile rose. A cold sweat broke out on her brow. What she was doing was wrong. She felt it in every fiber of her being, but she continued.

What she had done once before to a demon in error, she did now with intent. Tears trickled down her face as she commanded the pieces to knit together. "Live. Breathe."

The tortured creature on the floor screamed.

Lexi ran to him. "I'm sorry. I'm so sorry, Devon. I have to stop her and to do so, I have to know what you told her."

The old man extended a hand and wiped a finger across her wet cheek. He looked away, then pointed to a blood-spattered painting on the wall before he screamed again. "Reese me."

She understood. *Release me.* "Go to your wife. Go to Wanda." She unmade the spell, zipped the bag, and wept into her hands.

With her eyes closed, she reached out to her seeing ball. She saw Dolores, Scott, and Phil. They hadn't moved Bryan and he was still in the maze.

The sorcerer went to the picture and took it down, expecting to see a safe behind it or a crevice with something hidden. There was nothing and she examined the back of the picture. There was no envelope taped there and no message in code. She looked for a glamour but found none.

I have to find his message. I can't do that to him again.

She stared at the painting itself and put it onto his desk with the desk lamp shining over it. Lexi grabbed the white cotton gloves Devon used to handle rare artifacts. She wiped the blood from the glass and stared at the picture. It was of only two people, a man and a woman standing in front of a building. Her gaze moved around the image and back to the people. She squinted her eyes to look at the man. He was young but familiar.

That's Devon. I'd bet my katana on it.

Quickly, she snapped a few photos with her cell phone, but she couldn't understand what she was supposed to learn from a picture of two people in a doorway.

The cell in her hand rang and she almost dropped it in surprise. "Scott's back from the…place where he was," Dick told her. "He says the thing you asked him to do is done and we're ready to do the other thing." He sighed. "I hope you understood that. I confused myself. How's it going your end?"

"I think I have a clue but honestly, I'm not sure. There's a picture of Devon standing in front of a building but I can't tell what building it is."

"There are no clues at all?"

"It's merely a red brick building with a canopy over the door. I can see the number is two-two-two. There are two interwoven letters over the door."

"H and C?" the vampire asked quickly.

Lexi was dumbfounded. "Yes."

"Come back. I know where that is."

She replaced the painting on the wall, took hold of the body bag, and translocated home.

A short while later, she and Dick stood in the kitchen. The map of New York was spread across the counter and Scott's laptop was open to a picture of a doorway.

Lexi looked from the picture on her cell phone to the screen. "That's it."

Dick looked at the laptop. "The Hotel Chelsea. 222 W23rd Street, New York. Built in the 1880s. It closed for refurbishment around ten or so years ago." He looked at the picture on Lexi's cell phone. "Nice painting. The brushwork is quite familiar but I can't place it for some reason. Is it signed?"

She checked the image. "No, I don't think so." She raised an eyebrow. "Do you know all the hotels in New York?"

Dick was still staring at the screen. "No. The Chelsea was... special. He smiled as though memories were drifting across his mind before he sighed and focused his attention on her. "I had an apartment there back in the day."

Lexi did a mental eye-roll. "Of course you did."

Scott came downstairs. "I've encased Devon in a block of ice in the tub but we should bury him soon."

Lexi nodded, closed her eyes, and connected her mind with the seeing ball. After a moment, she smiled. "Good girl!"

"What's happening?" the mage asked.

"Alicia's put the ball in front of the TV so I can see what's going on through Azatoth's eyes." She frowned when she saw her sister lying on her bed with her back to the TV and wondered if she'd seen what Azatoth had done to Devon.

The young sorcerer watched out of the demon's eyes as Eric and Millicent walked ahead of her down a staircase.

"Where is she?" Dick asked,

"Walking down some stairs. Eric and Millicent are with her."

"What does the balustrade look like?"

"I don't know, she's not looking that way. Oh, wait. It's fancy...black and looks like iron."

"She's at the Chelsea." The vampire sounded confident. "You won't go there while Azatoth's there are you?"

"We'll have to wait until she's gone. I have the distinct impression that she's almost ready to do something bad to me. When she caught me outside the archives, I could sense that she was weighing her options."

Scott frowned. "She must think she's close, then. You'll be next on her list if she can manage to leave Alicia's body."

CHAPTER TWENTY-FIVE

Lexi closed her eyes again.

Azatoth looked carefully at the hallway ahead of them and followed it to a solid wall beside the stairs. They walked forward. The floor groaned as they stepped on it and Millicent squeaked and jumped to the side. She held a hand up and muttered as she passed each doorway. When they reached the end of the hall, she turned. "Here."

Eric opened the door to what was unquestionably a janitor's closet. He stepped back and closed it.

Millicent muttered an incantation and he opened the door again. This time, it provided access to a huge, cavernous room. The mage stepped in first. Again, she muttered and tossed a glowing ball into the air. It hovered to give them light. The walls were blackened and empty bookshelves lay on the floor.

Azatoth hissed in frustration. "It has to be here. This must be a glamour. Find it and break it."

They circled the mostly empty space several times but found nothing.

Lexi reported what she saw to the others.

The demon pinched the bridge of her nose, then sighed and

turned to Millicent. "Right. I need to think. I want you to spell the room, then I'll spell it myself with a little surprise should a certain shadow mage show up."

The woman raised an eyebrow. "Do you think she knows about this?"

"No. The old man swore he'd never told a soul where the hidden archive was. But I've been surprised by Lexi before." Azatoth gazed around the room and set her lips into a thin line. "I was so certain I'd found it that I almost pulled the girl's guts out. Now, I'll have to make nice because I might still need her."

Lexi continued to watch as they left the room. Eric stood back as first Millicent, then the demon cast over the entrance. They returned along the hallway to the exit.

Finally, she opened her eyes. "They found the old archive but it's empty."

Dick looked from her to Scott. "Does that mean there's nothing there? Or it's there but they couldn't find it?"

Scott shrugged. "We'll have to take a look."

"They've booby-trapped the room with spells," Lexi told him with a frown.

His expression matched hers. "That's inconvenient."

"I don't understand. I thought she needed me alive to open her portal, but from what she said, she intended to kill me tonight. I don't think the spell to get out of Alicia is the only thing she's looking for."

The mage scowled. "I guess there's only one way to find out. Is she leaving the hotel?"

She closed her eyes but saw her front door from outside. Her eyes snapped open and she turned to face the entrance. She started to speak but someone knocked before she could. They all gazed at the door for a moment before reality clicked in. Lexi pointed at the maps.

Dick snatched them in his arms and scrunched them in the process.

Scott stretched a hand to the vampire's shoulder but paused. "Oh!"

"It's fine, do it," Dick snapped.

The two of them disappeared.

Lexi went to the door, took a steadying breath, and opened it.

"Did your little friends have long enough to run away or should I give them some more time?"

She looked at Azatoth and decided she didn't want the demon in her home. "Let's sit out at the pool."

They sat outside and although the sun had gone down, it was still uncomfortably hot.

The visitor looked at the water and seemed mesmerized. "I haven't been for a swim since I've been here. This world has so much to offer. I should take a few days off."

Lexi was used to this side of the demon—pretending to be normal and pretending to be deep. Merely a girl in a big new world. It was laughable.

Azatoth smiled awkwardly. "I wanted to apologize."

"For what?"

"I didn't know you liked the old man. If I'd known…"

She could guess how that sentence ended. *If I'd known I'd have made you watch.*

"The thing is, we have a problem. Other demons are trying to get through here." The entity inside her sister sighed. "This is all my fault. They have sensed me here and now they're coming. The old man was working with them. They'll destroy this dimension if they get through."

Lexi played her part. She looked shocked. "I didn't know he was working with anyone." She leaned forward and nodded as though she believed every lying word.

"There's only one way they can get through—a kind of gateway in Las Vegas."

"A gateway? Like a portal? Here?"

Shocker.

"That's why there have always been wards here. They were in place long before the casinos—before anything, in fact. This was a desert when the portal was first discovered. Now, they've somehow disabled the wards. Look, I know you have no reason to trust me."

Ya think?

"But I feel like we've become friends. Like you're the only one I can trust."

You are fucking delusional if you think I believe this bullshit.

"I promise I'll find another vessel. You can have your sister back."

"You said she was gone."

"I know, I'm sorry. She's in here, jabbering all the time. Frankly, she gives me quite a headache sometimes."

The young sorcerer almost freaked out for a moment. *The demon knows she's there. No wait. Azatoth's a liar.*

"Is she lonely in there?"

"No, we chat often."

Now she knew without a doubt that the demon was lying.

"Where's the portal?"

"I don't know exactly where it is. I've been looking for it. I didn't want to drag you into this but the fact that they've been able to disrupt the wards means they're getting close. I've come to like this world and I don't want to think what they'd do to it."

Lexi nodded. "How can I help?"

Azatoth stood and stepped closer to her. "Alicia wants me to hug you. Do you mind?" She put her arms around her and squeezed. Fighting rising bile, the sorcerer returned the embrace.

The demon stepped back and stroked her hair. "She's been bugging me to do that for weeks."

Lexi took the demon's hands and looked into her eyes as though she thought she was looking through them to Alicia, which she was. "I miss you, sis."

The intimacy seemed to freak Azatoth a little and she stepped back. "Anyway, I think you might be able to help me find the portal. You seem to have some talent in that direction. But it might be that to find it, you need to be one hundred percent shadow mage. No light mage magic can exist within you. It will hamper your innate abilities."

She nodded at the obvious wisdom. "You've tried to warn me about that all along and I haven't listened."

The demon smiled. "I thought you'd come to understand it eventually. Get some sleep. I'll see you tomorrow and we'll talk more."

Lexi walked into the condo, closed her eyes, and watched through the seeing eye as Azatoth walked out to the street and around the corner to where Eric and Millicent waited.

"You can go. I put a tracker on her. I'll know if she translocates anywhere."

Scott and Dick appeared in the hallway in front of her. The mage twirled his finger.

"Can we talk now right?" the vampire asked warily.

The young man nodded.

Dick rubbed his forehead. "What a huge…steaming…pile of utter bullshit. I can act better than that on my worst day."

Lexi ran past them into the bathroom and threw up. She washed her mouth out and wiped it. "I need to get changed." Hastily, she pulled off everything but her underwear. Scott and Dick turned and faced the kitchen and she threw the clothes at their backs. "Check them for anything…unusual."

"I'll do it." Scott muttered over them. "Nothing. What are you expecting?"

"She's put some kind of tracker on me." She remembered the demon touching her hair. "Can you check my hair?"

Dick, still with his back turned, asked, "Me too?"

"Yes. All hands on deck." She stood in the hallway in only her panties.

The vampire turned and saw her. "Oh!" He spun away again.

"About face, soldier. You're looking in my hair for...I don't know.

They each took a side and ran their fingers through her long hair. Scott muttered as he filtered the strands cautiously.

Dick stopped. "Hang on. What's this? I can feel something here but I can't see anything."

The mage walked around and mumbled a few words. The invisible spec glowed. "Yes, that's it."

"Should I pull it out?" The vampire narrowed his eyes

Scott held a hand up. "Wait. It needs to stay connected to Lexi's hair so a few hairs need to come with it."

"Righto." Dick tugged a few hairs out at the root and held them out to the young mage.

"Ow!" Lexi rubbed her head and gave him an evil stare.

He smiled. "My work here is done." He looked down. "It must be those leather pants."

She narrowed her eyes at him. "What?"

"Your thighs aren't as fat as I thought they were."

Rather than grace that with an answer, she simply stared at him.

"I'll be going, then." He turned and headed to the door.

"Not quite yet," she called. "She put some spells on that room to keep us out. But you might be able to get past them. You'll have to come with us, which means traveling in my dimensional pocket."

"Fine." He closed his eyes and his expression became one of resignation. "As long as I'm not supposed to be driving at the same time."

Scott looked puzzled. "Huh?"

Lexi chuckled. "So that is why you don't like the dimensional pockets anymore. I thought it might be."

"What am I missing?" The mage looked from one to the other.

"Let's hurry." Lexi went to the bedroom and pulled fresh clothes on.

CHAPTER TWENTY-SIX

The three appeared outside the hotel. Scott immediately murmured a spell to ensure that they weren't being watched and nodded.

Lexi opened the door and entered. The others followed closely.

The foyer was a building site. Plastic sheeting was suspended over entrance doorways. Cables hung down the walls, waiting to be channeled for sockets and light switches.

Dick gazed around and sighed. "Oh, my broken heart. How did you come to this?"

They went to the stairway and descended quickly. When they approached the bottom of the stairs Lexi glanced back as Azatoth had done to see the end of the hallway behind the stairs. She turned to where Scott walked ahead. "Careful. The floor's not safe."

He moved to the side but stopped a few feet from the end of the hallway. "What did they use to spell the room? I can feel it from here."

She nodded her agreement when she felt the energy coming from the room. "There's no way any of us can get in there."

Dick led the way to the bottom of the stairs again. "Something looks different down here." He shrugged. "I suppose everything is different."

They climbed the stairs.

Once outside, they stood on the doorstep.

Lexi shook her head. "Why did Devon send me here if there's nothing to see?"

She took her cell phone out and looked at the photo she had taken of the old man's painting.

Dick looked over her shoulder. "Well, look at that—the door's different."

Scott looked at the building. "This is, like, fifty years later and they're renovating."

"Not this door now. The door in the painting. It didn't look like that back in the day." The vampire drew his brows down in puzzlement. "Now I come to think of it, the door in this picture looks more like the back door. There used to be a more discreet way to enter and leave the hotel through one of the buildings on 22nd Street if one didn't want to be seen by the ever-present photographers."

A few minutes later, the three of them stood in front of the multistory parking lot on 22nd Street.

Dick frowned. "This wasn't here before."

They entered the parking lot, walked through, and peered at the rear of the old hotel building.

"The door was down there." The vampire pointed.

"I'll go look." Scott vanished and reappeared moments later. "It looks like the door's been bricked up."

"Can we see?" Lexi asked.

They translocated to the top of a small stairway beyond the back wall of the parking lot which led to a brick wall. It was clear that a door used to be there.

Dick stepped up to the wall and brushed the dirt and dust

away beside it to reveal an outline of two-two-two. "You can still see where the brass numbers were."

Scott turned to Lexi. "Do you feel that?"

The vampire froze. "Is it booby-trapped?" He stepped back hastily.

"I don't think so." The mage walked down the steps and held an arm out to the wall. "But there's something."

Lexi didn't need to move closer. "It's a portal but it feels different to any other portal I've felt."

Dick waved his arm out in front of himself. "I can't feel a thing."

She put her hands out. "Give me a minute." She closed her eyes and reached out with her mind. Cautiously, she tested the edges of the portal but tried to avoid going through into an unexpected demon realm. It didn't seem to be trying to suck her through like the last one had. She felt her magic resonate with it and finally, she opened her eyes to see a door had appeared where the wall had been.

"That's the old door." Dick grinned, stepped forward, and opened it.

Lexi had opened her mouth to stop him but he was right. It was simply a door. They walked into the building.

Dick stood frozen a foot ahead of her in the lower hallway. "I don't understand. We were here not twenty minutes ago and it didn't look like this."

She pushed past him.

The staircase beside them still had its ornamental balustrade. It gleamed in black iron and the parquet flooring shone with its lustrous oak coloring. "That's the staircase we came down and look at the door we came through. It was simply a blank wall before."

They walked along the hallway.

As she passed the bottom of the stairs, she heard a woman laugh and a door close several floors up.

Scott looked at her. "Ghosts?"

"There would certainly be some interesting ones," Dick muttered.

Lexi shrugged and turned to the mage as he approached the door. "Do you feel the spells on the room that stopped us before?"

"There's something there but it's not the same." Scott leaned forward and opened the door. It was a janitor's closet filled with cleaning materials and a mop and bucket. "This is a standard Kindred glamour." He closed the door, mumbled a few words, and opened it again.

The door opened into a large room with dark-green walls and floor-to-ceiling bookcases. The parquet floor was shiny and clean, and row upon row of bookcases were filled with books.

Lexi wandered in. "I don't understand. None of this was here before. How come they didn't find it when they came earlier?"

A young man walked out from the stacks. He studied the three of them and turned to Scott. "Who are you? You're not supposed to be in here. Is this a vampire? Have you brought a vampire in here?"

Lexi stared at him. He looked sixty years younger but it was the same man. "Devon? How are you here? Are you a ghost?" She stepped forward and poked his arm.

"Don't be absurd. I'm afraid I don't know you and I don't think you should be in here."

"You sent me here. From the archives across town."

"You're standing in the archi—" He stuttered to a halt. "You can't be a— What are you?"

"I'm what you think I am. You did send me. Except you were old."

Dick leaned forward. "And dead."

She stared at the vampire, unable to believe what he'd said.

"Sorry. I was trying to help." Dick turned to the young man. "Don't worry, you're very old and you go…peacefully."

Lexi tried to ignore her twitching eyelid. "Azatoth's been trying to find a—"

"What? Who did you say?" Devon froze.

"Azatoth. He's a demon. He's taken Kindred over and he's trying to find the spell to get him out of—are you okay?"

The young man dropped heavily onto a footstool.

She jumped at the noise it made. It was unexpected as she still half-thought he was a ghost.

Devon shook his head. "You shouldn't be here. There'll be a meeting in ten minutes and they can't find you here. I'll find someone to talk to you. Come back in a couple of hours." He began to shoo them toward the door.

Dick turned to him. "May I ask what year this is?"

The man's mouth made a silent "O." "It's 1968."

Scott's jaw dropped. "It was a time portal? I thought that wasn't possible."

The vampire turned to him. "Scott, seriously. Catch up. Sixty-eight—how thrilling. Come along, then. We can go upstairs to my apartment." He led the way up the stairs to the entry level and continued to climb.

After several stories, he finally led them down a hallway. He stopped abruptly. "Damn! Oh, I know." He backtracked a few feet and knocked on a door. "Janis darling, are you in?"

A man answered the door. "Hey, Will. How are you doing, man?"

"Leonard, hello. I'm great but I lost my key. Has Janis still got my spare?"

A hand and bare arm appeared from behind Leonard with a keyring dangling from one of the fingers. A dark-haired woman's face appeared on the man's shoulder. "Hey, Will. Do you and your friends want to come in and party?"

He smiled at her. "Maybe later."

Leonard glanced at Lexi and Scott. "Then enjoy your own beautiful party."

The door closed.

Dick continued along the hall and stopped in front of a door.

Lexi caught up with him. "Wait. What if you're in there?"

"I was out of the country for most of sixty-eight." The vampire opened the door, flicked the light on, and invited them in.

The windows were covered by huge artworks and bright pieces of furniture and fabrics were displayed casually.

An easel stood in one corner with a psychedelic painting on it. The sorcerer tilted her head this way and that but couldn't decide what it was meant to be.

Dick put the key in his pocket. "I knew something was going on between those two. Then Leonard wrote a song about it of course, and everyone knew."

Scott looked at him. "Oh. Are they famous?"

"Oh, my God!" The vampire groaned. "Janis Joplin and Leonard Cohen."

The young man's face remained blank.

"I swear…" Dick lowered his head to pinch the bridge of his nose. As he did so, he glanced at a table and his face lit up. He picked a gold ring up. "I thought I'd lost this. To be honest, I wondered at the time if Janis had taken it. She was the only one with a key to my apartment. I remember seeing some odd scratches on the lock when I returned, though, so maybe someone picked the lock." He slipped the ring onto his pinky finger and rubbed it on his jacket to restore the luster. "Coffee? There's no milk so it'll have to be black. I haven't been here for months. I'm traveling through Europe having a fabulous time."

Two hours later, they hurried down the stairs to the first floor. Lexi stopped. "Where's the front door?"

They stared at a blank wall where the door to the street had previously been. Scott shrugged. "Maybe we're not intended to leave the building."

As she contemplated that, a young couple appeared to walk through the wall into the hotel.

"It seems you're right. We can't exist outside of the hotel in this timeframe." Dick sighed. "That's a shame. I could have shown you a great time around the city."

They headed to the basement but the vampire paused. "Are you sure there won't be a dozen Kindreds waiting to gut us in there?"

Lexi tilted her head from side to side. "Maybe. I can't say it didn't occur to me too, but what choice do we have? Devon sent us here for a reason. He knows we have to stop Azatoth and his last act was to send me here."

Scott spoke the spell to reveal the room and they stepped through hesitantly.

Devon was clearing cups away and looked up when they entered. "It's okay. You can come in."

Dick looked around suspiciously. "Can you confirm that no one is waiting to stake me?"

The man held a book up. "That's a little too Bram Stoker for us. We're reading *The Time Machine* by HG Wells. It's much more appropriate, I think."

The vampire's face lit up. "Your meeting was a book club? How splendid."

"Have you read it?" Devon asked.

Scott grinned. "I saw the movie."

Dick elbowed the mage. "Spoilers, sweetie."

Scott rubbed his arm. "I know where you got that line."

Devon shook his head. "What year are you from? Wait, don't tell me. I don't want to know. Please excuse me. I'm going to see if my friend has arrived."

The young man stepped out of the archive.

Lexi drew a deep breath and blew it out abruptly. "I can't look at him without thinking about…"

Dick patted her back. "I know. And I didn't even see it."

Devon entered the room behind them and they turned quickly. "I'd like to introduce you to—"

"Dolores!" the three of them exclaimed in shared astonishment.

CHAPTER TWENTY-SEVEN

"Oh dear." The little fae woman raised her eyebrows.

Lexi's jaw dropped. "You already knew me? And you didn't say anything?"

"Oh dear, oh dear," Dolores repeated.

Dick picked at an invisible thread on his jacket. "I think you'll have to elucidate."

Devon indicated the table. "Let's sit."

They moved to the table and sat without protest.

The woman cleared her throat. "Firstly, please be assured that I've never met you before in my life—although it appears this won't be the last time. I'm sure the only reason I would have kept this from you is to preserve the timeline. I hope you're mindful of that the next time you see me. I think it's best for the sake of the timeline that we don't discuss anything that might change the future."

Lexi's gaze flickered involuntarily to Devon.

"Agreed. Nothing. Including my…" He glanced at Dick. "Peaceful end."

Scott shook his head. "But that's crazy. All we have to do is tell Dolores about…you-know-who in Palm Springs. Then maybe we could kill him before that entire clusterfuck even happens. What about all the lives it would save?"

Devon winced at his language.

Lexi sighed. "It could end up costing more lives. With him gone, Azatoth or some other demon could simply start grooming someone else to take his place. We might not know about it at all and millions could die."

Scott seemed to think about it before he hesitantly agreed.

Dolores laced her fingers in front of her on the table. "Right. Tell us the bare minimum."

The dark sorcerer took a breath and began. "A demon called Azatoth has escaped her—his—dimension and is trying to open a portal in…somewhere." It was difficult trying to not give them information they didn't need. "To bring holy hell down upon the earth."

Devon frowned. "How did he get out if the portal in Vegas is still sealed?"

Dick's eyebrows raised. "So you already know about the portal."

Lexi continued as if he hadn't spoken. "It seems she went the long way around. She spent hundreds of years slipping through the cracks of realms, then missed her one opportunity to get through physically but was able to possess—"

The vampire leaned forward quickly. "Someone."

She nodded at him, grateful for his intervention when she realized she'd been about to say her sister's name.

"But she can't get out of the vessel she's currently in," Scott explained. "A Kindred mage sealed her into it. She's been looking for the spell to find out what went wrong but it's not in the archives. From what we understand, she wants to get out and take over Lexi's body, we think so that she can find and open the portal herself."

Dick put his hand up. "I have a question. Why are we speaking with a curator and a fae and not the Kindred council?"

Dolores and Devon shared a look. "We belong to a group unknown to Kindred. The Order of the Shadow." The woman paused. She seemed to see that the name meant nothing to the three of them. "What do you know about Azatoth?"

Lexi counted on her fingers. "She's a psychopathic, lying, piece-of-shit demon."

Devon adjusted his tie and she smiled. He truly didn't like their language.

Dolores seemed puzzled but continued. "And why are you here?"

"If the demon wants the spell, I want to be certain she never lays eyes on it. But if it can tell me how to exorcize her without becoming the next vessel, I'm all in. You were going to tell us about Azatoth."

"The first thing you need to know is that Azatoth isn't a demon. Not fully, anyway."

Lexi frowned at her. "Then what?"

Dolores began her explanation. "I'm sure you know that in the 1600s, an infection of what seemed to be pure evil spread through the magical communities. It impacted the witches worst. They were possessed and became careless, practicing magic in the open and cursing people."

Scott interrupted. "That's when the magical community came together to create an organization to police them. That was the birth of Kindred."

The fae nodded. "Correct. The sorcerers were much less affected by the affliction so they were chosen along with partners who were imbued with the combined blood of the magical races."

Lexi nodded. "The legacies, who were supposed to keep the sorcerers honest."

Dick raised an eyebrow. "Best laid plans."

She made a mental eye roll but noticed a hint of a smile on the other woman's lips.

Dolores continued. "Two hundred years later, it happened

again. Once more, the witches were consumed. Kindred discovered a thin place existed between our world and a demon realm. A creature known only as the Darkness had been pushing again at this thin place when the dimensions moved close together. This time, Kindred decided to fix the problem once and for all.

"Thirteen shadow mages created a portal at the thin place. Their magic was fed by sulfur instead of by air. They were immortal and were to cross over to destroy the Darkness. When they had won the battle, they would return to this world through the portal which, as a precaution, could only be opened by shadow mage magic.

"The thirteen were translocated to the location. They created a portal that spanned the thin place, opened it, and went through. The portal was then sealed on both sides."

Scott narrowed his eyes. "So, what happened?"

"Soon after, one of the shadow mages tried to open the portal again, which is when they discovered they had been deceived by Kindred. The portal could not be opened from the other side, and when the last of those who had created it had gone through, it had also sealed from this side."

Dick straightened. "That's awful. They were stuck there for eternity, unable to die? Why?"

"The council feared the power and immortality of the shadow mages. They didn't want them to return to this world, so there they stayed. The few people who knew about it were forbidden to try to communicate with them or even speak of the portal again."

Scott looked sickened. "Couldn't other shadow mages have helped? And where are the others if they can't die?"

Devon patted his arm. "The thirteen were the last of the shadow mages."

Lexi looked up. "Then how do I exist?"

"I have no idea. But if, as you say, Azatoth has escaped, perhaps others did too."

The mage frowned. "I thought sorcery couldn't be passed down through blood."

"It seems there is much we don't know about shadow mages and their magic."

Dick leaned back. "Did they kill the Darkness then?"

Dolores answered. "They learned that the Darkness is non-corporeal—"

Scott stood abruptly. "This is monstrous." He walked away and spun back. "So they could have been there for two hundred years, fighting a creature that can't be killed and unable to contact home."

Lexi felt a wave of nausea and empathy through their bond link.

Devon shook his head. "Not exactly. They tried to contact Kindred but every avenue was blocked. Which is where we came in—the Order of the Shadow. A few mages along with other magical creatures like fae and witches defied the edict and formed the order to continue to communicate with them.

"Together, they worked to try to open the portal but it was impossible. Without knowing the exact location, they couldn't concentrate their efforts in the same place and probably wouldn't have succeeded anyway."

The young sorcerer was confused. "If your order has been communicating with these shadow mages for two hundred years, shouldn't you know if any of them made it back to Earth?"

"The contact hasn't been consistent because of the dimensional orbits. The realms drifted too far apart to communicate with them for decades at a time."

Lexi tried to pull the conversation back to something that could help them. "This doesn't explain what Azatoth is."

Devon sighed. "While the shadow mages will heal physically, the damage to the psyche was too much for one of them to bear. He went mad within a few months of arriving. He left the mages and wandered off alone. When he returned, he had joined with the Darkness. He was physically altered, proclaimed himself to be Azatoth, and swore vengeance upon Kindred. He joined the battles against the shadow mages but eventually, he wandered away, seeking another way to the human realm. Through the years of never-ending battle to keep the Darkness from the portal, more mages grew weary in their hearts. Most of them lost the hope that they would one day return to their world. Over time, more joined with the Darkness. There are only a few shadow mages now and they continue to battle against demons, the Darkness, and their former comrades."

Dick tutted. "Seriously, after that betrayal, I'd have been chipping away at the portal myself."

Dolores looked at her watch. "To throw the portal open would be to sacrifice the families they left behind to the Darkness. Most of them have forgotten that but some still remember." She stood. "I've told you as much as I can. I have to be somewhere else and I can't allow my timeline to be altered by your visit. Good luck." The fae woman left.

They were left with Devon. The curator sat for a moment in thought. "How did the demon possess this person?"

Scott frowned. "A mage was working with him. I don't know exactly how he did it."

Dick shuddered. "It involved copious amounts of disgusting animal fat."

Devon raised his eyebrows in surprise. "Animal fat? That can't possibly be correct. Surely you mean sandalwood oil."

"No. Because sandalwood smells delightful and the place where he prepared the vessel smelled like an abattoir."

The man nodded. "I don't think it's a true fusion. He can be removed."

Lexi spluttered. "Seriously? How?"

The curator leaned forward. "He could be returned to the body he abandoned."

"I killed that body." She frowned. "I ripped its heart out."

He chuckled. "You haven't been paying attention."

"What?" Lexi narrowed her eyes at him.

"Shadow mages can't be killed," Dick interjected.

Devon looked at the two young people. "Who created the portal that brought you here?"

The mage shook his head. "I assumed it was you. I didn't know such things were possible."

Lexi added, "You directed me to a painting in the new archive that held a clue to the location of the portal."

"I did it? How marvelous." The curator looked delighted. "I've been curious about portals for a few years but my goodness, time portals. I appear to have a new hobby, and it's great to know I'll succeed." The young man grinned, then frowned. "But I suppose I'll never be able to tell anyone."

Scott was shocked. "Why not? It's an amazing achievement."

"It will be easier to hide the time portal I'll make for you if no one knows it exists." He shrugged. "Follow me."

He led them through the stacks.

"The location of this archive seems to have been lost over the years," Lexi told him. "I wonder how that happened. It doesn't seem so secret if you're hosting book club nights."

"I'm afraid that's in the future and is not currently my problem. But if Azatoth is unable to find the grimoire of Greater Spells, it might be for the best."

"Caleb must have seen it as he performed the spell." Scott put his hand over his mouth. "Sorry."

Dick wagged a finger at the mage. "I think you mean You Know Who."

"Shit! This is hard."

"Please don't cuss in front of the lady." Devon changed direction and pointed a book out to Scott. "This should be the next book you read."

The young mage turned his head to read the title. "*The Legacy's Book of Etiquette and Fine Manners*. Erm… No thanks."

Dick snorted. "I bet that's a popular read."

The curator twitched an eyebrow. "I firmly believe the spine has never even been cracked and probably never will be." He stroked the book. "It's a first edition, too." He led them back on their previous course through the stacks until they finally reached their destination where the young curator pulled out a book wrapped in leather, placed it on a table, and opened it. The book seemed to fall open on the page he wanted. He turned it toward Scott and Lexi. "This is the only spell for permanently binding a demon to a human. You see here? It says sandalwood oil, not animal fat. Read it and learn it. It's not to leave this archive."

Lexi noticed the engraving tools on the table. "Your engraving equipment." She smiled at the thought of how long he'd been doing it.

"I've recently taken up the hobby. I do enjoy it." He walked away.

Scott took his cell phone out.

She put her hand over it. "I don't want any evidence of this. We do what he said— read it and memorize it."

"And change it, of course," Dick added.

"Huh?" She looked at the vampire in surprise.

"You said it yourself, Scott. If only one such spell exists, Caleb must have seen this book at some time in the future. If we leave it as is, he'll get the correct spell and we need him to get the wrong one." The vampire grinned. "But perhaps you could swap it for something that smells nicer, like cocoa butter."

"Let's not fuck the timeline up. Animal fat it is." Lexi tapped her head. "But no dimensional pocket evidence."

Scott nodded and they got to work.

After they'd spent ten minutes with the book, she looked at her friends. She put a hand on the book, where it now referred to tallow instead of sandalwood oil. "With this, we could get

Azatoth out of Alicia and be rid of him for good." They closed and returned it, then walked to Devon at the front of the archive.

She shook the curator's hand. "Make sure you take the etiquette book to the new archive. If anything happens that you think I should be aware of, drop a note inside it for me. We can test your theory about it never being opened."

"Surely if there were something so important, I'd have told you when we met."

Lexi chuckled. "You'd think so, wouldn't you? But you didn't say a word about any of this."

Dick joined them. "I have another request. Please look out for a framed painting appearing in the hallway out there. The man in the painting will look uncannily like you. Keep it on your office wall always."

Devon nodded. "Ah yes, the painting you mentioned."

"I should take it from the archive," the sorcerer commented.

The vampire smiled. "There's no need. I understand now why the brushwork was familiar. I painted it."

They went to the portal at the end of the hall and stood beside it.

"Oh, look." Dick picked up a framed canvas that lay against the wall. He turned it. "I already did it. How efficient I am." He handed it to Devon.

Scott smiled. "And you found out who stole your gold ring."

He looked at the ring which was still on his finger. "It was me. I stole it from myself. Good grief, I need a drink."

CHAPTER TWENTY-EIGHT

The next morning, Lexi didn't even manage to reach the training room. Azatoth put a hand on her shoulder the moment she stepped out of the elevator.

The air was acrid and made her eyes water. She had been brought to the demon realm again.

"I take it we're no longer in Kansas."

There was no answer and she sighed as she turned a three-sixty.

She's left me here again.

A little more calmly this time, she examined her surroundings. She wasn't in the cave and the land around her was barren and deserted. From what she could see, she'd have to walk for hours to find anything that looked like it might house a portal home. The sky was a yellowy gray and foreboding. She couldn't sense a portal anywhere near her and wondered if the demon had simply left her there to die.

The atmosphere was hot and oppressive and her skin began to feel itchy. Not knowing what creatures might inhabit this realm, she felt like a sitting duck simply standing there and decided to start walking. But in which direction?

Lexi closed her eyes, centered herself, and breathed slowly the way Scott had taught her. She pushed her awareness out around her and followed the ripples of magic in the same way her mind followed the seeing ball. Rather than with sight, it was as though she searched with her fingertips. After a few minutes, she sensed something calling to her magic from far off.

At the same time, she sensed something else much closer. It was moving and it was behind her. A moment later, the katana was in her hand and she spun with the blade outstretched. It glided through the middle of what appeared to be a dog-sized slug that had been poised to strike. She retained the katana in her hand, mostly because it was covered in monster gunk and she didn't want to put it away like that. It was time to move.

She set off and began to follow her senses. Over the next couple of hours, she had a few encounters with similar creatures that tried to attack her and dispatched them easily, but for the most part, she tried to steer clear of the local inhabitants as this wasn't her world. She continued to follow the magical pull which remained consistent but didn't feel like it was getting any closer. After another hour, she began to tire and noticed the skies had begun to darken.

This isn't a place where I want to be stuck in the dark. She increased her pace.

Finally, in the fourth hour, she reached a rocky formation that protruded from the wall of the valley. As she drew closer, the pull of the magic was stronger.

When she found the entrance to the cave, she knew without a doubt that it was the right one. She stepped into the entrance and the air inside changed dramatically. Cautiously, she grew an energy ball in her palm and hovered it above her to provide light. She stepped out of the cave and brightened the orb before she directed it into the shadowy interior.

Several creatures scuttled out into the open. She waited for a few moments before she stepped into the cavern and to where she knew the portal was. Once there, she sat on a rock, not because the magic in the portal tried to dissuade her from approaching it but because she realized what going back meant.

If I go back, Azatoth will know I'm capable of finding the portal. If I don't, though, I don't think I'll last the night.

Lexi shook her head. *One problem at a time.* She closed her eyes, walked toward the gateway, and opened them again in the training room.

Azatoth was lying across a desk blowing big, pink bubbles of gum. "You made it." The demon straightened with a grin, then frowned. "You look awful. I don't think the climate suited you."

She remained silent and simply stared at her.

"But on the bright side, you're ready to find that portal. Let's go now."

She was past caring if this monster wanted to rip her apart. "No."

Azatoth's eyes flashed yellow. "No?"

Her jaw set. The demon needed her and so wouldn't kill her yet. She assumed she still had time to put some kind of plan together. "I'm tired and hungry and my skin feels like it's on fire."

Alicia's body slid off the desk and strode closer to her. "And your hair's a fright." Azatoth put a hand on her arm. "You're right. Get some rest. We can do this tomorrow. Well done today. You did great." She disappeared without waiting for a response.

Lexi sighed. The demon had said all the right things but her fury was palpable. She knew she hadn't bought herself much time. Wearily, she shook her jacket out and sat on the desk to pull off her boots one at a time and tip sand and stones onto the floor. She took the hairs and tracker from her pocket and smirked as she dropped them amid the mess.

The young sorcerer left the building and texted as she walked down the street.

Heading your way now. She sent the text to Dolores and continued to the coffee shop.

When she stepped into the fae's apartment, Dick was already there.

The vampire looked up from the sleeping puppy in his arms and gasped. "What the fuck happened to you?"

Marcel woke up and jumped onto the floor.

Lexi looked at her arms. Her skin was mottled red with burns.

"I spent the afternoon stuck in a demon dimension with acid in the air."

His face was aghast. "But your hair's so frizzy. It's a fright."

"That's exactly what Azatoth said." She shook her head. "Where's Dolores?"

"She's out back. She has a visitor."

The young sorcerer stepped into the bathroom and looked into the mirror. Her hair was a fright. She healed the burns on her skin but her breathing was shallow. There wasn't much she could do about her clothes other than a glamour and they looked ready to disintegrate. She tied her hair back and turned at a knock on the door.

Scott entered. "I was coming to find you but you texted that you were on your way."

She put a hand out but instead, he put both palms on either side of her neck and gazed into her eyes. Her lungs cleared, the pain in her throat disappeared, and she blinked as her eyes became less scratchy, then clear.

He remained close and didn't move his hands for a few more moments. He seemed to become aware of the intimacy and stiffened before he stepped back. "There you go. Better?"

Lexi nodded and surprised herself when she realized she was blushing.

That wasn't...horrible.

They walked through the apartment. As she got closer to the back door, a pungent smell grew stronger.

Scott proudly indicated the bench outside the shack on the lake. "Look who's here. I said I'd find him and I did."

Sam waved awkwardly. He sat beside Dolores and looked very flaky. Limpet lay in his lap. "Your pet's very affectionate."

Lexi stared at the little demon with an eyebrow raised.

His expression said, "What?"

She walked into the apartment and took the glass of bourbon Dick had poured for himself. Ignoring his spluttered protest, she knocked it back and narrowed her eyes suspiciously at Scott. "How did you find him?"

"Edward texted me. Sam turned up at his property in San Bernardino. It seemed he tried to visit Dick's home but was chased off by an angry young man in gold shorts with a baseball bat."

Lexi raised an eyebrow. "When you say you found him…"

"I lied."

She sighed with relief, then fixed him with a questioning look. "Have you called Adele?"

"Yes, she'll meet us at our place. They can plan their next steps while we have the conversation we need to have." Neither of them looked at Dolores but the fae woman gulped so loudly that they heard it from fifteen feet away.

Lexi walked out of the apartment into the condo. "Give me a few minutes to change."

Scott gave Sam instructions. "Adele and Krish are on the way here. Make sure it's them before you open the door. Don't go out and don't remove your cloaking charm. There's food if you need it, and here's the TV remote. We'll be back in an hour."

She opened the front door which led to the fae apartment, and the mage followed.

Marcel and Limpet rolled around the floor play-fighting over a ball. The dog dropped the ball and ran to them.

Dolores had a coffee jug and two cups in her hand. She smiled at them. "Dick, bring the bourbon, please."

The three of them sat quietly and waited for the fae to join them.

She held two glasses.

The silence was almost deafening.

The woman passed one of the glasses to Dick and kept the other in her hand. "How did it go at the Chelsea Hotel? Did anything interesting happen?"

Lexi smiled sweetly. "I think you could say something interesting happened…Dolores."

"Thank the gods. Finally." The fae took a slug of her bourbon and sighed.

The young sorcerer folded her arms. "You knew us all that time and you didn't say anything—not even a hint."

"I couldn't say anything. You must understand that."

Dick shook his head. "Oh, Dolores, I'm very disappointed in you."

Scott tapped a finger on his cup. "Is this why you've always been so unflappable? Because you knew we weren't going to die in Palm Springs or New Orleans or any of the other dozen places we've all been since we've known you."

"I knew no such thing. You traveling back could have completely changed the timeline. I suspected it probably had. So every time any of you have been in mortal danger, I've wondered if this was it—the moment where one of you dies and can't travel back to meet me. Of course, it occurred to me that five of you could have traveled back, then time changed and two of you died but I wouldn't know as the timeline would have changed—"

Lexi held a hand up. "Okay, stop. You're blowing my mind."

Dolores knocked back another bourbon and Dick slid the bottle to the other end of the table.

The fae woman continued. "I could never be sure what would happen in the future and couldn't take anything for granted. If I had said something, it could have changed the timeline to a future where everything went wrong." She leaned forward, grabbed the bottle, and poured herself another.

Scott put a hand on his fae friend's arm. "It's okay. We understand."

Lexi looked at her. "How long did you know Devon?"

"His father was in the Order of the Shadow before him. I knew him as a boy."

She squeezed the woman's hand. "I'm sorry you lost your friend."

"Thank you, dear." Dolores made a call on her cell phone. "It's me. We're all caught up. It's time. Let the others know we're coming."

A few minutes later, she stood and opened her front door.

They entered the gambling floor of a casino. "Where are we?"

The fae spoke as she walked purposefully through the building. "It's a casino on the edge of town, well away from downtown and the Strip. It's mostly frequented by locals and conferences."

The three of them followed her as she strode past slot machines, elevators, and restaurants. She stopped at a set of doors next to a large sign indicating that a conference for accountants was taking place inside.

Lexi grimaced. "An accountancy conference?"

Dolores smiled. "It says whatever you're likely to be least interested in."

Scott looked at the sign and grinned. "Vegan conference."

They stared at Dick.

"I'd rather not say." He stepped up to the door and held it open for the others.

The room held a few hundred people who were separated into groups.

Lexi identified witches, sorcerers, and various fae creatures.

A man broke away from a group and walked toward them. "Lexi. How nice to see you."

Scott's jaw dropped. "Louis. You're in on this too?"

The sorcerer looked from the old man to her fae friend. "Hey, wait. I thought you two had never met before a few weeks ago."

Louis laughed. "That's true. I only joined within the last year. While I was recommended to the order by Dolores, we never met until the day the demon awoke. This is all quite something though, isn't it?"

Lexi shook her head. "I don't even know what this is."

A voice spoke from behind her. "Let's sit and we can talk about it."

As she turned, Scott stepped in front of her and raised a shield. "This is the guy who attacked me in LA and took the mage's body."

CHAPTER TWENTY-NINE

Lexi stepped around Scott. "Sebastian. It sounds like you have some explaining to do."

"That's exactly what I suggested." The mage turned and walked to the coffee set up on a side table near the door. He took a cup and worked the lever on a coffee urn to fill it. She did the same.

The young mage looked furious. "That's Sebastian? The guy who laid me out? I don't think—"

Dick pointed at the table. "Would you look at those cookies? They must be the size of my face."

Scott's head snapped toward the table, then back to Lexi. "I'm still annoyed." He marched to the cookies.

She smirked and muttered to Dick. "Nicely done."

They sat around a table with Sebastian and Louis.

"So what's all this about?" the vampire asked.

Sebastian tore a sachet of sugar open. "Firstly, I'm very sorry. I did my best to not cause you any serious damage. I know it was a dick move to hit you when you weren't looking, but I was under Dolores's instructions to interact with the two of you as little as possible before you'd been to the Chelsea."

Scott broke a giant cookie in half. "Don't worry about it. Only my pride was hurt, and doing the same to you in Chihuahua made me feel better. We've worked out that the mage was Francesco. Who was the woman? Who killed them?"

"Francesco killed the woman. He was one of the demon's inner circle. Oh… We don't use the demon's name here." Sebastian waited for them to nod their understanding. He looked at Lexi. "The woman was Susan, a legacy. She was your mother's best friend. Eric and Millicent found out about Susan and wanted her memories extracted. They thought she might know where the demon gate is. Devon sent me to protect her. I was too late, however, and Francesco had already killed her. I did the next best thing."

Lexi finished the thought. "You killed him."

He nodded. "I managed to kill him before he could tell anyone what he'd learned but before I could get rid of his body, the goons arrived. I've seen them around the office. I think Eric has them on retainer so I had to get away before they saw me. As it stands, I don't know if they got a look at me in the church."

Scott leaned forward. "They didn't. Eric arrived seconds after you left and they were unable to tell him anything about you."

Sebastian looked relieved.

"I waited for a chance to get Francesco's body again but I saw the zombie go in. He hurried out about ten minutes later with the goons after him. Then I had to decide if I would go in for the body or follow the zombie. In the end, two of the goons followed him and I followed them. The next time I saw the house, it was engulfed in flames so I had to snatch the body from the morgue."

The young mage narrowed his eyes. "What were your intentions toward Sam?"

"To counsel him if I could. I've never counseled a zombie and I don't even know if it's possible. If it wasn't possible…" Sebastian shrugged.

"Kill him?" Scott didn't look happy about that.

The man immediately defended his position. "If he has the location of the gate and the demon gets hold of him, we're fucked."

Dolores put a hand over Scott's fist on the table. "I'm sure that between us, we have something that can take those memories from his mind."

Lexi knew Sebastian's comments didn't sit well with Scott, but he said nothing more.

She glanced around the room. "What is all this?"

"At first, we were trying to get the wards up but she's too strong. This is the whole order and everyone we know. Now, we're concentrating on flooding Las Vegas with magic to interfere with the cabal's efforts to find the gate."

The sorcerer smiled. "I know that's working so keep it up." She turned to Sebastian. "Why do you think my mother knew where the gate is?"

Louis took up the story. "Do you remember when I told you the ancestors had asked me to rat you out to Dick?

Lexi nodded.

"That request didn't originally come from my ancestors."

She frowned at him. "I'm confused."

"All I knew at the time was that my ancestors asked me to help yours. And a good boy always does what his grandma tells him to."

Her frown deepened. "Go on."

Louis leaned forward. "Your mother's name was Amelia."

"I was told her name was Elizabeth—Liz."

"That's what they named her when they found her. She had forgotten her life before she was found wandering aimlessly around Las Vegas."

"Az—the demon said a mage took her memories."

"That was an assumption. Given what they were working with, it made more sense than the truth."

"Which was?"

"Your mother was Amelia and your father is Jonathan."

"Is? Are you saying my father's still alive?"

Louis nodded. "He is most certainly still alive."

"And he's a dark sorcerer too? I thought I was the only one." She raised an eyebrow. "I have to keep reminding myself that I got all my information from the demon."

"You are a shadow mage because your father was a shadow mage. And he was a shadow mage because the Kindred council made him one."

"Kindred can create shadow mages? So why hasn't the demon done that?"

"Every council has been made up of the most powerful mages on earth, but when they discovered the thin place and attempted to seal it, they could not so they made a different plan. They chose thirteen of the best mages from the rest of Kindred and worked a spell on them. When they awoke, they were changed. At first, it was believed the spell had failed and their magic had diminished, but when they were taken to the demon realm, they became incredibly powerful. The plan was that they would create a powerful portal across the thin place."

Dick took his flask out. "We're familiar with this part of the story. The bastards tricked them into going through the portal but they were never able to return. And assuming their immortality stemmed from the spell, they're possibly still all there, except Aza...thing, who is now here."

Lexi sprinkled sugar into her coffee. "I think I've been to the portal they practiced with. The demon has been teaching me to open portals."

"We know," Sebastian grumbled. "Dolores told us."

"I suppose Lexi's lucky you didn't simply think to kill her," Scott muttered.

"Don't think that hasn't been suggested." The older mage looked away.

Lexi felt Scott's temper rise.

Sebastian continued. "Calm down. Dolores said she'd cut parts off me I'd rather keep. Also, we are in an unusual situation. Lexi's our biggest liability because she alone can open the portal from this side. She's also our best hope because shadow mages were created to fight the Darkness."

Dick smoothed a perfect eyebrow. "Except they seem to have failed spectacularly at that for two hundred years."

Lexi was beginning to get murderous vibes from Scott and changed the subject quickly. "Louis, are you saying my parents were and are two hundred years old?"

"Yes and no. Your father is. Your mother tried to hide in his dimensional pocket as he went through the portal but when the last of them went through, the portal began to close. She was torn between the worlds. When the portal spat her out, it had been mere seconds for her but she had been dropped into nineteen-ninety. There is a little more to her story but it's not my place to tell. It wasn't until she reached the other side of the veil that she remembered who she had been before."

The young sorcerer nodded as things began to fall into place. "The veil. The ancestor realm?"

He nodded.

She stood, then sat again. "This is so much to process." She thought for a moment. "How did the demon know who my mother was? She had a different name."

Sebastian answered again. "Devon told me that Eric had taken her file to the demon's office. There would have been a picture and because Liz was the legacy of one of the thirteen, she must have recognized her."

"What was the demon's name when she was a mage?"

"Mortimer Bergen."

Lexi looked around the room, her mind working furiously. She returned her gaze to Sebastian. "You need to get your people working hard at this. She won't be put off any longer and wants me to find that portal tomorrow. We'll need you to run as much interference as possible." She turned to Dolores. "We have to resolve that other issue." She was hesitant to mention Sam in front of Sebastian in case he decided to opt for plan B where the zombie was concerned.

The fae nodded her understanding.

At the condo, Lexi looked into the living room. "Sam?"

There was no answer.

Dick ran to check upstairs.

Scott shook his head. "The place is empty."

She frowned. I don't see any sign of a struggle. I guess Adele arrived and they simply left."

"Scott," Dick called in his high-pitched there's-nothing-wrong-but-there's-something-wrong voice.

The young mage hurried upstairs.

Lexi could hear them having a whispered conversation for a few seconds before they fell silent. Scott had helicoptered a bubble of silence around them.

She didn't like that and walked up the stairs. When she stopped halfway and stared at them, they returned her look but neither of them said anything.

"What?"

Dick grinned so hard it looked scary. "It's probably nothing. Let's go open a bottle of something very strong."

Lexi continued up the stairs. They were blocking the way into the bathroom. "Excuse me."

Reluctantly, they moved.

The first thing she saw was an empty body bag in the bath and several blood-stained napkins in the trashcan. She trembled reflexively and her right eyelid immediately started to twitch. She turned to her friends. "Dick. You're a betting man."

The vampire sighed. "Oh, God."

She enunciated each word clearly. "What would you say the odds are that Sam ate Devon?"

"Personally, I wouldn't bet against it."

Scott punched him in the back of the shoulder.

"She asked a very clear question, Scott."

Lexi looked at the mage and quoted his earlier comment to Sam. "There's food if you need it and here's the TV remote."

The young mage facepalmed.

She stormed past them and down the stairs. "In case you want to watch the game after you've eaten Lexi's friend." She snatched a beer from the fridge and sat on the deck. Tears rolled down her face.

Scott came out with a beer in his hand followed by Dick with his flask. The mage opened his mouth several times but couldn't seem to find the words.

Finally, she sighed. "I brought him home for a proper burial." She wiped the tears from her face, shook her head, and finished with a brittle laugh. "Fuck me! You couldn't make this up."

She held her bottle out. "To Devon. It's not the funeral he deserved but it's the one he got."

They clinked bottles and flask.

Both men responded. "To Devon."

CHAPTER THIRTY

A loud crash yanked Lexi from sleep. She was out of bed in a second to face the chaos around her. Scott was unconscious and slumped between two men she recognized as members of the cabal. Her katana appeared in one hand and an obsidian energy ball in the other. She hurled the ball and tried to hit the guy on the right but also keep the blast away from her friend.

The magical projectile seared half the guy's head off. He dropped like a stone as the young mage disappeared with the other man. Belatedly, Lexi realized she wasn't alone. Before she could strike out at the third man, she was blasted by a force of energy that blew her into the wall.

Water splashed in her face. "For God's sake, Lexi. Wake up." Dick's voice was shrill.

She was on the bed, she realized, and when she put a hand to the back of her head, she found a towel there.

The vampire's brows furrowed. "Careful, you're bleeding."

The sorcerer looked at him. "How long have I been out?"

"Maybe ten minutes? I got here seconds after you tried to crash through the wall. Where's Scott?"

Lexi sat quickly. "They took him. I got one of them but—" She frowned as she looked at the floor. There was no body. "I thought—"

The vampire's lips drew into a thin line. "You did. Limpet took the trash out."

She placed a hand gingerly on her head and muttered the spell Scott had taught her to heal herself. That done, she stilled herself and thought about her next moves.

Dick watched her. "I assume it was Azatoth."

Her mind raced through her options, knowing the demon would be several moves ahead as she always seemed to be.

After waiting for a few seconds, the vampire tried again. "Should I call Dolores?"

Lexi's gaze darted around the room as she played scenarios out, but she didn't see the room. Rather than seeing her surroundings, she visualized moves and counter-moves. She knew she had to be careful. They would expect her to go after Scott, of course. What could she do that they wouldn't expect?

The wall shimmered and Limpet came through. His huge eyes met hers.

Dick tried again and sounded nervous. "You're very quiet. What are you thinking?"

The little thinner demon jumped across the bed and climbed onto her back.

Lexi stood. She drew a breath and blew it out slowly, now utterly calm. "They took Scott. If they hurt him, I will tear them apart. Hell, I'll tear them apart anyway."

"Stop right there! Don't you dare disappear without me. Put some thought into a plan with a little more detail and I'll get Marcel. We'll have to leave him with Albin." Dick left before she could argue.

Lexi dressed in seconds. She took a sulfur vial out and clasped it around her neck.

The vampire returned to the condo as she came down the stairs. "Are you in the bedroom? Good. Lexi will drop him off now." He paused for a few moments. "Me too." He disconnected.

She took her cell phone out and called Maggie. She felt certain her unit sister would answer a call in the middle of the night and she was right. The woman's sleepy voice came on the line. "Lexi?"

"Is everyone okay?"

"No one's pleased with you and we're on a knife-edge here. People have been watching us."

"Azatoth's made her move. You all need to get somewhere safe. She'll be looking for more leverage against me."

"More leverage?"

"She's taken Scott. I'm going to get him back." There was nothing more to say and she was about to disconnect when Maggie called her name. She returned the device to her ear. "Yes?"

"I need to see you. It's urgent."

"I'll be there in a few minutes. I'll meet you in your room." She cut the call.

Lexi took the puppy and a squeaky ball from the vampire. "Come on, little man."

Marcel licked her nose.

She translocated to Albin's apartment and put Marcel on the floor.

Albin's voice came from a bedroom. "Look after him for me."

"I'll bring both of them home." Lexi threw the ball and disappeared as Marcel raced after it.

When she arrived in the room, Maggie was waiting. She turned to the woman. "You should be out of here by now."

"We're heading out now. I wanted to give you this." Maggie reached into her dimensional pocket and pulled a sword out.

"Harpe? But how? I thought Azatoth took it."

Maggie smiled. "It was Bobby. He's a little kleptomaniac."

Lexi took the sword and felt the weight of it. "I still hope I won't have to use it. But it's good to know I have it, if it comes to that." She put it into her pocket and hugged her sister before she stepped back to look at her pregnant belly with a grin. "Get my niece or nephew somewhere safe."

Back in the condo, she took brass knuckles from her pocket, slipped them on, and flexed her fingers. "I can feel Scott's rising anxiety. He's waking up."

Dick raised an eyebrow at her hand. "Can he feel your fury? I bet that won't help his anxiety."

She took a few breaths and released them slowly in an effort to calm.

Limpet jumped onto her back and she grasped Dick's shoulder. "Let's see if the head archivist has high enough clearance to bring a vampire into the archives."

"What will happen if you can't?"

"We'll probably appear across the street."

They appeared in the archives.

Dick spun hastily, looking for danger.

Lexi put a hand up. "No one's here."

"How do you know?"

Lexi puzzled over it for a moment, then shook her head. "I don't know. I merely do." She closed her eyes, seeking her seeing ball.

It connected and she watched through Azatoth's eyes as the demon walked through scrubland. Ahead of her walked Eric and Millicent and someone else. Although she couldn't see clearly, she had a good idea who it might be. "Azatoth's not here. She's outside somewhere with Eric and Millicent."

"How many can we expect?"

"There are twenty-six in the cabal. I've only managed to count twenty-five on both occasions I've seen them but we can't rely on that. With Eric and Millicent away and the half-faced guy at the condo, that leaves us with twenty-three."

Dick swallowed. "But how many people are in the building? Could there be hundreds?"

"I think they're trying to keep this under wraps but yeah, I guess they could have the whole organization after us."

He rolled his eyes. "There's a comforting thought."

A pain seared through Lexi's head and she grimaced as she grasped her arms. It felt like she was being stabbed all over. "They're doing something to him." She reached out to Scott with her mind. He was terrified and feeling claustrophobic. Her thoughts immediately went to the Iron Maiden. She tried to locate him through the link but the cabal had put wards around them that interfered with the connection. When she felt a warmth from the ID card hanging around her neck, she knew without a doubt that the Iron Maiden was in the executive conference room.

She looked over her shoulder at Limpet. *Stay with Dick.*

The little demon dropped to the floor.

"Stay here," she told the vampire.

He held a hand up. "Wait. Don't—"

Lexi translocated to the conference room. She didn't look for Scott as she knew he was there from the screams. They were waiting for her as she knew they would be. They assumed she'd go straight for her mage, but they were wrong. Two legacies moved to disarm her but the katana in her hand was merely for show. Both would-be assailants went down in flames in the same moment in which they moved.

A mage screeched incoherently as he aimed a killing blast where she appeared to be standing in front of them. Two other mages redirected their spells at him. He might have been able to survive one attack but two had the effect of crushing his skull.

They must be under orders to not kill me.

The cabal cast spells at her which seemed to have no effect

because she was no longer standing there. She appeared in the corner behind them, flicked her gaze around the room, and counted nineteen. Her count was completed with a glance toward the large metal object. Scott and two female mages were behind a shield designed to stop her from escaping with him. She plunged a dagger into the back of the nearest mage's skull and bounced down to the archives.

"There were twenty-two," she told Dick. "Now, there are eighteen but I need to tweak my plan."

Dick looked surprised. "There's an actual plan?"

She led him to the relic room and used her ID to reveal the door before she turned to the vampire. "You need to stay outside this room." Signal me to let me know if anyone comes into the archives."

"What if they simply appear?"

She indicated her ID. "I'm the only one who can do that." She stepped into the relic room and walked to the recall button on the plinth, tapped it with her foot, and stepped back.

The Iron Maiden appeared but so did the two women who were guarding it. She threw a shuriken as she ducked out of the way behind a display, barely in time to avoid a streak of lightning that struck a dunking stool and blew it apart.

Neither of the women moved to follow her and chose instead to stay behind their shield.

One of them thumped the huge metal device and Scott moaned. "We're having fun with your handsome young friend. Although he might not be so handsome if he ever gets out of this."

Lexi clamped her jaw. She needed to get the women to drop their shield and sent a text. *I need your help. I need to separate Scott from his guards.*

She watched the dots flash for a few seconds, indicating that a response was coming, and it appeared a moment later. *I'm ready. Please remember to keep your hands to yourself.*

Lexi smirked. She aimed a blast of energy at one of the women. As it bounced off the shield, she translocated to Albin's apartment.

A wave of desire came over her as she took hold of the incubus' arm and returned to the relic room. They appeared out of sight of the Iron Maiden and the mages guarding it.

Albin would know why he was there. She didn't risk speaking to him and appeared on the other side of the door with Dick.

"What happened? Have they drugged you? Your pupils are huge and your heart's beating like—" He stopped speaking when he heard a familiar voice.

"Well, hello, ladies."

Dick's eyes bulged. "You have Albin in there? With whom?"

"Two female mages guarding Scott in an Iron Maiden. Albin's going to distract them so I can free Scott."

The vampire raised an eyebrow. "Unless they prefer each other."

Albin's voice came through the door. "Goodness, one at a time. Who wants to be first?"

The fight broke out after a moment's silence. Lexi listened as the two mages hurled blasts at each other. "I think we're good."

She darted into the room behind the Iron Maiden. The women were now on the floor, tearing each other's hair out while Albin stood nearby reading a book. She glanced at him. The full effect of the incubus was breathtaking and she took a step toward him until a cry of pain from Scott brought her to her senses. She shook her head and turned away. Quickly, she pulled the door to the device open and the mage tumbled forward into her arms. He was covered in blood. She translocated him to the other side of the door where the vampire waited. "See if you can stop the bleeding."

She stared from Dick to Limpet and back. "No eating Scott."

A blast erupted in the relic room. "If I can't have him, no one will."

A moment later, Lexi appeared in front of Albin to protect them both with a shield as they faced the women.

One of the mages shouted something in Latin with her arms outstretched. Flames launched from her hands and struck the shield. They rebounded and caught the other woman full in the face. Within the space of a second, her visage was reduced to a skull and she fell.

The remaining mage looked at her friend in horror. Lexi took advantage of her shock and blasted her without holding back. "Another two down."

She returned the incubus to his apartment and bounced out immediately to Dick, who was seated with Scott.

"Albin's home. How's Scott?"

The mage raised his head. "I'm healing."

Her shoulders slumped with relief. "Your cheeks are pink. I guess that's a good sign."

He grinned. "I think that was the bourbon."

Dick's jaw dropped. "Scott, you swore you wouldn't tell."

"I did?"

Lexi heard nothing in the stacks. "No one's been here?"

The vampire shook his head. "I'm surprised the noise in there didn't bring the entire building down here."

She shrugged. "This is a strange building. Nothing's where you think it is."

As if on cue, the door to the archives creaked.

"Maybe we should get out of here," Dick whispered.

Lexi nodded.

Limpet jumped onto her back and she placed her hands onto her friends' shoulders. Unfortunately, they didn't go anywhere.

"They must know where we are," she whispered. "They've locked the building down. We can't get out."

CHAPTER THIRTY-ONE

Dick cracked his neck and prepared for a fight.

"I have an idea." Lexi looked at Scott. "Can you move?"

He nodded. She was concerned, though, as he didn't seem to be healing as quickly as he should.

The thought was pushed aside as she led them into the stacks. The archive was enormous but somehow, she knew exactly where to go. She felt the ID card pulling her to the correct aisle.

Finding the ladder was still in the same place, she shared a nod with Dick and they both took a firm hold of the struggling mage.

Dick's eyes bulged as he took in the small, seven-step ladder. "If this doesn't lead to Narnia," he whispered, "we're in big trouble."

She began to hear the sounds of people moving around in the archives, then looked at the thesaurus and remembered the conversation with Devon.

This is a book you'll want if you're ever stuck in a difficult situation.

Despite her joke at the time, she hoped he had been speaking literally. She reached out to the rail at the bottom of the ladder as

Scott staggered beside her, propped up by her arm. He seemed preoccupied with the pain and she felt it too. She was grateful for that because she didn't think he would quite believe that she was dragging him up a ladder to nowhere. She and Dick hauled him up between them and she looked at the vampire and shrugged as she snatched the *Roget's Thesaurus*. The moment she put her hand on it, they were in a different place. They had somehow translocated to a dimensional pocket.

Dick took Scott's weight and lowered him carefully onto the floor where he passed out. She crouched with a hand on the mage and began to heal him. After a minute, she knew she'd done everything she could.

Lexi stood and examined her surroundings. The room was sparse with little more than a chair and a desk on which the thesaurus and a soda bottle rested. She thought it best to not touch the book. It seemed a fair bet that touching it would take her outside. Beside the table stood a full-length mirror on a stand. Scott groaned and she went to check on him.

Dick gazed around. "Where are we?"

"It's a dimensional pocket but I don't know whose."

"Could it be Devon's?"

"I don't think they continue to exist after someone's died. Maybe the archives has one of its own."

Scott opened his eyes.

Lexi was relieved that he looked better.

He sat hastily. "They snatched me from the condo."

"I know."

He scrutinized their surroundings. "What's the situation?"

"We're in the archives in a dimensional pocket hidden in a book. The cabal is stalking the aisles trying to find us. I suspect it's the full contingent of cabal mages and legacies. I'll have to deal with them."

Limpet padded to the mirror, sniffed it, then licked it.

Lexi narrowed her eyes. There was something unusual

about it.

She stood and approached it. The closer she got, the more she could feel the magic coming from it. She turned to the others "This is a portal."

Dick helped the mage climb to his feet and they joined her.

She put her hands up to it, closed her eyes, and felt the portal giving up its secrets.

The surface of the mirror shimmered, became hazy, then cleared. It reflected the room they stood in but not them. It showed the desk, but the chair wasn't empty. Devon sat reading a book.

Lexi looked at the empty chair and then at the old curator. She stepped through the mirror and the others followed.

The man closed the book and stood. "I thought my little hints had fallen on deaf ears and yet here you are."

She stepped closer to the old man and put her arms around him. "I'm sorry, Devon. I'm so sorry I wasn't here to save you."

He raised his eyebrows and nodded as he patted her arm. "So it's happened then."

Scott gazed around. "When did you create this time portal?"

"A few minutes after Lexi left the archives on the day she brought me a sandwich." He turned to her. "Which was very nice by the way. I can assume you are in a dire situation?"

"The cabal is after us. They took—" Lexi felt a tremor through her bond with Scott and turned in time to see him collapse. "Scott!"

The old man crouched and felt the mage's head. "He's burning up."

She put the back of her hand to his cheek as pinpricks of blood began to appear on his face. "I don't understand. I healed him."

Devon lifted Scott's t-shirt. It was clear that the wounds had not healed. "Was this the Iron Maiden?"

Lexi nodded.

"I see. The spikes in it were poisoned. Don't worry. I know what to do." He walked to the desk with the thesaurus on it.

Dick looked at the old man in horror. "Wait. You can't go out there."

Devon smiled. "It's the same day as the sandwich for me, remember? I'll get the antidote for him. When you leave, you must go back through the mirror first." He placed a hand on the book and disappeared.

Scott groaned.

"How long do you think he'll be?" The vampire paced in agitation

Lexi touched her friend's forehead. "Fast, I hope. This looks bad." She put a hand on Dick's shoulder. "Can you look after him? I'm late for my math class."

He frowned. "Math?"

"I'm working on subtractions."

She took Scott's hand. "Devon will be back to help you and you'll be okay. I have to get rid of some pests." She stroked his face.

He opened his eyes. "No. They'll kill you."

"I have to go out there and finish them. We can't get out of the building and it won't take them long to realize we have a bolt hole here." As she went to move away from him, he caught her wrist.

"What are you—" She realized what he was doing. He was pulling his magic out of her and leaving her with only the shadow magic.

He gazed at her unhealing scar and the swirling black energy within and smiled. "That should give you an edge." His eyes closed.

Limpet looked fascinated. He stared at her with his huge amber eyes.

Lexi knew her eyes were black. The sulfur pendant around her neck glowed and she felt the magical energy flow into her. As she stepped through the mirror, she held her katana in one hand and her short blade in the other. She reached out to the thesaurus and found herself staring at the desk with the thesaurus and the bottle. Confused, she turned and looked at the table in the past.

After a moment, she shook her head. "I'm an idiot."

Dick stood and looked at her. "What's wrong?"

She snatched the bottle up and handed it to the vampire. "Devon hates Gatorade."

The vampire snorted. "We're both idiots. I should have realized that it's the only thing that's different. Good luck. Hopefully, we'll be right behind you."

Back in the archive, she turned and stood face-to-face with a cruel-featured woman who immediately stabbed her in the chest. The cabal member opened her mouth to call to the others but Lexi had snapped her neck before she could utter a sound. The shadow mage pulled the knife from her chest and watched in fascination as the wound healed before her eyes and grinned. "Oh, I am here for this."

With a careless gesture, she dropped the woman's blade onto her body and inched silently to the end of the aisle. She felt rather than saw someone creeping across the aisles toward her and crouched, waiting for them to appear. As the man rounded the corner, she struck upward as she stood and thrust her katana through his chin until the blade struck his skull from the inside. She slid it out and he dropped soundlessly. "Fourteen."

Lexi crept farther into the stacks. She paused at the sound of whispers. At first, she thought it was cabal members but the quieter she became, the better she understood what she was hearing. It was the ghosts of the archives. They were angry, and they were warning their new archivist that more were coming.

She had to admit that her training sessions with Azatoth had been very useful. Now that she relied only on the shadow magic, she understood what the demon had been trying to show her. She could sense the magic more clearly. A man snuck around the corner and she used her magic to encase him within a black bubble as the demon had done to her. She could see instantly that he was blind to his surroundings and he waved his blade around wildly.

The shadow sorcerer darted beneath the blade and as he spun, she stuck him through the chest, a fatal wound. *Thirteen to go.* It was becoming abundantly clear that they had been told to take her alive, which limited their options. It was unfortunate for them because she had no intention of doing the same.

An urgent voice whispered to her from the dark. "Lexi…Lexi is that you?"

"Nora? What the hell are you doing down here?"

The woman approached and her heels clicked noisily on the floor. Lexi did a mental eye-roll.

"Azatoth called. She told me to come down here and let you know that she was going to rip me to pieces if you don't come out. For God's sake, Lexi, please do what she says. I don't want to die."

When the woman got close enough to see her face clearly, she froze. "Your eyes are black. What's happened to you?"

"I've given up all the white magic, which I guess makes me immortal now. Azatoth got what she wanted after all."

Nora's jaw dropped. "Immortal? You can't die?"

"Correct." She put a finger to her lips and listened to the whispering ghosts. Someone was around the next corner, waiting for her. She stepped quietly into the closest aisle and stood before the bookcase. Without her having to do anything, the books moved aside silently and allowed her to see the outline of the man lying in wait for her. Books began to fly from the opposite shelves and struck him in the head. He stood with his back to the shelves between them and she thrust her blade through the bookcase and into his neck. She didn't wait to watch him fall.

With him dealt with, she turned to Nora "That's over half of them gone."

"You've killed half the Kindred Council? Are you mad? Azatoth will destroy you. She'll kill us both."

Lexi pushed her short sword into the woman's hand. "Do you know what to do with this?"

The secretary took a step back. "I can't."

"Nora. This is the point where you're either on the side of humanity or the demon."

The administrator stared at her, then glanced at the sword and took it. "I might be a little rusty. It's been some years since I was in the field."

"I'll go first," Lexi whispered. She crept along the edge of the bookcases and looked back a few times to be sure no one was sneaking up behind Nora. As she moved, she reminded herself of how many were left. She counted again. There had been twenty-two cabal members in the conference room. The cabal, as with the council, was made up of thirteen sorcerers and thirteen legacies. Without Eric and Millicent, that made it twenty-four. She'd eliminated one at her condo but there had only been twenty-two in the room. Could another sorcerer or legacy have gone with the demon? It occurred to her to ask Nora who the last member of the cabal might be.

She was a moment away from turning to ask when everything slotted into place. With a groan, she realized who the last member of the cabal was.

The dark sorcerer left the image of herself in Nora's mind and appeared behind the woman in time to see her stab the short sword where she had been a moment before. The secretary realized her error and tried to spin in time to save her life but it had already been taken. As she turned, she sliced her throat against the katana in Lexi's hand.

Nora clawed at her throat as she slid down against the end of a row.

Lexi pulled the short sword from the woman's grasp as her eyes glazed over. "What a waste of latte."

CHAPTER THIRTY-TWO

Lexi reached an intersection of five aisles. She tried to move quickly across the exposed area but seemed to be frozen to the spot. A lattice of energy strings held her in place.

Several shapes detached themselves from the shadows. She tried to twist out of it but only succeeded in sending the short sword clattering to the floor.

Next, she tried to leave an image of herself trapped there and translocate out of it, but she couldn't escape from the trap.

The man in front of her pulled the cord tightly. "Don't bother. This is made for your kind. There's no way to escape it." His gaze dropped to her unhealing scar. "I see the poison finished your mage off. You're free of his magic. If you'd simply done as you were told, we'd have left him alone. Azatoth will be pleased. She's gone to confirm the location of the portal. Then she'll be back for you."

"I thought she needed me to find it."

"She found another way."

Lexi grinned. "Thanks for the information."

A woman to her right spoke. Her voice was thick and heavy

with grief. "If she can't die, let's simply hack at her while we wait."

Someone else added. "How does it work? Could we take parts off and see if they grow back? Azatoth won't need her to be whole."

The guy in front pulled tighter on the string. "You've upset many of us today." He glanced around. "Someone call Nora. She can update the boss."

Lexi's lip twitched. "Sorry. Nora's not available to take your call."

The grieving woman stepped forward and created slack in the string, allowing the captive to move a little. "We should—"

"Hold your position," the guy at the front snapped at the woman and the string tightened again. He looked at Lexi. "Nothing to say?"

"I'm merely trying to decide if I have enough information. Is there anything else you wanted to tell me before I go?"

"Surely you've already tried to translocate out of the lattice. You know you can't get out."

She smiled. The weak link had already been identified and she glanced over her shoulder at the woman. "Which one was your match? The one I blasted in the face? The one I stabbed through the neck?"

The woman snarled and stepped forward, slackening the trap again. It was all she needed. Before any of them could react, she stepped out of the trap and sprinted into the stacks.

"No!" the grieving woman shrieked. She dropped her string and raced after her, followed by the man who had wanted to cut parts off her and the rest on their heels. Of course, they ran after no one because Lexi had still been held captive until they dropped the strings.

The trap dissolved and she walked the other way.

She decided it might be time to try to double back to the

portal when running footsteps approached her. It was Scott and Dick.

Lexi held a hand up. "Could you two be any louder?"

The mage grinned. "Not without making them suspicious."

Dick shushed him. "They're coming."

It sounded like the five she'd gotten rid of. She readied her katana and the runners moved closer. A moment later, shrieks were followed by screams that sounded like they were going into the distance. Lexi frowned in puzzlement as she walked to the end of the aisle and peeked around the corner. A portal in the floor was closing as Limpet's limbs shrunk to their regular size. When it finally snapped shut, the distant screams cut off.

Scott came around the corner. "Were they still falling?"

She nodded. "That must have been very high up. Maybe it was a soft landing like a dumpster realm."

The little thinner demon looked at her and shook his head, then gazed sadly at the floor.

Dick scratched the creature's head. "Perk up little guy. I'd guess there are still a few more tasty heads around here."

After two decapitations, three throats ripped out, and one blown to bits, Scott suggested it might be time to leave.

Dick counted on his fingers. "Are you sure we got them all?"

"I think so." Lexi attempted to translocate but couldn't. "There must be one left. And I assume it's the one who spelled the archives to stop us from translocating."

The vampire shrugged. "I don't think we're in much danger from a cabal of one. Perhaps we'll run into him on the way out."

They headed toward the front of the archives. Dick paused and signaled that he could hear something. He mimed ripping paper. They moved cautiously and when they were close enough, he peeked out. His wave moved them back and his face was a mask of fury. "He's sitting at the front desk, tearing pages out of books. What a savage."

Lexi frowned. "If he's at the front desk, he has visibility of the door and every way into the stacks. He's certain to have a shield."

Scott folded his arms. "We won't get near that door without risk."

The vampire shrugged. "Why is he simply sitting there? Surely he must be wondering where the rest of his little friends have gone."

"None of them strike me as the caring type," she pointed out.

"But what is he waiting for?" Scott scrunched his face in confusion.

After a moment's thought, the three of them said, "Azatoth," at the same time.

Dick adjusted his shirt collar. "Let's not do that again. I would hate to inadvertently summon her."

Lexi smiled. "Let's give him what he's waiting for then." She closed her eyes and focused on how the demon had looked the last time she saw her.

The vampire put his hand on her shoulder and she opened her eyes. "What?"

"Make sure you don't accidentally take over her body. There are already too many people in there."

Lexi frowned at him, then chuckled softly. "I'll do my best. Don't worry. This is only a glamour."

She placed the picture of an empty floor gently into the mage's mind and walked up to the side of the desk as he continued to tear pages from the book. It was the paperback Devon had been reading and she swallowed a flare of anger.

She allowed him to see her. "Well? Where is she?"

The man's feet flew off the desk. "How—"

"And how was I able to step through here? It's supposed to be locked down."

"It is. It was."

Lexi smiled. She conjured the sweetest, most disarming smile she could manage. Anyone who knew the demon would know that smile preceded violence. "Where is she? In fact, where is everyone?"

"I think she might have killed them all."

She was ready to go crazy eyes on him when he added. "But you said the others weren't important so—"

"They were important until I had that pathetic excuse for a shadow mage. Everything's prepared. I'm ready for her."

"She must be in here somewhere."

"Because she couldn't translocate out of here?"

"I don't know how that—"

"Go and look."

"Where?"

She glamoured a pair of black and yellow eyes. "Everywhere."

"Right away, my lady." He bolted into the stacks.

Lexi waited and was rewarded by a loud crunch.

"There. Now we can get out of here."

Limpet raced out of the stacks and jumped onto her back. She waved a hand. "Eww…crunchy head breath." She grasped Scott and Dick and again, nothing happened. "You have to be fucking kidding me. Come on. We'll have to take the elevator."

She stepped out of the archives and stopped, face to face with Ian Baskerville in the hallway.

He sneered at her. "I see you've discovered there's only one way out."

Her smile contained an edge of menace. "Yes, and I see it's through you."

Scott and Dick walked into the hallway behind her.

Baskerville glanced at the mage. "You're supposed to be dead. I destroyed the only vial of antidote myself."

Scott shrugged. "It's the weirdest thing. It seems Gatorade is a perfect substitute."

Lexi rolled her shoulders, ready to fight. The cabal member stepped toward the three of them and jets of fire flashed from his fingers.

The young mage shielded Dick and Limpet and Lexi launched a blast of energy toward their adversary. Before he could retaliate, she thrust her katana straight through his chest and the jets of flame became sparks and their smoke fell far short of the mark.

He thrust his hands out repeatedly and seemed to think the fire was still being released.

Dick smirked. "Oh dear. He's firing blanks."

Scott turned to him. "Do you think we should tell him?"

The vampire stepped around the failing mage. "Let's not ruin the surprise."

Lexi called the elevator and her two friends stepped in. She retrieved her katana from the dead Baskerville and joined them.

They stepped out of the elevator and walked through the lobby. The security guy at the desk gazed in horror at the blood-spattered trio and their cat as they walked through the security gate and out the door.

Lexi stepped onto the street. "I need a coffee. Let's go get a coffee."

Dick pouted. "But I don't drink coffee."

She pointed at the vampire. "Then you, my friend, can watch." She remembered the sword Maggie had given her and turned to Scott. "Hey, you won't believe what turned up unexpectedly."

A familiar voice said, "Hi."

Lexi turned and her heart skipped a beat.

Azatoth snaked her hand out and caught her wrist.

Her last view of Scott was his face registering shock as he stepped toward her, his arm outstretched. The air around her grew heavy and gray for a few moments before it cleared to reveal dry scrubland barely lit by a half-moon. Her first thought was that she had been taken to the demon dimension, but while the atmosphere was heavy with heat, the air was breathable.

She turned to see the city lights of Las Vegas behind her.

CHAPTER THIRTY-THREE

"Why are we in the middle of nowhere?" Lexi asked Azatoth.

The demon grinned. "I think you know why. It's close. You can feel it, can't you?"

She raised her head and looked into the darkness, letting her gaze shift this way and that. "Nope. I can't sense a thing."

"Come with me. I think I have something that will sharpen those senses." The demon dragged her along and she made no effort to resist. She suspected that Azatoth would have prepared a welcome party and needed to know who was in it. Several people had gathered farther up the hill.

Eric and Millicent stood with three figures seated on the ground. As she had suspected, it was Sam, Adele, and Krish.

The legacy gave her a vicious smile before he turned to Azatoth. "He became more helpful when Millicent arrived with his sister."

Sam looked at him. "You promised you wouldn't hurt them."

He kicked the zombie in the stomach. "Do I look like the kind of person you can rely on?"

"Don't even get me started on that subject," Millicent muttered.

Azatoth rolled her eyes. "Save the lover's tiff for later." She looked at Sam. "So where is it?"

He coughed and pointed at the ground. "Here. This is the exact place Susan remembers. Liz stood here with her and told her this is the first place she remembers being. She thinks she must have walked here but she didn't know from where. Susan said, 'Are you sure you weren't dumped here by the guy who got you pregnant?' Liz said, 'No I feel strongly that I walked here but not a great distance.' That's the whole conversation."

"And over to you." The demon stared at Lexi. "Not a great distance. I feel like you can feel it. Come on Lexi, you've trained for this and I've been beside you every step of the way."

The shadow mage glanced at Eric. Sam was a crumpled mess on the ground at his feet. "Sam, are you okay?"

The crumpled mess sat. "I'm okay. I'm sorry I couldn't keep it from them."

Eric shrugged. "It wouldn't have hurt so much but we lost our best counselor."

Lexi strode toward the legacy. "What the hell is wrong with you?" She stepped over the zombie and stood nose to nose with the Grandfather of Colorado and stared into his white eye.

His face was smug. "I'm in mourning for my son."

"Warren was a fucking psychopath. Like father like son. Have you even noticed that Lucy died? I think you should have. She got a face full of manticore venom right in front of you."

"Lucy was weak. She was always a stand-in for Scott."

In her peripheral vision, Lexi watched the shock register on Millicent's face.

"Scott would rather have died than bond with that lunatic." She turned to face the other woman. "I wonder who you're a stand-in for." She turned her attention to Eric and pointed at the three prisoners. "Why are they even here?"

"It appears that your unit can't be found. But you're right, we don't need all of them." He took a step closer to Adele and touched her forehead to release a bolt of energy through her. She fell without a sound.

Sam screamed but Eric held him back.

Krish swept her up. "Adele?" She lay with her eyes open but utterly unresponsive. He rocked her in his grief.

Lexi left a vision of herself standing still in Eric and Millicent's mind while she bent closer to Adele. She didn't know if it would work with a zombie or not but she put a hand on the girl's chest and brought her power forth. "Live."

The girl didn't move or respond in any way.

She became aware that someone was leaning over her and looked up. Azatoth was staring at the girl too.

The demon frowned. "Oh, never mind. You seemed so sure. I thought for a moment it might work. That would have been quite exciting. But as Eric says, there are still two to go. Who next?"

"Fine. Let's find your fucking portal." She stood and started to walk farther up the hill.

"Lexi," the demon called.

She turned to face Azatoth, who pointed at Eric and Millicent where they still stood frozen. "Don't make me clean up after you."

Lexi wasn't sure what she'd done. She waved a hand at them and they both jerked and spun to look at her and Azatoth.

The demon frowned at them. "Do keep up. You're letting the side down." She pointed at Sam and Krish. "Bring them."

The young sorcerer led the way. With each step, she considered and dismissed plans and wondered if her mind trick would have worked on Azatoth. She suspected that it might have given that she was now fully shadow mage, but she'd be guarding against that now. If she simply vanished, they'd kill Krish and Sam and look for more innocent people to kill until they got what they wanted from her. She considered killing herself but there would be nothing to stop the demon from laying waste to the Earth out of spite.

Lexi heard electronic beeps from behind as she walked. She turned to see Millicent with one hand on the back of Krish's neck. The mage pushed him forward and her face lit up from the light of her cell phone screen. The shadow mage turned away with a smile on her lips.

The electronic tones continued as they walked, then intensified as Eric joined the dialing and texting.

Her smile deepened and when she glanced at Azatoth, she was smiling too.

Quickly, she looked away. She kept the smile on her lips but she realized she'd been played. The demon's intention had been to force her to give up Scott's magic. First, they'd kill him, then she'd use all the remaining reserves of his magic to kill the cabal who, as it turned out, would be expendable with the portal open.

She had some gems and a battery pack in her dimensional pocket. She could use them to refill her reserves but then she'd be powerless against Azatoth. Sam and Krish would be dead for sure.

Unintentionally, she quickened her pace. As much as the portal might try to drive her away when she got there, the magic powering it drew her closer.

The unanswered calls continued behind her. Finally, Azatoth had enough. She spun on her heel to face Eric and Millicent. "Enough already. They're dead."

He froze. "You killed them?"

The demon sighed and rolled her eyes. "Not me. Lexi gets the credit for those."

"All of them?" Millicent's jaw dropped.

"Yes," Lexi added. "All of them. Your boss wanted me to use Scott's magic and revert to my innate shadow mage magic, so she sent the cabal after me to force me to use it all."

"All of them?" the woman repeated. "Including—"

She rolled her eyes. "Yes, including Nora."

"What?" Azatoth looked visibly shocked. "But she was your friend."

After a big, dramatic shrug, she continued toward the portal.

The demon followed her. "You've seriously managed to upset me. Do you know how hard it is to get good secretarial support? She even did shorthand. No one does that these days."

Lexi didn't turn to look at her. "I don't know what to tell you, Az."

Finally, they stopped in front of a cave. The entrance wasn't much taller or wider than a person.

Azatoth stepped forward. "It's in here?" She walked up to it and took a couple of steps inside, then came out.

Millicent threw Krish down then bent over with her hands on her knees, tired from the climb.

Lexi looked at her. "Seriously? Who goes hiking in FMPs and pantyhose anyway?"

The woman didn't respond. She looked quite nervous now and didn't seem to know who to be more concerned about. Eric had admitted to not caring that a young, female mage in his care had been killed, Lexi had murdered the whole cabal and Azatoth had planned it, and she was now out in the middle of nowhere with them.

The demon tried to shoo Lexi into the cave. "In you go. Let's get on with it."

She sighed. "You've walked through it twice. It's across the entrance to the cave."

Eric and Millicent left Sam and Krish on the ground and moved forward in curiosity.

Azatoth narrowed her eyes. "Just like that? You've given in? Surely you have something planned. What's your move, Lexi?"

The shadow mage turned to the creature with her sister's face. She wondered if Alicia was watching this play out.

The demon continued, "Come on, we're here. What's your last

big play? Some more mind games? Will you run? Do you want to fight? Do you think you can take me on?"

Lexi was very sure she could take Azatoth on but that meant killing her sister. She looked around. "I seem to be out of options. Ideally, I'd like it if someone took those two away to safety." She looked at Millicent and Eric. He scoffed but the woman turned to Azatoth to see what she wanted.

Azatoth nodded. "I give you my word. When you open the portal, they'll go free. I'll even pull Eric's guts out for killing the girl without my permission."

The man stepped back with a look of discomfort. He too seemed quite unsure of his footing in all this.

But Lexi hadn't been speaking to the three of them. She was speaking to Scott who had appeared behind them. He bent silently to Sam and Krish, touched the two of them, and they all disappeared.

Lexi turned to the demon. "Well, if you promise, that's all right then."

She faced the portal, closed her eyes, and put her hands out. Immediately, she felt the edges of the spell hiding the portal. It fought back and she was surprised to discover that the magic that had hidden it was light magic similar to Devon's portal.

Azatoth gazed wide-eyed at the cave and seemed to be lost in a memory. "It was like this last time. The portal was created across the naturally thin place but it didn't want to be opened."

The young sorcerer looked at her. "There were more of you then. It can't have been that hard."

She smirked inwardly as the demon narrowed her eyes at her. Her expression indicated that was wondering how she would know that.

Good. That'll give her something to think about.

Lexi closed her eyes and continued to tug at the edges of the portal.

After another five minutes, Millicent hissed a breath. "I see it."

A blue halo had begun to show. It was coming along nicely. She made the last few adjustments and finally, the portal appeared.

"You did it," the other mage whispered, her voice full of fascination and dread.

She glanced at the woman. "It's not open yet. I have to touch it."

Azatoth marched forward and took Lexi's arm with one hand and grew sharp talons on the other. "Touch it and step back or I'll rip your guts out."

Lexi extended her hand and touched the portal. The dark cave disappeared and a strangely colored daylight appeared at the other end of a short tunnel.

"You did it. You were true to your word." The demon gazed at the portal as she called to Eric and Millicent. "Free the prisoners." She paused, then smiled. "But free them in the direction of that." She pointed at the portal. "I want to see them get safely to the other side before I call my friends through."

"Where's the zombie and his friend?" Eric demanded. "You were supposed to be watching them."

Lexi turned to see he was addressing Millicent. "You were supposed to be watching one of them too. You truly are a shit." Turning to Azatoth, she added. "So are you. They ran off about ten minutes ago. That was my last play."

The young sorcerer felt Scott through their bond. He was back, unseen and watching while he waited to see what she would do. She felt sad for him and stared at the portal while she sent a message from her dimensional pocket.

"It doesn't matter," the demon said. "I can feel the portal is truly open. I am merely a fraction of what I should be. The other shadow mages I joined with will come through and my non-corporeal essence will join with others. I didn't lie. I won't let any other demons through. There is only me in all my shapes and shadows, and I will flow across the land like a rolling storm and destroy everything in my path." Her eyes were closed and she stood with her arms extended.

Lexi looked behind them to where she knew Scott stood. He could feel her resolve but wasn't sure what she intended to do.

Unaware of his presence, Azatoth continued to twitter on. "I will lay waste to this world."

The young sorcerer smiled at Scott. Suddenly, he saw it and his mind screamed at her.

She translocated to the edge of the portal which she knew would close when the shadow mage who opened it went through.

The demon's eyes snapped open. She threw a bolt of energy at her but it bounced off the shield she had created across the gateway.

Lexi smiled. "Suck it, Mortimer." She stepped through the portal and saw the demon's horrified face and behind it, like a mirror, was the face of her mage with sorrow in his green eyes.

The gateway was gone and in its place was a dry and dusty landscape.

CHAPTER THIRTY-FOUR

Scott stood frozen in his dimensional pocket.

Krish held onto Sam, who looked like he was about to collapse. "We need to go back for Adele. We can't leave her lying there."

"Lexi's gone." The young mage felt the absence of his Kindred match immediately. "She went through the portal. She's gone."

"I'm sorry." Krish grasped his shoulder. "We'll get her back."

He felt that he should explain there would be no way to bring her back now that the portal was closed but he couldn't say the words. "Let's get Adele."

Scott appeared with Sam and Krish farther down the hill. The three of them turned toward the trail as the sound of Azatoth howling like a furious, wounded animal echoed to them.

"Where is she? She was here." Krish stared at the ground.

"Sam?" Adele's voice came to them.

Her brother and friend ran down the hill toward her.

Scott walked behind them. "We need to get out of here."

No one answered. The two men stood motionless, staring at Adele.

The young mage narrowed his eyes. The young zombie looked different.

She stared at her hands. "I don't understand."

Lightning began to erupt from the top of the hill.

Scott took one look, grasped the three of them, and translocated to the casino where the Order was working.

They entered the hall.

Dick rushed to them. "What happened? They said the portal opened, but—" He stared at Adele. "Your heart's beating."

Krish still couldn't keep his eyes off the former zombie. "I think Lexi did it."

The vampire shook his head. "That's astounding. Where is sh —" He gazed at Scott's pale face and fell silent.

"She went through. The portal closed behind her." The young man could hear the shakiness in his voice.

He went to sit and pulled out the message Lexi had sent in her final moments on Earth.

Don't be mad. Okay, I know you're mad. There wasn't anything else I could do. You have the spell. Get that demon out of Alicia and put it into a brick or something.

If you're still alive when the dimensions come close enough, maybe we could talk. Ask Dolores how that works.

Don't be mad at me forever.

Scott wept.

Lexi realized how sorely lacking she was in shadow mage skills. She hadn't achieved the ability to maintain a shield as she slept and almost lost her head on the first night. While it appeared that she did indeed require no sustenance, she did need sleep. Neither could she corporeally enter her dimensional pocket.

She had managed to snatch minutes of sleep here and there during the day, but the nights brought horrors. Huge crab-like monsters sprayed her with poisons that burned her flesh but she recovered quickly and fought back before they had the chance to eat her.

Experience taught her that it was best to walk through the night as it kept her alert. She didn't want to stray too far from the portal. While she had no hope that it would open again, she simply didn't know which direction to walk in. All of them looked the same.

It also didn't help much to remind herself that there were twelve shadow mages there. Eight had joined with the Darkness and four were still mages but they had been there for two hundred years so she didn't hold out much hope for their mental state.

The Darkness had made its presence known from the moment she arrived. Its constant whispering was maddening and she wondered if Mortimer had joined with it simply to shut it up.

The crab-like creatures became her greatest resource. She marked out a perimeter by burning their bodies and walked the boundaries through the night.

After a few weeks, she'd lost count of the number of the giant crabs she had killed and burned and hit upon the idea of making a den out of their shells. The bastards were so tough, nothing else could get through their shells, which allowed her a little more sleep during the day.

She used the hollowed-out shells as armor and as protection from the sun during the day.

The worst part was that she lost track of the days and felt certain that they were longer there than they were on earth. Possibly only by a couple of hours, although she wasn't sure.

With no familiar yardstick, she tried to estimate the length of her stay by how long her hair had grown or how much her nails were growing. Her monthly cycle had gone for shit. It had simply stopped when she got there like her body had said, "I don't know what a month is anymore. I give up." It was fine with her.

Lexi missed her friends and would imagine conversations with them.

She would say, "I think I'll leave the portal today and start exploring farther afield."

But Dick would respond, "You're going out dressed like that? What if you meet someone you know? Your reputation will be in tatters."

"Yeah, fuck you, Dick. You know I get my clothes from Target."

Sometimes, she'd imagine she was seated on the bench

outside Dolores's shack, looking at the setting sun reflecting on the lake. She missed the water.

While she tried not to think of Scott because it hurt too much, she couldn't stop the dreams. They were always holding hands in her dreams—not transferring energy, merely holding hands. *What's up with that?*

One day, she began to walk. She reached her perimeter and continued beyond it. The rough, sandy terrain began to change and so did the creatures. She was surprised to discover that not everything wanted to kill her and made friends with a beetle that was the size of a football. She was worried at first but it seemed to only eat plants. That made her realize that she hadn't eaten anything since she arrived. It must have been about a week before she accepted that she didn't need it. There was so much sulfur there that everything smelled like rotten eggs, but she felt it nourish her magic.

She walked until she was tired, then took the two giant crab shells from her dimensional pocket. It had taken her a while to find two that fit so well together. She would put one on the ground, lie on it, and pull the other over her until they fit snugly like an oyster.

After traveling with Boris the beetle for a couple of weeks, she noticed he was now the size of around four footballs. "Hey, Boris, you're getting fat. You need to cut back on those plants."

He didn't answer and simply moseyed along beside her as she walked.

A few days later, she yawned, stretched, and put her shells away before she started to walk again. After a few steps, she noticed that Boris wasn't shuffling beside her. She stopped and turned back. "Hey, Boris, what's up dude?"

She plucked a plant and waved it in front of him, trying to entice him to eat.

A long, thin, snake-like tongue shot out and stung her hand. "Boris, you fucker. We're not friends anymore."

Lexi started to walk away but within minutes, she was dizzy.

She fell to her knees and her vision blurred. As if from a distance, she could discern something dark coming toward her but in the next moment, she fell face-forward into unconsciousness.

Water dribbled into her mouth. Fresh water, she realized, something she hadn't tasted for months. Warily, she opened her eyes. Something loomed above her and it took several minutes for the features to arrange themselves into a human face.

"Where am I?"

"You're in my home," the man said.

As she blinked away the blurred vision, she focused on a man in black pants and a matching button-up vest. His vest seemed crisp and white. He had his back to her and she heard the sound of pouring water.

Lexi was still a little dizzy and confused. "Boris stung me."

The man turned to face her. "I beg your pardon?"

"Boris. He was my pet beetle. We were traveling together and suddenly, he up and stung me. The little shit."

"Oh dear. I'm afraid you misinterpreted the relationship you had with the beetle. But we do call them companion beetles."

"He was vegetarian," she explained.

The man chuckled. "To begin with, he was a she. When she finds a good food source for her offspring, she stays with it until her young—which have been growing and multiplying under her shell—are ready to hatch. She paralyzes the food source so it—or in this case, you—can't escape, then around five-thousand of the little beasts burst out to feed on you."

"Oh, Boris." Lexi shook her head. "I have to say I'm a little disappointed."

He proffered a wooden cup to her. She took it and drank. "Where did you get water from?"

"I make it. Are you hungry?"

"There's something here to eat that won't kill me?"

He looked puzzled. "I see from your scar that you're a shadow mage. Do you truly believe something could kill you? How long have you been here?"

"A few months I think."

"How did you get here?

"I came through a portal in Las Vegas."

The stranger sighed. "I feared as much. Many people have suffered to keep that closed."

"Well, your friend Mortimer had other ideas. But I'm happy to see that two hundred years here hasn't driven you crazy. Who are you?"

"My name is Jonathan."

Lexi stared at him. "You're Jonathan? You probably won't believe this…"

Happy New Year! I hope that you had a great Christmas and the coming year brings you health and happiness. If you're reading this in November, Hello from the past. I hope the year went well.

First, I want to thank those of you who follow me and review the books on Amazon, Goodreads, Bookbub… etc. You are my tribe, and I deeply appreciate you.

So, I'm trying to get back into keto after Christmas. Well, I say "trying" but to be honest, I could try a little harder. I lost 27lbs before Christmas, I'd like to shift another 20 if possible. I've discovered a couple of downsides to losing weight. 1. My butt has disappeared and sitting down is now uncomfortable. 2. I'm starting to look like a Shar Pei puppy.

But… Since we're back in lockdown, I just had KFC delivered for what is basically breakfast. I sort of regret it; not just because I shouldn't be eating that lovely coating, but because you can't request exactly what you want with delivery. I'm a drumstick and thigh girl. I reached into the bag and pulled out a piece of ribcage, then a wing with a bit of side boob. "Oh goodie!" Said no one ever!

Result! Pieces 3 and 4 are a drumstick and thigh, all is not lost... except I kind of filled up on the not-so-nice pieces. I see now that the hot wings were overkill.

Even though I've been stuck in one room for the best part of the year, it has been an eventful one. My Prosecco intake went up considerably due to the number of boozy zooms I've been on, some lasting 8 hours! I published 4 books and co-wrote a short story in the Hellcats Anthology with Jon Evans, author of the Royal Marine Space Commandos sci-fi series. I was thrilled that our story was accepted to the charity anthology, it was for a great cause and writing sci-fi was fun.

I'm lucky to have finished this book, I've had a really distracting couple of months. First, I binged the first four seasons of The Vampire Diaries (then jumped straight to the last episode because it was disappearing from Netflix), then all of White Collar, then I watched The Queen's Gambit 3 times, then Bridgerton (spicy!). I guess I was just feeling like the well was empty and I needed a recharge. By the way, I'd be delighted to receive recommendations of good shows to watch.

Oh... quick question... did anyone make the recipe from the last book? Let me know.

ACKNOWLEDGMENTS

This book could not have been written without the support of so many people. My sincere thanks to the wonderful people who make LMBPN the great organization it is. Michael, Judith, Kelly, Jen, Steve, Judah, Lynne, Jen, Grace, and Moonchild for the beautiful covers. Huge thanks also to the beta readers, Rachel Beckford, Larry Omans, Kelly O'Donnell, and John Ashmore, who took the time to read and feedback my errors and inconsistencies, and to the JIT team who repeatedly save our skin in the neck of time.

To Micky and ladies (and honorary ladies) for LMBPN. What an absolutely cool group of humans you are.

Thank you to Phil the non-Minotaur, who stops the world around me from grinding to a halt, and for keeping me fed with awesome food and who doesn't judge me when I work until 6am then sleep for half of the day.

Thank you to the good friends who drag me forward with them, and stop me from losing my shit on a daily basis. Anne, Erika, Fatima, Kate, Craig, Sam, Jon, Nat, Sarah, Chelle, Alice, Chrishaun, Pat, Kasia, Merri, Las, Sine, Robyn, Chris, Susan, Marion, Clare, Caroline, Emilia, Kristin, Josie and Meg.

https://www.bookbub.com/authors/michael-anderle